The
Irish Bride

Lynn Bailey

JOVE BOOKS, NEW YORK

THE IRISH BRIDE

A Jove Book / published by arrangement with
the author

PRINTING HISTORY
Jove edition / February 2001

All rights reserved.
Copyright © 2001 by Cynthia Bailey-Pratt.
This book, or parts thereof, may not be reproduced in any form without permission.
For information address: The Berkley Publishing Group,
a division of Penguin Putnam Inc.,
375 Hudson Street, New York, New York 10014.

The Penguin Putnam Inc. World Wide Web site address is
http://www.penguinputnam.com

ISBN: 0-515-13014-1

A JOVE BOOK®
Jove Books are published by The Berkley Publishing Group,
a division of Penguin Putnam Inc.,
375 Hudson Street, New York, New York 10014.
JOVE and the "J" design
are trademarks belonging to Penguin Putnam Inc.

PRINTED IN THE UNITED STATES OF AMERICA

10 9 8 7 6 5 4 3 2 1

One

To be a traveler is to be beset by a swarm of tiny annoyances, petty in themselves, but accumulating into a large sense of frustration. This feeling drove Nick Kirwan on toward home despite the fact that the sun was dropping toward the west. "Not long now, my boy," he said, patting the silken brown neck of his horse.

His voyage from France had been delayed by a storm in the Channel. Then his ship's captain had taken ill and the first mate had been a fool who had miscalculated his course to Wexford Harbor and had been too stubborn to admit it until they'd spied the shipping at Dublin. Next, Nick's horse, which had carried him through half a dozen campaigns including Waterloo, had come up lame after only a day on the cobbled streets of Dublin. Nick would sooner abandon his head than Stamps, so he waited until he was fit again. And these were only the largest of the frustrations that had harried him.

He'd set out two weeks ago to cover the hundred and sixty-odd miles between Trinity Street and his home,

Greenwood. The same current of delays, small and large, had held him back. Now, however, he was but five miles from home. Every foot of stone wall dividing the landscape into crofts and yards held memories of his childhood. The scents of cow byre and sheep pen spoke to him of long days spent riding over this very country, sometimes to visit tenants with his father, sometimes in wild steeplechases with his friends.

Involved in memories, it was only the sound of a lady in distress that made him look up. He saw a carriage fallen to one side, the two horses being held by a boy, and a man and a girl standing in the road. Despite the man's burly looks, it was plain from their postures that she was giving him a piece of her mind.

"Oh, it's too bad, John Garrity! Can't you fix it?"

"No, Miss Blanche, and asking me twenty times in a minute won't make my answer change none."

"But I can't stand in the road all night. I'll catch cold. Or there might be robbers!"

"Your sister's gone to beg you some shelter for the night. Then I'll to Galway and have your father send out the landaulet."

"Rietta may relish the thought of spending the night in some smelly peasant hut, but not me! I won't! I won't!"

She turned then and saw Nick, and Nick saw her. He'd never seen a flowerlike face, for all the poets might say, but he saw one now, glowing like a white rose against the deep green hedge behind her. She was pale, but with pink charming her round cheeks. Her hair was a deep rich gold, hanging beneath a piquant bonnet to the middle of her back. Nick began to feel much better about this delay.

Walking Stamps up to the oddly assorted group, he asked, "May I be of some service?"

The beautiful girl clasped her hands with an almost childlike expression of delight. "Oh! You look just like the knight in my book! Except your horse isn't white and you don't have any armor on."

Nick smiled down into her eyes. "I am indeed a knight, though my horse be brown. Sir Nicholas Kirwan, at your service."

The coachman, a burly figure in a stuff weskit and heavy overcoat, touched his forehead with two fingers. "We had a bit of an accident, as your honor might see. The rear wheel's unpinned itself as we came around the corner."

"How awkward," Nick murmured, staring with fascination into the lagoon-blue depths of her eyes. The pink in her cheeks increased and she looked down at the ground, only to smile sideways at him like a born flirt.

"That it is. T'lad ain't strong enough to raise the wheel, while I lift the coach up."

Nick looked a little harder at the coachman. He was a square figure with powerful thighs and a broad torso while his coat sleeves bulged over muscles as well developed as Nick had ever seen. "You can lift the coach?"

"John Garrity, Sir Nicholas, formerly of Penlow's Circus. I was strongman there for over twenty years."

"Pleased to know you, Mr. Garrity," Nick said. He turned again to the dainty face of the girl. "And you are?"

She turned her pretty head to the side as if embarrassed and said cooingly, "Miss Blanche Ferris of Galway, Sir Nicholas."

He swung himself down purely for the purpose of raising her soft white hand to his lips. "An unlooked for, but much appreciated, pleasure, Miss Blanche."

She simpered, an undoubted outward push of the lips and a little wriggle that set her enchanting hair swinging. Ordinarily, he would not be pleased by such a fatuous trick but in one so lovely surely much must be forgiven.

"Oh, sir. I can no longer count this accident as anything

but the kindness of Providence as it has brought you in our way."

"And here I am thanking Providence for it myself," Nick said and found her giggle surprisingly delightful.

What promised to be a delectable flirtation was cut short by her expression of very real distaste focused, not on himself naturally, but on the woman walking none too elegantly down the hill. "My sister, Rietta. My *older* sister."

"If she is half so charming as yourself . . ."

"She isn't."

"Now what was I thinking? Of course, she couldn't be."

Lovely Blanche giggled again and said frankly, "I like you, Sir Nicholas, but she won't."

Rietta Ferris was taller than her sister, longer through the waist, and presented a much less girlish figure to a gentleman's eye. Under a close-fitting bonnet, her cheeks were flaming from her exertion. She stood in the road a moment, catching her breath.

Nick saw that she took in his sudden appearance with a flash of her eyes, but it wasn't until she could speak without gasping that she approached. By then, she'd apparently had her fill of looking at him, for her attention was entirely given to the carriage.

He could, therefore, study her. Though not as instantly striking as her sister, her face was modeled on the same lines of delicacy and harmony. She had perhaps a tad more chin than a lady really needed and a way of carrying it, high and haughty, that boded ill for anyone who crossed her will. Nick couldn't catch even a glimpse of her hair color, but her eyebrows held more than a hint of red. His theory that she was a high-spirited red-haired woman was further proved by her translucent skin, the color only now fading.

Blanche said, "Come meet Sir Nicholas, Rietta."

"Has Sir Nicholas a family name?" she asked, her voice husky compared with the lilting tones of Blanche.

"Kirwan, Miss Ferris. Sir Nicholas Kirwan."

Rietta recognized the name. Indeed, one would have been hard-pressed to find someone from Galway who didn't. The Kirwans belonged to the Fourteen Tribes, the semimythical founders of the town. Names of some of the Fourteen had been lost in the mists of the past, leaving no descendants, but others went on, up or down with the turning of Fate's great wheel.

This Kirwan did not look as though life had been treating him very well lately. His face was thin and far more tanned than became a gentleman. Though he spoke and moved like a young man, there were lines carving the skin around his mouth and shadows haunted his blue eyes. Yet he smiled with something of a devil's charm when he looked at Blanche. Rietta sighed as she recognized the symptoms of another man instantly slain by her sister's allure.

She turned to the driver. "Well, Mr. Garrity?"

"It's a right to-do, miss. But if the gentleman would be so good as to help me, we may yet see home this night."

"With pleasure," Sir Nicholas said, but he was gazing only at Blanche.

Rietta thanked him and stood back. He stripped off his coat and laid it with a smile onto Blanche's extended arm. Rietta took it from her before she committed the impropriety of nestling it to her bosom.

"Isn't he handsome, though?" Blanche whispered.

Rietta had already noticed Sir Nicholas's strong arms when he'd taken off his coat. Nor was it tailor's padding that made his shoulders so broad. Beneath his hat, worn at a jaunty angle over straight brows, his hair was black, but with a touch of frost that again struck her as odd in such a young man. She would put his age at no more than thirty, despite hints to the contrary.

"Is he? I hadn't noticed."

"You should have your eyes seen to! Such address, such a way of looking . . ."

"Don't be mooning over some chance-met stranger, Blanche. Think of Mr. Mochrie."

"He hasn't enough money to buy a candle in church."

"Then think of Mr. Joyce. He has fortune enough."

"He'd never be able to help Garrity by lifting a wheel. He can hardly lift those books he reads all the time."

"I suppose it is useless to urge you to consider Mr. Greeves, then?"

"He may be rich but if I marry him, I'll never be a lady. I've been wondering if a title wouldn't suit me. 'Lady Kirwan . . .' 'Lady Kirwan of . . . of . . .' Let's find out if his property has a name."

"He probably doesn't have a property. The one doesn't necessarily follow the other."

"Of course he does. A big, grand house with a twisting staircase that I can come down whenever we give a party." Blanche gave a blissful sigh and looked so completely angelic that she could have been mistaken for a saint in the throes of spiritual ecstasy.

Rietta rolled her eyes toward heaven for quite another reason as she saw her sister fall in love yet again. Blanche had fancied that she'd found the perfect man on countless occasions, from the accordion player at an inn they'd stayed at when she was fourteen to her latest whim of thinking it would suit her to be the darling of an elderly, wealthy man. Somehow she managed to keep three notable gentlemen on her string even though she'd given none of them either a yes or no once the inevitable proposals were made. To be fair, she had a gift that turned flirtation into an art.

Rietta tried to look disapproving as she watched Sir Nicholas's muscles strain under his shirt as he lifted the wheel into position. Though not as muscular as Garrity, his body showed that he had not spent any time recently sitting at his ease in comfortable chairs. The faded stripe on the outside of his riding breeches told the tale.

Now that England's war with France was over, many soldiers were coming home. Ireland had been officially neutral, though national sentiment inclined toward France rather than the old enemy. Yet many Irishmen had served in England's army and navy. Rietta wondered what side Sir Nicholas had chosen.

To Rietta, the soldiers' return meant there'd be even more opportunities for Blanche to lose and regain her ever-elastic heart. Would one ever come to win her permanent affections? Sometimes she wondered if Blanche didn't enjoy the chase so much that she never would consent to be caught.

In her own heart, she wished Sir Nicholas Kirwan, already showing signs of being smitten, all the luck in the world. If only she did not have to be there to see the romance unfold in the usual style.

Blanche stood by until the men had finished, then tripped nimbly forward to offer a lace-embellished handkerchief to Sir Nicholas so that he might wipe his brow.

"Thank you," he said, and tucked it into his sleeve.

Blanche simpered. "Oh, but you must give it back!"

"So I will. When I call upon you."

She pressed her lovely hands to her bosom. "Oh, will you?" she cried, showing her delight like a child.

His gaze went past her to Rietta. "May I?"

"I see no way of preventing you, sir."

"You might refuse to give me the address."

Rietta found, to her surprise, that she was not yet entirely immune to charm. She liked that he did not plead with her, or make any overt attempt to win her approval. He only looked at her with a dancing challenge in his sharp eyes, daring her displeasure.

She knew perfectly well what he saw—a starched-up

maiden lady, duenna to a winsome younger sister. It was an appearance she worked hard to project and it rarely pained her anymore. Yet if she was to be honest with herself—and she always was—she could wish for a different appearance in his eyes.

She smiled, thinly, tightly, for it was against her will that she smiled at all. "Naturally, sir, whether you call upon us must be left to the judgment of my father."

Mr. Garrity coughed meaningly. Rietta shot him a narrow-eyed glance so that by the time Sir Nicholas looked around, the coachman was the picture of innocence.

"We live on Prospect Hill," Blanche said quickly, taking advantage of the pause. "Anyone might tell you the way. My father is Augustus Ferris—the mill owner."

"Tell him I shall look forward to meeting the father of so lovely a—a pair of daughters." He handed Blanche into the coach and waited, hand held out, for Rietta.

Approaching, she put his coat into his hand. "Thank you," he said, "but may I assist you?"

He laid the coat over the open window of the coach and took her hand in his. His arm came about her to steady her. Their faces were as close as two people's could be without kissing. He had just done the same for Blanche with a smile that promised much. There was no smile for her, just a straight glance that seemed to penetrate the depths of her soul. Then she was in the coach, still feeling his hand on her waist. Even more lingering was the strange disturbance he'd caused in the tone of her mind.

Nick felt Stamps's gait begin to quicken as they came to the last hill, as though his master's eagerness drove him without any overt command. Night had begun to gather around them, filling the valleys like a wave rushing in from the sea. Nick heard the flutter and fuss as the birds settled in the hedgerows for the night and saw cottagers closing their doors against the dark.

At the top of the hill, he drew rein for a moment and Stamps blew hard through his nostrils. "Now, then, have patience. Let me look my fill."

Down there, nestled against the bosom of this land, was Greenwood. The coppice that gave the place its name had been planted by his great-grandfather to shelter unseen generations. Now the trees stood straight and tall, like soldiers guarding the future for the next generation of Kirwans, a generation Nick could only hope for as yet.

And the house, to his relief, looked just the same. Greenwood was not some palatial residence of soaring columns and wide wings sweeping out like a woman in a court gown dipping a deep curtsey. It was a four-square house of a fifty-year-bygone fashion, the yellowish stucco a bit weathered, the brick chimneys stained with smoke. Yet welcoming lights shone behind the tall windows and the faint drift of peat smoke came wafting toward him on the dying evening breeze.

Ireland was home. His countrymen's expansive speech and purring accent were enough to make him feel that he'd reached some kind of haven. But Greenwood was *home*— the place he had been born. The place where his children would grow up. The place—God will it so!—where he'd die.

Not in Belgium, where so many friends had been killed on that hot day men now called Waterloo. Not in Spain nor in France, where fat Louis could be deposed again for all Sir Nicholas would stir in the business. Nor in Austria, either, where the victors would soon be dancing themselves to death. So long as it came for him here, right here at home, he'd meet death gladly, aye, and shake his bony hand to boot.

Nick clapped his heels to Stamps's sides. With a shake of his noble head and a whinny that must have pricked every equine ear in the county, the horse raced down the hill, the man on his back whooping with a delirious sense of accomplishment. He'd survived the war's horrors and come home at last.

The front door opened before a single hoof had struck a spark from the cobbled courtyard. His mother came out, arms outspread, crying and laughing together, reaching up for him before he'd even dismounted.

Then he was in her arms, feeling like a boy again, though his mother had been shorter than himself since he was thirteen. She hugged him tightly about the waist, her frail arms seeming to gather strength from her happiness. She was even tinier than he remembered, the top of her linen cap hardly reaching his heart.

"You've come back," she said, over and over. "You've come back!"

Why had it never occurred to him that she had worried about him? Her letters had always been lighthearted with an emphasis on how proud she was of his service. Though there'd been tears sparkling on her cheeks the day he'd left ten years ago, he'd callowly accepted her explanation of suffering a slight cold, for she'd smiled and laughed with him up until the moment he'd rode away.

For the first time, Nick realized his mother had probably been afraid that she'd never see him again. He'd been home on leave twice since then. Had she faced her fear anew each time he'd gone away?

"I'm all right, Mother," he whispered, knowing the words were inadequate, bending low to kiss her cheeks, soft as suede and scented with flowers. "A little tired from the trip."

"Oh, sir! Oh, Master!"

Old Barry was there, groom for thirty years, his face as wet with tears as was his mistress', sharing her elation, even as he reached for the headstall of his young master's horse.

Clinging to Nick's arm, Lady Kirwan said, "He's come

back to us, Barry. Bring up a barrel from the cellar and the whole household will drink with us."

"Yes, yer ladyship. Thanks, ma'am." Even as she spoke, he was running an expert eye over the horse. "Fine fellow he is, Sir Nick! Takes his jumps flying, or I'm no Barry of Connaught. From foreign parts, is he?"

"You're right. I had him from a rascally Austrian count who should learn to count his aces."

His gaze lifted to the two young women who stood hesitating on the doorstep, surrounded by the golden yellow lamplight. He smiled at them and shy answering smiles warmed their faces. It had been so long since he'd last come home that he couldn't help being a little surprised to find them grown into women. Somehow he'd gotten it into his head that nothing would change here while he was off on his grand adventure of war. But time had not stood still for any of them, least of all himself.

As he walked into the house, his mother clinging to his arm as if afraid he'd vanish should she let go, he saw that even more had changed. The two paintings of horses that had hung on either side of the hall were gone. Instead of an ornate silver-gilt candelabra on the console table, there stood one of pottery. It was pretty, all white and blue, but it obviously belonged to a bedroom. The red carpet was worn almost to the drab drugget liner beneath.

His mother escorted him into the drawing room, where a cheery peat fire burned, sending the incense of Ireland through the room. A few candles—too few— burned close to the chairs, leaving the rest of the room lost in obscurity like the background of a time-blackened oil painting.

The tea tray, just brought in, to judge by the crumb-free plates, was scantily supplied, only enough for the girls. The glass case against the wall, once so full of small treasures and amusing objets d'art, now held only a few things, and they were the least valuable of the lot.

Most damning of all, his sisters had obviously been darning, for the sewing basket stood by the threadbare settee, and a sock, perhaps hastily thrust inside at the sound of his approach, dangled a shredded toe over the edge.

"Mother . . . ," Nick began, then halted. Now was not the time to bring up any subject except his delight at being home.

"You must be ravenous as a lion," Lady Kirwan said. "Emma, ring the bell. Tell, Jean to bring the ham . . . oh, and a bottle! If we had but known you were coming today, Nick, we would have set out a feast."

" 'Tis a feast for my eyes to see you, Mother." He kissed her hands in their thread-net mittens. "Still the prettiest girl in the county. . . ."

"Did the Belgian ladies fall easy victims to your Irish tongue, my son? You've been practicing somewhere."

"Everywhere," he said, grinning at her. She laughed, bringing color into her cheeks, and told him that he'd not changed.

Turning, he held out his hands to his sisters. They stood together in the doorway, one with tears sliding in glistening trails down her cheeks, the other smiling at him with a grin so like his own that he was taken aback. Then they came and put their hands in his.

"Greenwood grows the fairest flowers," he said.

"Oh, Mother, you were right," the younger said. "He has the gift, sure enough. We'll have to keep our friends away from him."

She tossed a bouncing head of curls and laughed at him. Amelia still possessed a youthful plumpness of cheek and chin but her audacity had increased by leaps and bounds in his absence. Nick liked it. She'd always seemed a little in awe of him on his earlier visits.

"Minx," he said, and Amelia just laughed.

"Now tell me how much I've changed."

"That would take all day and half the night, Amelia. You've grown to be a fine-looking woman." She dipped a thank-you curtsey, then stuck out her tongue. "Or perhaps you've not changed so very much. Do you remember telling me that you'd not be a lady, no matter what your governess said. What was her name? Miss Talent . . . ?"

"Miss Tanager," Amelia said. "I haven't thought about her in an age. I will tell you, Nick. I'm as good as my word. I'm afraid I never have been a lady."

"Amelia's been as good as the son of the house while you've been away, Nick. 'Tis she who scolds Barry, sees to the marketing, and tallies the accounts."

"And it's glad I'll be to be shut of that," she said fervently. She added, "My head for mathematics has never been strong."

"When I did it," Emma said, "it took me days to find a shilling I'd misplaced while adding up."

Nick felt that his sisters were attempting to convey something of importance, but it had been a long day and he was too tired to work it out.

He turned to his other sister, the quieter, graver elder. After kissing her cheek, he held her hands and swung them lightly while he studied her. For a moment, he was afraid she would cast herself on his chest and howl. But instead she sniffed, wiped beneath her eyes, and gave him a tremulous, half-drowned smile. Tears had little effect on her smooth, nearly colorless skin.

"It's good to see you looking so well, Nick. When we heard of your fever . . ."

" 'Twas nothing compared to the time I took the typhus," he said. For his mother's benefit, he added, "I only had a mild case, thank God."

"Thank God," Emma echoed.

He looked around. "It's good to be home at last," he

said. Then he noticed anew the shabbiness of the room and
how many things were missing.

"Mother," he began, "what has happened to . . . ?"

Amelia kicked him lightly on the ankle. Lady Kirwan
didn't see it happen but Emma looked shocked, and giggled.

"You'll have to wait to find out about your old sweethearts, Nick," Amelia said brightly. "Come and have a
wash before you eat. You may not know it but your hands
are all-over mud."

He glanced down. "I helped a lady in distress—two
ladies, come to think of it."

"Someone I know?" his mother asked.

"I doubt it. Their father's a mill owner. Their name was
Ferris. Blanche and Rietta Ferris." His three ladies looked
blank. Nick added, "Blanche Ferris is possibly the most
beautiful girl I've ever seen."

"We shall have to call on them," his mother said with a
decisive nod. "Ferris? Yes, I believe Mrs. Halloran mentioned that family. Highly respectable."

They could not do enough for him. Amelia drew off his
boots, falling over backward with a laugh, while Emma
brought down a pair of slippers she'd been embroidering
against his return. His mother sat with him while he ate
and gazed at him as though she could not look at him
enough. Nick enjoyed being spoiled almost as much as his
family seemed to enjoy spoiling him. Yet after his mother
had kissed him and gone to bed, he rapped gently at
Amelia's bedroom door.

"Come in, Nick," she called.

He opened the door and saw both his sisters, Emma
seated before the glass and Amelia standing by the window. She said, "You've come to find out the truth, haven't
you?"

"I'd like to know why Mother has been selling things.

Half the silver seems to be gone, as well as pictures, furniture, and other oddments."

The girls exchanged glances. Emma rose to her feet and came to take Nick's hand. With tears welling up in her eyes, she said, "I'm afraid it's bad news. Father . . ." Her voice trailed off.

"Let me," Amelia said. "Father began gambling again just before he died."

"Gambling? He swore to me the last time I was home that he'd given it up."

"He swore that often enough," Amelia said, bitterness clear in her tone. "And that's not all. There was a woman."

"We don't know that," Emma said in protest. "It's all conjecture."

"True, but what else could it have been? Money just vanished like water poured into the desert sand. It was bad enough before he died, but afterwards even what little income we had dried up."

"Does Mother know about his 'woman'?"

Amelia shook her head. "Mother doesn't say anything to us. She wouldn't tell us a word, as if it weren't so obvious that she has no money. She's tried hard to keep up appearances but I'm afraid people are beginning to talk."

Emma gave a sudden, convulsive sob and turned her face away from her siblings. Amelia put her arm about her sister's waist. "It's harder for Emma than for me. She wants to marry and there's no money to give her her rights under Father's will. The money's just not there."

"Who do you want to marry?" Nick asked.

Emma sobbed again. "It doesn't matter now. He's leaving Ireland. I'll never . . ." She broke from Amelia's comforting arm and bolted from the room.

"Why wasn't I told?" Nick demanded. "I could have come home sooner."

"Mother wouldn't hear of it. When you couldn't get

leave for Father's funeral, she said that the army had first right to your time."

"I could have gotten leave," Nick said, thudding his fist into his hand. "But things were heating up in the Peninsula and I wanted to be with my battalion. I should have come home after Napoleon went to Elba. There was no need for all this sacrifice on your parts."

"It's all right, Nick," Amelia said. "You're home now."

"Yes, I am. First thing in the morning, I'll want to see the account books. I'll talk everything over with Mother. I'm sure the situation isn't as black as you've painted it. Go tell Emma she'll get her inheritance if I have to cut down every tree at Greenwood. You'll get yours as well. I don't suppose you've a young man waiting?"

"As a matter of fact . . . ," Amelia grinned. "But my case is even more hopeless than hers. She wants to marry a gentleman—I'm going to marry a farmer."

"Have I anything to say in the matter? I am head of the family."

She shook her head with a gleeful grin. "We're quite used to making our own decisions," she said. "You have only to approve them."

Growing serious again, Amelia added, "You won't distress Mother, will you? None of this is her fault. It's all Father. Why, oh why, wouldn't he stop gambling?"

"I've known officers like that. It becomes more to them than a battle or their honor. It's like a hunger that can never be satisfied."

"Do you gamble, Nick?" Her eyes were intent as she worried a fold of her dress between her hands. He owed her his honesty.

"From time to time. But there's no lust in me for the cards or racing. It's an occasional pastime; nothing more."

Her sigh was one of relief. "We didn't know, you see. You're something of a stranger to us."

Nick put out his hand and shook hers. "I won't be a

stranger anymore. I need you to put me in the way of things here. Do that, and the Kirwans will be a paying proposition in no time."

He was not so certain come the morning.

Two

Nick spent the morning poring over the accounts. After an hour, his head was pounding like the hooves of a charging cavalry squad. Neither his mood nor his headache improved when he discovered his father's diaries in the back of his wardrobe.

With a resigned sigh, Nick tied a cold towel about his brow and began to read the diary for the last year of his father's life. As it was written in the not-very-difficult shorthand that the late Sir Benjamin had invented, which Nick had first to decipher, it was not until Amelia came to tell him about luncheon that Nick closed the book.

"Have you found a thousand pounds lost in my arithmetic?" she asked with a hopeful laugh.

"Unfortunately, no. Not even that lost shilling."

Amelia's brow wrinkled as she bit her lip. "It's bad, isn't it, Nick?"

"Bad enough. But cheer up! We can always take in washing."

"Or I could hire out as a maid of all work," she said, responding to his tone. "And Emma is a marvelous cook, you know, though Mother doesn't like her to do it. If it weren't for Mrs. Beattie being in the family so long, we should have replaced her with Emma."

Nick encouraged her to prattle in this light spirit as they came downstairs. He saw his mother look up and smile, the worried lines fading as she heard him laugh. Not for the world would he reveal what he'd read in the diary.

In addition to betting heavily on horses and losing large sums at cards, Sir Benjamin had been an adulterer. He had paid for his pleasures with diamonds or, more indirectly, with "loans" his estate could ill afford to make.

Reading between the lines, Nick had realized that his father's wildness came partly from his nature and partly as a way to assuage his growing fears about his wife's health. The notation of a dizzy spell or a visit from the doctor would be followed shortly by a visit to the mistress of the moment or by a romp with a stranger. Nick had often seen soldiers fend off thoughts of mortality by such a debauch; he could almost sympathize with his father. Nevertheless, it was Sir Benjamin who had fallen down dead of an apoplexy while his wife survived, indifferent health or no.

After luncheon, Lady Kirwan followed him into the study. She entered hesitantly. This had been Sir Benjamin's sanctuary against domestic upsets and neither she nor her children had ever been welcome.

Nick stood up as soon as he perceived her. "Sit down here, Mother," he said, bringing her to the chair behind the desk.

"No, that's your place now. This one will do for me."

"Nonsense. You're not a tenant behind in the rent. You sit there, and I shall sit here." He put aside the feeling that he was committing an act of sedition and perched on the edge of the desk, one leg dangling to the carpet.

His mother clasped her mittened hands in her lap and looked up at him. "In what case do we stand, son?"

"Well enough." He spoke lightly, hoping to put her off.

"No, do not treat me so. Take me into your confidence."

"I am, Mother. Believe me. All will be well. Father did play heavily, but he was honorable about his debts. Except for what he owed on the last night he played—"

"The night he died," Lady Kirwan said levelly.

"Yes. Except for those debts and a few bills from tradesmen and the like, he left nothing for me to pay. I confess I was afraid I should find myself owing more than that. Most of those debts I can pay immediately through what I made in the war."

"I am relieved to hear it. Yet I wonder, what are we to live on?"

"You're not afraid of starving, Mother? Things are not so dire as that. We shall have to be careful of expenditure for a few years until our estate regains its health. I shall have to look into matters more deeply to be certain, yet I believe that if we are thrifty, we can regain our former status within four years."

"Four years?" Her mild eyes filled with tears.

"Come. That's not so long. There's nothing to be afraid of."

Lady Kirwan shook her head, her jet earrings swaying. "Yes, there is. I'm afraid for the girls. If we are impoverished, how are they to get husbands?"

"Early yet to think of such things. They're hardly out of the schoolroom."

"They have been out longer than you realize, Nick. Besides, what has that to say to anything? I was married myself long before I reached Emma's age."

He took her hand and kissed it. "And it's grateful I am to you for it."

Nick had done it to make her smile and so she did, though the tears still stood in her eyes. "But my father had a thousand pounds to go with me. How shall we find them decent young men without a like sum?"

"It sounds uncommon like you have someone in your

eye, Mother. Tell me who it is. I knew most of the young men for forty miles around before I went away."

"It is less who I have in mind than who it is your sisters have chosen."

"Have chosen?" Nick echoed. "Can it be they've already given their promises?"

"Oh, no," Lady Kirwan said. "No, I don't believe it's gone so far as that. They would have told me so if it had." She smiled proudly. "I cannot think of many mothers who have such confidences from their daughters as I have. These last months have drawn us ever closer."

"Mother," Nick said. "Why didn't you write to tell me things had become so bleak? I would have come home at once. Wellington had enough officers and to spare without me."

"I couldn't have asked it of you. My father said that every man should have his war to fight if he was ever to hold up his head among men. I couldn't have stolen your war from you."

Her eyes glowed with such loving pride that Nick could hardly bear to meet her gaze. He knew too much about himself to feel any arrogance about his war service. Yes, he had acquitted himself well time and again. He'd been mentioned in dispatches and had the right to wear more than one decoration. Once, after a particularly hideous affray, the great Duke, despite his dislike of the Irish under his command, had shaken his hand.

Yet his clearest memories were of the fear, loathing, and hatred toward his enemy that had filled him again and again, combining to turn him into something less than an animal. He'd looked into men's eyes as he had killed them and known no remorse. He had picked his way over the bodies of his comrades to close with the enemy and had never given the groaning wounded a second thought.

He'd committed no atrocities, nothing that contravened the laws of war, but he'd washed blood from his hands and sponged it from his uniform over and over. If he could have killed Napoleon thus, breast to breast, he would have done it and rejoiced, but killing instead the emperor's duped soldiers left him feeling soiled, weary, and sick.

"Yes," he said, staring out the window. "I have had my war."

Lady Kirwan laid her hand on his knee. "What is it?"

He couldn't tell her. She had never experienced the horror that would have given her common ground with her son. No woman could understand what he had seen and done. Even now, the memory of his war service was sharper than his memory of last night's homecoming.

"You were going to tell me the names of my sisters' suitors. Dare I hope even one of them is rich as Midas?"

"Neither of them," she said with a sigh that seemed yet to have something of happiness in it. "Emma is very fond of Robbie Staines, Lord Bellamy's youngest boy. It will never do, of course. I'm afraid he's so very shiftless that they are sending him to his uncle in Boston."

"That sounds like Robbie. He's some years younger than I am but I never heard any good of him. How did Emma come to grow fond of such a shabby fellow?"

"She is bosom friends with his sister. They were much thrown together when Emma visited Belmont last summer. I'm afraid her heart is deeply engaged. I believe that if she had the money, she would follow him to America."

"Then that is the first good to come out of our lamentable situation. And Amelia? She, I know, has had sense enough to choose some man of property."

"She has not said as much to me, yet I feel there is some thought in her mind of—"

"Yes?" He felt sure Amelia had picked someone even less eligible that Robbie Staines. There had been so little good news of late that he would not have been surprised to find her enamored of old Barry the groom.

"On St. Brigid's Day, she visited our neighbors as my

representative, for I was taken ill with a fever. She stopped
to see Mrs. Daltrey, who had fallen the week before. The
dairy floor was wet and she slipped down. Wrenched her
back so that she could hardly walk."

"Mother . . . ," Nick began, when it seemed as though
she'd pause on this point forever.

"It was at his mother's cottage that I'm afraid Amelia
met Arthur Daltrey." She seemed reluctant to mention his
name, as though fearful of making the man himself appear.

"Arthur Daltrey? I know that name. One of our farmers,
isn't he?"

"He was. He now owns Badhaven."

"Owns it? His father rented from us."

"I'm afraid your father sold it outright when he lost a
bet to one of his cronies. Which of two raindrops on a window would reach the sill first, I think." Her voice held no
distaste. He heard rather a fatalistic acceptance of whatever came her way. Only for her children's sake could she
rouse herself to take an interest. Nick realized the true cost
of his father's improvidence and vowed that no wife of his
should ever have cause to weep over his thoughtlessness.

"I wouldn't have thought Amelia would fall in love
with a farmer," he mused. "A poet, perhaps, or a revolu-
tionary. Someone utterly humorless to balance her own
merry spirits."

"I have not seen him, but I have heard that Arthur Daltrey could turn any girl's head. He's said to be the handsomest man in the county and perhaps he was, before
yesterday." She fluttered her lashes at him, like a girl teasing a boy.

"You'll make me blush," Nick said.

"I say it without prejudice—or at least, not much. I have
the handsomest son in the West."

"Why not the whole of Ireland?"

"I haven't been to Dublin for some time so can't speak
to the truth of it. But from Cork to Ballina, there's no finer

man than Sir Nicholas Kirwan, now that he's come home. And Arthur Daltrey can just whistle for the girls now."

"Amelia can't be serious about him. One of our own farmers?"

"It's difficult to know with Amelia," Lady Kirwan said. "She doesn't show all she feels. I don't believe she has seen him often, but I myself saw them together two weeks ago. She'd been out riding but they were standing with their heads together, talking under a tree."

"I'll have a word with her."

"Carefully," Lady Kirwan warned. "Remember Romeo and Juliet. Sometimes all love needs to blossom is opposition."

"I'll bear it in mind. Well, m'lady, since neither of my sisters seem poised to bring the family fortunes up to snuff, it may well fall to my lot."

"What will, Nick?"

"The necessity of marrying for money. Show me a woman with three or four hundred pounds of her own and I'll wed her out of hand."

"Oh, Nick. Don't joke about such things. Someone might think you are serious."

Desperate for fresh air and movement, Nick went out riding in the afternoon. Stamps, used to constant exercise, greeted him with an impatient whicker the moment he entered the sunlight-strewn stables. Nor did Nick care to stay in, hunched over his father's crabbed handwriting any longer. The mist that had hung over the hills in the morning had lifted, leaving the air cool and soft. Nick took great, gulping breaths of it as he rode, finding it more heartening that a dram of poteen fresh from a cottager's still.

He found moments from yesterday's meeting playing in his mind as they trotted along the lanes. Blanche Ferris gleamed in his imagination like a gilded goddess in the dark recesses of a temple. She seemed to possess all things

desirable in a woman—beauty, charm, a sweet helpless-
ness that left a man feeling the stronger for her weakness.

If she had faults, they were girlish and would be eradi-
cated by the joys and sorrows of womanhood. And if her
father should prove to be as wealthy as promised by that
mill owner so simply mentioned, then surely heaven had
marked Blanche out for his bride. "Providence set her in
my path yesterday," he told a cow looking over the gate.

Nick decided then and there that he would call upon the
Ferrises tomorrow. Assessing himself, he knew he could
offer little beyond a title, yet such things had considerable
merit in the eyes of the merchant class. The title was hereditary, so that Mr. Ferris's grandson would have that all-
important "sir" before his name. *Hell, I'll even name the
lad . . . wait. She said her father's name was Augustus. No,
I'm damned if I will.*

A shadow showed against the gray stone wall as he
came around the corner. It slipped among the tangle of
trees where the wall ended.

Even in the depths of reverie, his soldier's senses,
honed by ambush and melee, never slept. Instantly on the
alert, Nick gripped Stamps hard with his knees, keeping a
deceptively loose hand on the reins. He let his right hand
fall with apparent casualness to his thigh, but in truth he
was feeling for the pistol butt in the holster by his knee.
His father had taught him that it was never wise to travel
without the means to put one's horse or one's enemy out of
his misery.

Nick went forward, refusing to be frightened by a
shadow until he knew whether it be that of man, boy, or
sheep.

The other horse broke from cover, crowding Stamps in
the narrow lane so that he backed, half-rearing. With knees
clamped tight, Nick forced him down, controlling the
horse's instinctive swerve in order to present his pistol
over Stamp's neck.

The other rider laughed as he, too, brought his mount to a standstill. "I was going to say 'stand and deliver' but 'tis you who keeps the upper hand."

Nick held his aim over the other man's heart. "David? By the Lord, man, there must be easier ways of committin' suicide."

"And easier ways of starvin' than bein' a highwayman in Ireland. Pickings are always poor for the fraternity at this season."

He pulled away the muffler he'd wrapped around the lower part of his face, revealing a countenance both boyish and brash. His smile seemed to have three corners while his bright green eyes laughed even more than his lips. For the rest, he had hay-colored hair, a bump on the bridge of his nose, and a few scars about his mouth and chin from a youthful bout with smallpox.

He should have been ugly, but the whole of his face was more than the sum of its parts. Women of mature years were strangely susceptible to the combination of youthful enthusiasm and manly prowess. Or so the rumors had flown, some fostered by David himself.

Nick eased off the hammer and slid the silver barrel into the holster. He turned Stamps alongside David's silver-gray mare and reached across to shake his boyhood friend by the hand. "Have you been traveling with the Gentlemen so that you know their complaints?"

"No. I'm not hard up enough as yet to take to the High Road."

"I am." He hadn't meant to admit it, but the sight of David Mochrie seemed to take him back to a day when they had no secrets from one another, nor would ever have thought of keeping one if they had.

"Came out of the war poorer than when you went in, did you? I heard Napoleon was paying a bounty for every Irishman who'd join his Grand Armèe. I know a few lads who took him up on his offer." He lay his finger alongside his nose and winked.

"That must have been when he wanted to make Ireland the same sort of running sore in the side of England that we'd made Spain for him. He'd have won, I think, if he could have fanned the flames from the '91."

"I would wager no one's sorrier that he didn't pull that off than the man himself. I hear St. Helena's such a drab spot that it makes the stony ground of Connaught look a paradise."

"All the same, it's too good for him," Nick said sharply. "I'd seen what *Liberté, Egalité,* and *Fraternité* did in France, Spain, Austria, and everywhere else he laid his foul paws. Ireland would not have escaped."

"Better Napoleon than the English."

"You only say that because you weren't there."

"Well now," David said with a shrug that could not have been bettered by a Frenchman, "you chose the winning side in the end. You were right not to take the advice of 'helpful friends.' "

They were interrupted by a girl herding a flock of sheep up the road. She glanced curiously at the two men on their horses. As she passed, it was as if she took all talk of politics with her.

"Where are you going today?" Nick asked.

"To your house, of course. It's all over the county that you've come home. So after a trifle of business, out I came to seek you—and a glass of old Barry's beer."

"Come on. He's been keeping a barrel of the best for me."

In comfortable sloth, boots off, feet on the fireplace fender, Nick drank to David's toast. "May peace bring you better fortune than war."

They talked a bit of old times, then David sat silently, staring into the heart of the fire. Nick, too, saw pictures in the crumbling peat bricks. Then he became aware that his friend kept flicking appraising glances at him, as though weighing him for some judgment.

"What is it, man?" Nick asked at last.

"I was only wondering—did you find a bride while abroad?"

"A bride? No, of course not. Oh, there were women enough, but none I'd keep."

"Good." Again, David fell silent. Then he chuckled.

"You've not changed," Nick said. "I can still tell when you are plotting some mischief."

"No mischief, but a good turn for my old friend. At least, it may prove to be a stroke of good luck for you. The benefits outweigh the dangers."

"That's what you said the day we tried to cross the pasture to reach the apples. That bull took a different view of the matter."

David waved that memory away with a flick of his fingers. "You are neither married nor pledged? And you'd thank the man who put you in the way of even a thousand pounds?"

"I'd thank the man who showed me the way to a few hundred. What's in your mind?"

David sat up and leaned forward with his fingers steepled before him. "Nick, I'm in love with the fairest girl in Ireland—nay, the world. She's as sweet-natured as she is beautiful—a bride in a million. Though she is modest, I have experience enough of the female sex to know that she favors me above all the others."

"Good luck to you, then," Nick said, sipping from his glass. He'd seen David Mochrie in love before this. Each time, whether through fate or a father's investigation of his standing, it had come to nothing. "Make your proposal and marry the girl."

"It's not that simple."

"It never is. What prevents you?"

"Her father, though wise enough in most things, has taken to heart an old tradition. The youngest daughter may not marry before the eldest."

"A foolish custom. Though my own sisters love one another dearly, such a tradition would only breed resentment. I would not honor it."

"I would you were my love's brother. Maybe you could convince her father to give me what I want without waiting until a miracle occurs."

"Then the older girl is so ugly that no man wants her?"

David hesitated, biting his knuckle. "I'll not hide the truth from you," he said, making his decision. "She's fair enough, if you like red hair. In addition, her father has promised a thousand pounds dowry to the man who marries her."

"She sounds a prize," said Nick, thinking more of the money than of her virtues. "But you've more than hinted that there's a catch."

"Plainly spoken, the girl's a shrew. Everyone in the house goes in fear of her viperish tongue. Even her father, who should be able to school her, dares not take a second egg at breakfast without reference to her. She even has the temerity to put her nose into his business. I forgot to tell you that the family is in trade, but that should not signify."

"You are not thinking that I should marry this woman to make your path clear for the younger?"

David nodded, his eyes hopeful. "If someone doesn't marry her, Blanche will die a virgin."

"Blanche?"

"Blanche Ferris," David said as though the words were honey in his mouth.

"I met the Misses Ferris yesterday," Nick said slowly. "Their carriage had thrown a wheel."

"Then you've seen Blanche? Isn't she an angel?"

"She was quite attractive." Nick held up his hand to stem David's raptures. "I met the elder Miss Ferris as well.

She seemed a trifle severe, perhaps, but she did not impress me as being so very shrewish."

"You must have seen her in a soft mood; something rare with her if gossip is to be believed."

"Oh, if this report of her is mere gossip . . ."

"Gossip rarely lies. Besides, I have heard hints from Blanche as well. It makes my blood boil to think how she is mistreated!"

Nick tried to picture Rietta Ferris. Though she did not shine in his memory the way her sister did, he could recall a straight nose and determined chin. Perhaps she'd been somewhat forbidding, but he'd hardly noticed her. He imagined himself married to her, then tried to imagine himself married at all. On both accounts, he failed.

"Sorry, David. I'm not so hard up as that."

"You said you'd be willing to be a highwayman—marriage is an easier fit than the noose."

"I may have said it, but no one has come to me with a detailed plan to rob the Royal Mail, either. I'd say no to a proposal of that sort just as I do to yours."

David sat back and picked up his glass. "It was worth a try. If you hear of any other man of equal poverty and fewer scruples, send him my way."

"I will. Come to think of it, my sister has a suitor I should be glad to see fobbed off onto another."

"Who's that?"

"Robbie Staines."

"Oh, no. Rietta wouldn't look at him."

"You mean, he tried—"

"That he did. All but hanging on the knocker. But his reputation preceded him. By all I heard, she had some harsh things to say about wastrel second sons. That is why you would be ideal. Title, property, everything handsome about you—even your person, in some lights, is not too terrifying. The girl needn't wear a veil to bed to block the sight of you."

"You're too kind."

David grinned. "Always happy to oblige a friend. Well, if you won't, you won't." He drank. "Seems a pity, though. If it weren't for Blanche, I'd have a go at Rietta myself. I'd soon school her to keep quiet."

"You'd marry for money?"

"I'd marry for a barrel of herring, the way things have been. The price of everything has been inordinately high since the war, and my little income is hardly enough to cover it all."

"At least I'm not alone in my predicament."

"No. There's a hundred in the same boat with you. Regrettably, few of them are desperate enough to marry a viper-tongued wench."

When Lady Kirwan awoke from her afternoon nap, she greeted Mr. Mochrie and pressed him to stay for dinner. "My neighbor below stairs thanks you," he said with a bow.

"Why should he?" David Mochrie could always make her laugh.

"I've been cadging dinners off him for the past three nights. He knows when my quarter-day pay rolls in I'll repay him twice over, but three nights in a row is a bit far to stretch anyone's good fellowship."

"Not ours," Lady Kirwan said. "I hope you'll dine with us whenever it pleases you. There is always room at this table for friends of Nick's."

"You'll see a lot of me here," he said, inhaling the steam spiraling up from the soup. "Especially if you give me such wonderful things to eat."

Nick admitted that David earned his soup. He kept up a stream of jokes, gossip, and inconsequential chatter that kept his mother laughing and even caused Emma to look up and give a slight, watery smile. Nick was distressed to see by her swollen eyes and red nose that she had been crying.

When Lady Kirwan took David outside to hold her basket while she cut some roses, Nick sought Emma. He found her in the morning room, sewing desultorily at a worn sock. When he touched it to admire the work, he found it damp, as if she'd dabbed at her tears with it.

"I suppose," she said with a sniffle, "that Mother has told you all about it."

"Something of it."

"No doubt she's shown Robbie in the worst possible light."

"I wouldn't say that."

"Oh, I don't blame her. He hasn't always been wise in the things he's done. He's often played the fool. But I believe he can change. He's promised me that he will."

"His family doesn't seem to believe it. Why else would they send him so far away?"

Emma's chin trembled as she tried to keep from breaking down again. "He doesn't mind that. He's even glad of it. You don't know what it has been like for him, living here. Everyone knows that he hasn't been a satisfactory son and sometimes it is as if everyone in the world has heard the gossip about that girl from Westport."

"You defend him very ably."

"I just don't understand why people can't be fair. How can he prove himself a changed man if no one will give him a chance? They all look at him as if just waiting for him to make another mistake. He's not the kind of man who can stand up under that."

"And you think he'll be more likely to change his manner of living in Boston?"

"Isn't that what a colony is for? A place where people prove themselves?"

"I doubt our American cousins would describe their nation in just those terms, but there is some justice in what you say."

He touched her hot cheek. "But if Robbie's going to America, what comes to you?"

"He promises he'll send for me as soon as he has the money. If only I had it right now. I'd go with him. You see, I know him so well . . . he's not strong like you are. He means to be but he loses his head when he's in company. He spends too much time and money on that lot of slug-gards who call themselves his friends. But are they at his side when he needs help? Not they. But if I'm with him, I can help him."

Nick shook his head slowly and Emma grasped his sleeve. "He's not a bad man," she said with a tight desper-ation in her voice. "There's such sweetness and even po-etry in him. He's almost like a boy, a boy who needs my help and guidance. If I let him go to America alone, I daren't think what trouble he'll get into. He's sure to fall in with bad companions. But if I were there, too, to work with him, to plan with him, I know he'll be respectable and happy."

He looked into her eyes and saw that she was burning with an earnest desire to help worthless Ronnie Staines create a useful life. Nick didn't approve of her wish to im-molate herself on the altar of the self-sacrificing wife.

If he'd been home more often, or if he'd known Emma better, perhaps he could have turned her from her purpose. As it was, he knew she'd bitterly resent the interference of a brother who'd been absent so long.

"How much do you need?" Nick asked, thinking of the inarguable numbers in the ledger, underlined with red ink.

"Five hundred pounds."

"So much? It can't cost that to cross the Atlantic even in a gold-plated boat."

"No, but Robbie's father is only giving him enough money to go to Boston. He wants him to go into law with his uncle but Robbie wants adventure. He has it all planned. We'll go to a place called Kentucky. It's a growing territory or state or whatever it is they call it there. Robbie feels that if we start some kind of manufactory there, we should do well. There are lots of rivers to run mills. But we'll need money to do it."

"Robbie has your future all planned then?"

"Yes. He's wonderful at making plans. He can always come up with a way out of a difficulty."

"So it seems. So he's going to Boston to earn enough money to bring you to America, where he will marry you and go to Kentucky."

"Yes. If only I could go with him now. But without the money, there's no reason for me to go."

"Do you believe, in your heart," Nick asked, his voice low, "that Robbie Staines will wait for you?"

His sister's face crumpled like a sheet of paper crushed in a careless hand. "No. He'll find some other girl the moment he lands. He'll hate himself for breaking my heart, but he won't be able to help it."

"And this is the man you want me to help you marry?"

"Oh, yes!"

"I'd be mad to give my consent. He'll bring you nothing but sorrow, my dear."

"He's what I want," Emma said fiercely. "He needs me so."

Nick looked into her reddened eyes and could not deny her. "Very well. You shall have your money if I must wring the estate dry. When does Robbie sail?"

"Not for some weeks," Emma said, her eyes brightening as though he'd handed her the keys to a magnificent castle made of precious stones and roses. "His sister is to be married and he has been permitted to stay for that."

"Matrimony does seem to be in the air," Nick muttered.

Then he smiled at her warmly and tapped her cheek. "Enough tears for now," he said. "Show Mother a smiling face."

He left her in raptures, eager to share the kindness of her brother with her mother and sister.

Nick went in search of David Mochrie.

"Where did you say those girls lived?"

Three

Rietta faced Blanche across the breakfast table, certain that if she heard one word more about Sir Nicholas Kirwan she would empty the sugar bowl over her sister's blond curls. For the past two days, she'd heard little but raptures over the gentleman's appearance, manners, and probable fortune. Blanche seemed to have discovered in him infinite food for discussion, despite the brevity of their association.

Blanche had already thought of a dozen witty remarks and answers she might have given him. It was only Rietta's inconvenient presence that made it impossible for her to say that she had delivered all that clever repartee.

Beside Rietta's place at table were letters and papers which she studied attentively. A ship's log lay beneath them and, from time to time, she checked a reference. When Mr. Ferris came in, she looked up from her work.

"Father, there's been a rise in the price of cochineal. When you see Captain O'Dea, ask him to sell back to us his share of the last voyage at the previous price. We'll have Ronald take it to market in the south, then pay Captain O'Dea seventy-five percent of the difference."

"Does the captain know about the rise?"

"If he reads the newspapers attentively . . ."

"But he has been at sea. He might have missed the announcement. Why not offer him the same price and then pocket the difference? We can always use a few extra pounds."

"Oh, yes," Blanche said. "I saw a bonnet in Mrs. Merrill's shop window—black silk with blue satin lining and strings in the new Waterloo shade. It's only twenty guineas."

"You shall have it," Mr. Ferris said, smirking indulgently. "Got to see my girl looking her best."

"I'm sure Sir Nicholas will be flattered if I wear Waterloo ribbons. Even if it should prove he wasn't in the engagement, he was in the army."

"Father," Rietta said patiently, returning to the subject, "Captain O'Dea is one of the best seamen in Ireland. He is very well respected by the other captains. If you cheat him . . . if you do not offer him a profit, he may feel cheated."

"That's his affair," Blanche put in, cutting off her father's reply. "You are too scrupulous, Rietta. It doesn't pay."

"Or," Rietta added, "he might sell his cochineal to another buyer and we shall lose even the twenty-five percent gain that I have planned."

"Why shouldn't he take his own dye to market?" Mr. Ferris wondered.

"His wife is ill and he cannot leave her at present. I know that his agent in London has not been satisfactory and that he has not found another as yet. If Ronald can sell the dye powder for him, we shall earn some money and much goodwill."

"Goodwill won't buy my little girl her bonnet!" Mr. Ferris frowned. He had a hairline that stopped inside his large ears and when he frowned he looked like a fretful baby. "I wish you wouldn't be so assertive, Rietta. I'm too tired to argue with you at breakfast."

"But you will see Captain O'Dea today, Father?"

"Yes, yes. Just as you wish. Now, what have we for breakfast?" He uttered little glad cries of surprise as he foraged among the dishes on the sideboard, though there was nothing there that hadn't appeared for breakfast every morning.

If her father was tired, Rietta was exhausted. She'd been up half the night reconciling the mill's accounts, making certain that no funds had mysteriously vanished, as had been known to happen in the past. Then there were bills to pay, letters to write for her father's signature, and orders given for the employee's half-holiday next week. After she fell into bed, she dreamed she was a navvy, spending all day pushing increasingly heavy crates into ships that shrank from moment to moment.

The maid, Arabella, entered, carrying a bouquet of white lilies over her arm. Their scent well nigh overpowered the smell of bacon and kidneys.

"Ooh!" Blanche squealed, holding out her arms.

"No, Miss Blanche," Arabella said. "They're for Miss Ferris."

"You've misread the card," Blanche insisted. "Let me see it."

Arabella gave a tiny sniff and handed the white pasteboard to Rietta, who lifted her head to blink dazedly at the small square.

"For me?" she said stupidly.

The handwriting was cramped as though hemmed in by the narrow margins: *May I call?—N. Kirwan.*

"Who brought them?" Rietta asked.

"A servant, ma'am. He's waitin' for an answer."

"Oh, who are they from?" Blanche demanded. "They must be for me. They're white—Blanche means white."

Rietta had nothing but misgivings about allowing Sir

Nicholas to become further intrigued with Blanche, and vice versa. After nothing had been heard from him in two days, she'd hoped that Blanche had somehow failed to ensnare him, that he was impervious to the arrow of her beauty. Most men wasted not a hour after meeting Blanche to pursue her. Sir Nicholas must have tremendous self-control to hold off for a clear forty-eight hours.

In truth, Rietta would have denied him for his own sake, if not for Blanche's, but her father took a hand. He read the card over Rietta's shoulder. "N. Kirwan? Would that be Sir Nicholas Kirwan? I've heard of him."

"So have I," Rietta said. "Rather a lot lately."

"His family is well known, of course. His father was something of a wastrel by all reports, but they have a pretty property—a very pretty property indeed, and I believe something will come to him through his mother. He has two sisters—they will naturally receive a daughter's rights but still—a most pretty property."

All too acutely aware that her father never noticed whether a servant could hear every word he said, Rietta drew his attention to Arabella, standing patiently while he discussed Sir Nicholas's prospects. "Ahem. Father . . ."

"Tell the fellow that Mr. Ferris will be more than pleased to see his master at any hour. Well, go on, girl."

Rietta inclined her head the merest degree. Arabella dipped a curtsey and left.

Mr. Ferris rubbed his dry hands together. "Well, puss, a fine fish in your net this time! A hereditary title in the family will look very handsome indeed. I shouldn't wonder if Mrs. Vernon will be most impressed. Like all ladies, Mrs. Vernon does love a lord!"

"He's not a lord, Father," Rietta said, her heart sinking at his evident wish to impress his mistress. "If his title's hereditary, he can be nothing more than a baronet."

"Fie," Blanche said vulgarly. "You would count yourself fortunate to catch an 'esquire,' if one could be found to take you."

Rietta could easily have retorted that until she caught even an esquire, Blanche would not marry. But she had not her sister's taste for a witty reply at the expense of dignity.

Instead, she gathered up her books and papers. "I hope you will remember to send for me the next time one of your admirers call. Mr. Greeves must have been very much shocked to have spent so many minutes alone with you."

"What's this?" Mr. Ferris sputtered. "Blanche, you sly puss! Have you made up your mind to take old James Greeves? He's a good man; a trifle long in the tooth, perhaps, but what does that matter?"

"He's only five years older than you are, Papa," Blanche said. "But ever so much wealthier."

"Ah, but there was money in his family. He did not start from nothing as I have done."

"No, Papa," Blanche said charmingly. "Tell me how you first began."

Nothing put Mr. Ferris in a better mood than recounting some interminable story about his early dealings, most of which seemed to skirt the very edge of double-dealing. As Rietta, who could not bear to hear the tale again, slipped from the room, she reflected bitterly that Blanche must be very determined to own that black-and-blue bonnet.

When the hour for callers came, Rietta jumped as the clock's chime and the door knocker sounded together. She'd been so engrossed in her work that she'd entirely lost her sense of time passing. She hurried to the washbasin to scrub ink off her finger and chin with a pumice stone and to pin straight the little lace circle she wore on the back of her head.

Though the men did not come to see her, she would not have it said that she was in any way untidy or eccentric in her dress. Yet as she looked in the glass, she saw not her own face but a pair of dark-blue eyes, a slightly wry smile and a thick pelt of dark hair. She faced the fact that it was not for Blanche's declared suitors that she endeavored to be more than neat. If Sir Nicholas should call . . .

A moment's calm reflection slowed her galloping heart and called down the hectic flush from her cheeks. "If he even recalls your face, he sees you only as a horrid, scolding wretch, jealous of her fairer, younger sister. What more could you expect? Or, indeed, desire?"

She emerged from her bedroom just as Arabella came up the stairs to call Blanche. "It's themselves again," the maid muttered as she passed. "The old 'un, the young 'un, and the wild 'un."

James Greeves rose as the two ladies entered. He was about sixty years of age, high in flesh, though not grossly fat. His corset creaked as he bowed. Two months ago, his hair had been quite white and his figure much less compressed. Then he met Blanche at the house of a wool merchant. Suddenly his hair bloomed again a deep red, some of which stained his scalp where the hair no longer grew, and his figure returned overnight to a youthful slenderness.

Rietta smiled with special kindness on the eldest of her sister's suitors. She felt so sorry for Mr. Greeves. For some weeks, Blanche had believed she would like nothing better than to be spoiled by a husband so much older than she. But the fancy was fading. Rietta knew it wouldn't be long before Blanche's kindness turned to impatience, and then came the inevitable rebuff.

Not just yet, though, Rietta was glad to notice as Blanche gave Mr. Greeves her hand. "Dear sir," she purred. "So very kind of you to call."

"Not at all, Miss Blanche," he said, patting the hand he held.

She smiled absently and slipped her fingers free to turn to the next man. Niall Joyce had youth, family connection, and some wealth to recommend him. Unfortunately they were allied to a face more noticeable for good humor than good looks. Niall was also rather overgrown, though never clumsy until he came into Blanche's presence. Then he tripped over his feet, spilled drinks, and developed a slight stammer. Rietta was afraid for him, should Blanche choose him. She herself could never be happy with a man she could not respect and she feared that Blanche couldn't, either.

"Mr. Joyce," Blanche said, "I hope I see you well?"

He murmured something incoherent as he bowed from the waist like a jointed doll. Blanche leaned back as he rose; she'd knocked heads with him before.

Blanche's smile turned so warm for the "wild 'un," that Rietta wondered at the other two for not seeing the difference. David Mochrie's father owned some thousand acres in the hills north of the city. The family was large and the land did not bear well. David was popularly thought not to have a penny to bless himself with. But the ways of fortune are balanced to a nicety. Niall Joyce had money but no charm; David Mochrie's lack of funds was supplemented by a smile that could give a woman too much conceit of her beauty. His eyes twinkled, making a woman believe in her own wit, while his voice made promises his words dared not express. Poor Niall could only sit by and glower when David Mochrie sat beside Blanche and made her laugh.

Yet rumor said that Blanche Ferris was not the first pretty girl of fortune that he'd approached. Nor would she be the last, if Rietta could in any way prevent it. Of the three men present, her choice for her sister would be James Greeves. Older, steadier, yet indulgent, he would perhaps not encourage Blanche to mature, yet he could offer her the security to grow wise later in life.

She turned to him now and offered him refreshment. "Arabella is just bringing in the tea tray, sir. May I pour you a cup?"

"Thank you, Miss Ferris. Two . . . ah, ma'am—how you spoil an old man!"

Considering he'd been taking his tea the same way every day for two months, Rietta hardly thought it remarkable she should remember to drop in two spoonfuls of sugar.

"Your father is not at home today?" he asked.

"Alas, sir. He is sorry to have missed you, but he had some business to transact this morning." She saw that David Mochrie had turned Blanche's palm upwards and was tracing her lifeline. "Tea, Blanche?"

"Oh! Yes, please. Did Cook make any Bath buns? I adore Bath buns. . . ."

With a sinking heart, Rietta saw both Mr. Greeves and Mr. Joyce writing on their shirt cuffs. She supposed they would now be inundated with buns from the best bakeries. The same generous impulse had led them to give Blanche pounds of soft-centered chocolates, a hothouse worth of white roses, and enough French perfumes to make a new ocean for Napoleon's stranded navy. Rietta thought Blanche made these seemingly artless pronouncements to provoke just such a generous response.

David Mochrie only smiled ironically. He had not money enough to send expensive gifts, but he could write passable poetry. Sweets, flowers, and scent bottles did not fit comfortably beneath Blanche's pillow, but Rietta had seen sheets of paper there.

Rietta tried to draw Niall Joyce into a conversation, but it was difficult. He sat with his ear cocked toward where Blanche entertained Mr. Greeves and Mr. Mochrie, leading him to answer Rietta very much at random.

Blanche's peal of laughter was cut short by a rapping at the door knocker so vigorous that it seemed to shake the whole house. She stood up and fluttered to the window. "Who can it be?"

While there, Rietta noticed, her sister peeped into the

mirror and tucked up a fallen lock of hair. Perhaps she had pinched her cheeks surreptitiously, for when she came to sit down again, her face was suspiciously pink. "I couldn't tell," she said in answer to Mr. Joyce's stammered question. "A gentleman, I think. I only saw the back of his coat and his hat as Arabella opened the door."

Yet it was enough to put her into an agitated state. Rietta did not need to see the card that Arabella brought in to know that Sir Nicholas had arrived.

"Yes, of course," she said to the maid. Her own heart had begun to beat faster, though she hoped she did not show it as Blanche did.

For Blanche had started across the thick blue carpet before Arabella had reached the door. She was standing behind her sister's chair when Arabella announced their new visitor.

"Why, Sir Nicholas." There could be no mistaking the delight in Blanche's voice. "I hardly expected you to call so soon—you must have so much to keep you occupied now."

She looked around prettily, drawing all her other suitors in with a glance. "Gentlemen, I want to make Sir Nicholas Kirwan known to you."

Going to him, she took him possessively by the arm and led him to each man in turn, pronouncing their names. "And this is Mr. Mochrie of Scardaun."

"Sir Nicholas is well known to me. We're old friends."

"I didn't expect to see you here today, David."

"This is the one place in all the world you may count on seeing me. For nowhere is the company more to my liking."

Blanche, who counted all conversation lost until it referenced herself—preferably with a compliment—sparkled when at last she saw David turn to her with admiration. "Tell me, Sir Nicholas, how you and Mr. Mochrie met."

Rietta heard the same coaxing tone Blanche had used

with their father that morning. She seemed to believe that the way to a man's heart was through showing a deep, if feigned, interest in him. Though Rietta scorned to play such games, she couldn't help looking up from her tatting to meet, surprisingly, Sir Nicholas's eye. At once, Rietta looked down at her fingers.

"Our fathers were friends and it was passed to us," he said. "I made my first trip abroad in David's company, when I was just a lad."

"Oooh," Blanche said, looking angelically wistful. "How I'd love to travel to France and the rest of the Continent. Tell me about it."

"We couldn't go to France," David said, "due to Madame Guillotine being so busy, so we headed into less civilized climes. Morocco, Egypt, the Grecian Isles— grand times."

"Which islands?" Mr. Greeves asked, turning about in his chair. "I spent some months serving in Ionian and Aegean waters when I was a ship's boy."

"I didn't know that, sir," David said with more respect than was usual when he spoke to the older man. "Did you go to Delphi? This lout . . ." He clapped his hand on Sir Nicholas's elbow. "He would hardly stir from the fleshpots of Athens to seek out the real Greek culture, but I persuaded him at last."

Sir Nicholas raised his hands. "Hold me blameless," he said with a chuckle. "David was mad for overthrown statues in broken temples, hiding in the most remote of mountain villages. Can I help it if I had a preference for clean sheets and decent food?"

"Did you find much of either in Greece?" Rietta asked.

"Enough to content me." He came closer. "Have you ever traveled outside of Ireland, Miss Ferris?"

"Never yet, sir, but I have hopes."

Mr. Greeves and Sir Nicholas exchanged places. Blanche was looking bored as the two enthusiasts discussed sights they'd seen. She seemed glad of the rescue of even Mr. Joyce, turning her petulant pout into a rather dark radiance as she pointedly turned her back on the others.

Rietta could only go on tatting as Sir Nicholas sat beside her. She began to work more quickly as she tried to ignore that they sat virtually thigh against thigh.

"What are you working on?" He took the strand in his hand and began stroking it with his fingers, trying to smooth it out.

"I hope to lay up enough trimming to edge some bed linen."

"A meritorious hope. Will you achieve it?"

"I believe I shall. I have already done one set for my father; this shall be for Blanche."

"You are very kind to them."

She could have sworn her entire attention was fixed on the white thread as she twisted and turned it in her fingertips, her needle a flash of silver. Yet how was it that she could see that his expression was sardonic?

"It is little enough. How do you find Ireland, Sir Nicholas?"

"You sail across St. George's Channel or the Irish Sea."

At this piece of nonsense, she turned her full attention on him with a tight-lipped expression of disdain. "I meant, after your travels?"

"Who says I've been traveling?"

"Mr. Mochrie—"

"That was years ago. . . ."

"And the state of your boots when we first met."

"They became muddy while I was helping your coachman."

"No. The road was dry enough for this time of year. Your breeches were gone in mud to the knee—and the stripe down the side told its own tale. Were you at Waterloo?"

"Yes, ma'am. You are rather observant. . . ."

"For a woman?" she asked, finishing his thought. "A woman must be more observant than a man because no one ever tells her anything. We must learn by observation and deduction if we are to learn anything at all."

"By God, a proponent of women's rights."

"By God, sir, a proponent of the notion that we have our own heads and the right to use them."

Rietta glanced toward Blanche who sat sighing, the picture of long-suffering femininity, while her three admirers discovered a like passion for the Greek theater.

"I am no radical, Sir Nicholas," Rietta said, lowering her voice. "We must each be satisfied with our lot in life."

"Must we? Why?"

"To rage against our situation is to deny the destiny that has been created for us."

"So you think we should all be born, live, and die on the same plot?"

"No, I—"

"I agree with you. Some day you must come to see Greenwood. Then you'd know why."

Relieved to have been rescued from the involved philosophy she'd been carelessly embracing, Rietta smiled. "I should like that very much."

"Come Wednesday. I'll tell my mother to expect you."

Four

Rietta could only stare at him, wondering if she'd heard him correctly. If she had, then he was quite the boldest of Blanche's suitors. Had she struck him so powerfully that he felt compelled to proceed in this hurried fashion?

"Oh, but we cannot," she said, after several false starts. "Blanche has her harp lessons and we must decorate the church."

"Your sister plays the harp? Well, she is an angel. What instrument do you favor?"

She wondered how he'd look if she confessed that her favorite instruments were the pen, inkpot, and ledger. Shocked and horrified, no doubt, for business sense was not a feminine accomplishment of which a woman boasted.

"I used to play the pianoforte, but I was thankful to surrender my lessons once it became apparent I had no aptitude."

"You may have been better than you know. I'm sorry I never heard you play."

"You would have been sorrier still had you done so. My

instructress threatened suicide, but she was ever highly strung."

He chuckled, though he seemed more obliged to be amused than in truth touched in his humor. Rietta studied him. He met her eye so steadily that she looked away first. His tone had been light, even bantering, but his eyes were as serious and focused as cannon mouths lifting inexorably toward their target. Yet his natural mark sat on the other side of the room.

Rietta quickly grasped the perfect explanation for Sir Nicholas's singling her out. He no doubt realized that Blanche was highly sought—five minutes here with her other suitors would have so informed a blind man. Winning her sister's approval might just be the feather that tipped the scales in his favor. With Rietta's approval, he might run tame in the house and if she could be brought to sing his praises, Blanche would soon echo them.

Perhaps that might be true in ordinary households, but Rietta knew he was wasting his time. No one had influence over Blanche, least of all her unyielding sister. Besides, even if she could act upon Blanche the way a breeze moves a feather, Rietta flattered herself that she was too downy a bird to be caught that way twice. *Never again,* she thought.

As the clock in the hall struck a deep note, Rietta gathered up her work. "I'm afraid that we must say good morning, Sir Nicholas. My father prefers that we entertain morning visitors for only half an hour at a time."

"That is customary, is it not?"

"I am surprised you know of that, sir, seeing how you have been out of the country," Rietta said.

"My sisters see to it that I stay reasonably well informed. I hope to see you at Greenwood very soon, Miss Ferris, and for more than half an hour."

He held out his hand. Rather clumsily, Rietta transferred all her supplies so that she might slip her fingers into his grasp. To her surprise, he bent his dark head low and brushed his lips warmly against the back of her hand. She felt as if dark wings had passed over her and shivered.

Nick felt her tremble. Though she had instantly suppressed the reaction, it had happened. He raised his head and thought how well the bright carnation in her cheeks became her. She was rather too colorless and pale, excepting her splendid hair.

He found himself strangely reluctant to let go of his one chance to touch her. Her skin was soft and lightly fragranced with lavender. His memory of her, overlaid by David Mochrie's unflattering report, had become distorted overnight until he'd been surprised to find her young, quite attractive, and pleasingly slender, rather than elderly, ugly, and painfully skinny.

Under the scrap of lace pinned to the crown of her head, her hair was more gold than red. Though ruthlessly pulled off her face and bound into a chignon, tiny sprigs had worked free to emphasize with natural curls the lines of temple and cheeks. She had a small cluster of freckles on her nose and eyes of so many shades of green that she could have given a few to Ireland. He had a sudden vision of her dressed in a low-cut gown of grass-green silk with nothing but her unbound hair for ornament. White muslin, however maidenly, didn't suit her.

Nick bowed over Rietta's hand once more, not merely brushing over the back but pressing there, showing more by a kiss than he'd intended for today. She pulled away with some strength and straightened. "Sir!" she said in a sharp whisper. He saw her glance toward the others but the men were clustered so close about Blanche that they had no eyes for anything else.

"Flirting with me won't help you reach your goal," she said frigidly. "I am not susceptible to the lures of gentlemen who wish only to reach my sister's favor."

Nick straightened. "The devil with your sister's favor.

She has enough moths to her flame. I'm a bit particular that way."

Her eyes widened. She took a step away, her hand fluttering up. He noticed, with pleasure, that she put it behind her back, pressing it against her waist as though to erase with another pressure the touch of his lips. "Absurd."

"Why?" He glanced at the others and saw David. Mochrie's eye flickered in a wink as he nodded encouragement. "You're not an antidote, you know."

"You never even looked at me the other day."

He smiled at her unconscious admission that she had been disturbed by this neglect. "I did. You wore a dark-green habit."

"No, I wore a black cloak."

"Yes. Over a dark-green habit. I recall perfectly, Miss Ferris. You cannot convince me otherwise. After ten years of army life, no camouflage can deceive me."

"That is neither here nor there. You cannot convince me that you took any notice of me whatsoever. Now to come here and play this game . . ."

"I assure you I am in deadly earnest."

The others came forward now to take their leave of Miss Ferris. She was plainly distracted by his standing there, yet she managed to smile and speak naturally to each of Blanche's suitors. He was not attracted to Rietta, he did not believe that he could ever love her, yet he could respect her self-control and her natural graciousness.

David, of course, he knew well. Niall Joyce was a stranger to him, though Nick thought that he'd once known his older brother. Mr. Greeves, though he smelled of the shop, had an air of respectability that charmed. Nick thought it a shame so good a gentleman should make a fool of himself over a so much younger woman.

"Sir Nicholas," Blanche hissed from beside him. "I'm sorry I didn't speak more with you. Stay behind the others, do!"

"Isn't our allotted time up?" Nick asked.

"For the others, yes. But you needn't run away."

"Your sister . . ."

"Oh, she's so fussy, it makes me cross. There's no sacred law that a morning visit can only last half an hour, is there?"

"Miss Ferris thinks so."

Blanche's alabaster brow wrinkled in a charming frown. "I know!" she said, brightening. "We'll go shopping soon down on Quay Street. Monsieur Andalouse's millinery shop. There's the dearest bonnet in the window. Meet me there. Anyone can give you the address."

"Will your sister accompany you?"

"Yes. But you needn't let that stop you. She hates shopping for anything interesting. She'll leave me to it and go to the bookshop—a dreary, drafty place. And the books are all dusty."

"Clarendon's?"

"Yes. You know it? Are you bookish, too?" From her expression, it was obvious that Blanche thought "bookish" was not at all what she expected from so dashing a figure.

"Only slightly," Nick said reassuringly.

"I suppose it's not so bad in a man," Blanche replied generously. "It's different for a girl. Rietta's only happy when she's reading some dusty book. They make me sneeze."

As agreed, Nick met David in a public house around the corner from the Ferris home. David already had a pint of black beer before him, the lacy foam clinging halfway down. He waved Nick over and before Nick reached him, the second half of the pint was gone. "Landlord, two more," he called.

Nick sat down across from David at the dark wood table, covered with an interlocking pattern of rings from countless glasses of stout.

"Drink up," David said. "Get the taste of that cat-lap tea out of your mouth."

Though it was a little early for Nick, he drank. "I've traveled a long way through the world and never had better beer than from home."

"Teach you not to leave it, then." He put his elbows on the table and leaned forward, dropping his voice to a conspirator's whisper. "Your wooing seems to have begun well, Nick. She cannot tell if she likes you or despises you."

"That's a good beginning?"

"Sure, man. Now you can nudge her in the way you want her to go. It's easier dealing with the darlin's when they don't know their own minds. Once she's made up her mind about you, you don't have a hope of changing it."

"I don't know if I've decided about her. She doesn't seem to be as evil-tempered as you suggested."

"You saw the best side of her, then. Perhaps I'm asking too much of our friendship. I shouldn't ask you to bind yourself for life to a woman of such vile temperament."

"I didn't come for your friendship's sake, David. I must marry sooner or later. Why not a woman of some property? I could go farther and fare worse than with this one."

"But without love?" David asked.

Nick laughed lightly. "I don't believe in it. I've seen women of every variety under the sun and never met one to whom I could say 'I love you' and mean it for more than a fortnight. No, a wise man marries for sensible reasons and he marries a sensible woman. Rietta Ferris is such a woman."

"You've come back a cynic." David shook his head and drank. "You're wrong, Nick. When I'm with Blanche, I'm a new man. A better man. She's so sweet and unspoiled. . . ."

Nick stared at David, amazed that any infatuation could so blind a man to a woman's faults. Perhaps underneath her flirtatious mannerisms and heedless indiscretion was a sweet girl, but unspoiled? Considered coolly, Blanche Ferris was probably the prettiest creature Nick had ever seen, but she'd never make anything but a perfectly maddening wife. He'd as soon marry Lady Macbeth.

"I still don't like the thought of my best friend marrying a termagant on my advice," David said.

"Absolve yourself," Nick said, summoning the landlord. "I did not decide until I saw her that I would have her to wife."

"You think her so beautiful, then?"

"No, as I said, I want a sensible woman. She'll be glad enough to marry me, if the rumors have frightened off all the other men. Every woman wants to marry."

"What if the rumors are true?"

Nick shrugged and drank. "What's a temper? I have a temper myself. If I can school myself to keep my own, I can soon teach her. My mother will still rule Greenwood, just as she does now. My wife will soon learn that I won't hear any criticism of my mother or my sisters. Let her rage; I'll ignore her. If she screams, I'll walk out. Does she throw things? I'll see to it that they are her own and not replace them. When she sues for peace, I'll treat her well. She's not a fool. She'll find it easier to be sensible."

"Better you than me."

"It's not so difficult. If her father had acted so, she would have been married long ago."

"Just as well then that he did not. Or you'd still be searching for your 'sensible' bride and Blanche would have been married long ago to someone less deserving than myself."

Nick couldn't help himself. "Are you certain she's the wife for you? If marriage to Miss Ferris will be difficult, what about your future life? She cannot have ever learned economy, and as for prudence . . ."

David looked black for a moment, then relaxed. "None

of that matters to me beside my love for Blanche. So she doesn't fit your notions of a sensible bride. I don't feel the need for such a one. A man and woman need passion between them if their marriage is to be successful. Without it, what have you to sweeten the dry crust of everyday living?"

"I may have come back a cynic, David, but you've turned into a poet. Is it love that worked the change?"

David's cheeks flushed. "I have written an ode or two to my love. Why not? Poetry is every man's birthright."

"Well, come down from the heights and be practical. Tell me where I may meet Mr. Ferris."

"Here."

Nick coughed as the beer caught in his throat. "Here?" he asked, his voice a notch higher than usual.

"This is his favorite place to stop in for a pint when Rietta lets him have pocket money." He looked around the barroom, the dim lamps reflecting poorly off the dark paneling. The small round windowpanes let in little light and let out nearly none of the smoke from the white clay pipes sprouting from the lips of half a dozen or so working men taking refreshment. "But I don't see him now."

"That," said a voice from the darkness, "would be because I'm sitting behind you, David Mochrie."

Nick's first glimpse of the man he had all but decided to make his father-in-law did not augur well for the future. Mr. Ferris's nose twitched when they met, as if sniffing for money.

His hand was damp, though in fairness that might have been the condensation from his glass.

The three men sat down together. "Am I to understand, Sir Nicholas, that it is your wish to marry my dear little Rietta?"

"I cannot deny that I have something of that in mind. I have only just met the young lady."

"She's a rare one. Not many girls are so serious-minded. She's not one to throw her cap over the windmill."

"I admire her for that quality."

Mr. Ferris's eyes disappeared when he smiled. "You'll find her a careful housekeeper. I've never encouraged her to waste money."

"You have obviously been a dutiful father."

"It hasn't been so easy, a man raising two daughters alone. M'wife—God rest her—was a Browne. You have some connection with that family, I believe."

So Mr. Ferris had checked on his family connections, had he? Nick glanced at David, who mimed innocent confusion. "Distant cousins only."

"Ah, the Tribes intermarried so! Important to keep good bloodlines, but all the more important to bring in fresh stock from time to time. There's little difference between improving a herd of sheep and people, Sir Nicholas." Mr. Ferris chuckled, shaking the crumbs of snuff loose from his waistcoat.

"Or horses," David said, grimacing.

"Ah, you gentlemen would know more of that than I would. Landlord!"

"No more for me," Nick said. The taste of the beer, the smell of the smoke, and Mr. Ferris's peering eyes and confidential tones combined in a whirl. He seemed to hear the faint whisper of a martial chorus and to see in the smoke the faces of his old mess mates. Someone laughed loudly, sounding just like Freddie Frobisher. Freddie had been shot through the ribs and had laughed and told jokes before he'd died.

"I am interested in your daughter, Mr. Ferris. However, a choice of wife is not entered into lightly or unadvisedly. I shall wish to see more of her."

"Come to dinner today. Just 'catch as catch can,' but Ri-etta sets a good plain table. You, too, Mr. Mochrie."

Nick stood up somewhat abruptly. "You're very kind; I should be honored. Good day, sir. David."

On the street, the fresh breeze from the bay revived him. He no longer felt as though he'd be sick, but was still shaken. Ghosts were all right in their proper places—graveyards by witch light, long halls in deserted castles—but they had no business leering over sticky beer glasses in respectable pubs.

David had followed him outside but, thankfully, seemed to notice nothing amiss. "You mustn't mind Mr. Ferris," he said. "He's not a bad old stick once you come to know him. If he was a bit overfamiliar just now, it must be the excitement."

"Excitement?" Nick echoed.

"Well, it's not every day a man lands a title for a daughter he's long thought unmarriagable."

"I don't understand you, David. Miss Ferris is an intelligent young woman, passably pretty, and more than a little charming. Yet you speak of her as though she were possessed of ten thousand furies."

"Just wait till you see her scold some poor serving wench for a fault. Don't make up your mind till then. For my own sake, I'd have you marry the girl tomorrow. But you're my friend and I'll not see you enter into such a predicament without your eyes being wide open."

Nick supposed he should have told David that Blanche would be alone at the milliner's. He had guessed that David, for all his confidence in the eventual happy outcome of his courtship, was not the favored one.

Blanche's pleased reception of him after having met him only once told Nick that his star was ascending in her eyes. No doubt she'd already created some fantastic deeds of heroism for him, turning him into a dream warrior from a fairy tale.

She'd been on the watch for him, obviously. He'd no

sooner emerged from the twisting alleys of medieval Galway than he heard his name shrieked as though by an operatic seagull. Blanche trotted up the street toward him, one hand holding on an untied hat. Her smile was brilliant.

"Hullo, I'm so glad to see you! The fiend of a milliner has brought out half a dozen hats, any one of which I'd absolutely die for, and I can't decide which one I should buy."

"I thought you'd had one in mind," Nick said, allowing her to take possession of his arm. She leaned on him as though she was unable to walk unassisted, despite just proving the opposite.

"Oh, yes, but I looked such a hag. . . ."

"You never could," he said gallantly, knowing what was expected of any male in Blanche's vicinity.

"Flatterer. But there's another one lined in crushed velvet that really is a marvel. Come see."

Nick spent fifteen minutes in the shop with Blanche, approving each hat in turn. He confessed himself unable to choose among them. "Yes, it is difficult," Blanche sighed. "Let me see that satin straw again."

"If you'll excuse me a few moments, Miss Blanche," Nick said. "I'll go down the street to the confectioners. I've been dreaming of Mr. Morton's caramels these past four years."

"Oh, aren't they wonderful?"

"Would you accept a box from me?"

She laughed. "My sister tells me it's wrong to accept gifts from men, but a box of caramels isn't exactly a diamond necklace or something valuable, now is it?"

"Has a man offered you diamonds?"

"Not yet," she said, half lowering her eyelids and looking as transparently sly as a kitten stalking a bowl of milk. Nick laughed and she pouted. Then, catching a glimpse of herself in the mirror, she leaned forward to admire her looks while Nick excused himself.

Clarendon's bookshop was a three-story building painted in chocolate picked out with cream. When he pushed open the door, a gust of dusty, slightly stale air surrounded him. He inhaled with pleasure. The only smell that spoke more enticingly of adventure was the sea on the morning of an embarkation.

From the dim depths, a small, bent figure appeared, pushing up a pair of sliding steel-rimmed spectacles. "Good afternoon, Mr. Clarendon."

"Who is it? Sir Nicholas, home from the wars?"

"That's right, sir. It's good to see you."

"And you, sir. Come, that copy of Pliny you wanted is waiting for you."

"Good Lord," Nick said. "I asked for that years ago."

"It was a trifle difficult to come by, but there was a sale of the late Lord Hardy's library in 1812 and he had a copy. Quite clean, barring a trifle of foxing on the title page, but you'll not mind that."

"Not at all. Tell me, is Miss Ferris somewhere about?"

Mr. Clarendon's jaw was slack, but his eyes behind their panes of glass were sharp. "Miss Ferris? She is a friend of yourself, Sir Nicholas?"

"I hope that she may be." He bore up under the bibliophile's study.

"Novels. Second floor to the rear."

"Novels?" Nick didn't like the sound of that. His sisters were fond of "horrid" books that left girls' emotions unsettled.

"She is engaged in reading the newest book by the author of *Sense and Sensibility*. I'm afraid Mr. Ferris doesn't approve of novels, either, so I permit Miss Ferris to read here." He pulled his watch from his vest and clucked his tongue. "Kindly tell her that it is nearly one o'clock, if you please. She shouldn't be late."

"Yes, of course."

"Thank you. I shall wrap up Pliny for you, Sir Nicholas."

She sat, half hidden by the wings, on a worn velvet armchair, her cheek leaning on her hand. A slight smile touched her lips as though what she read pleased her. The sunlight streaming in from the window behind her lit the golden dust motes that swirled about her like Titania's fairies.

Nick drew back into the shelves. He thought about what he was doing and why. He'd already exceeded his own bounds of taste and propriety by kissing her hand. A gentleman treated an unmarried lady always with courtesy and respect. He'd clung to that code in the midst of fleeing civilian populations and in noisy taverns, only to abandon it in a Galway drawing room. Did money mean so much to him? Was he such a mercenary beast that he'd drag an innocent woman into marriage with him just to achieve financial security?

Taking a second glance at Rietta, he knew he had no right to use her in such a way. David would have to wait for another suitor to remove the obstacle she represented.

He could have sworn he made no noise, yet she looked up. Seeing him, her full mouth tightened as if she forcefully restrained her impatience. The faint sound of her resigned sigh reached him and some resolve within him hardened. She had no gift for concealing her feelings as other women did. Was this the secret of her poor reputation?

"We meet again," he said, emerging.

"Indeed? It is strange to me, Sir Nicholas, that before two days ago I did not even know of your existence. Now you seem to be everywhere."

"I must say the same, Miss Ferris. Are you haunting me?"

"I? I was here first."

As he came closer, she rose to her feet, her posture defiant. In the daylight, her skin was unmarked, save for faint shadows beneath her clear eyes. She held her book, her finger marking her place, slightly behind her skirts, as if to conceal it from him. "However, now that you are here," she added, "I will take my leave."

"What are you reading?" He reached for the book; she swung it further behind her. His arm went around her waist. She caught her breath. There was no softening of her expression, no invitation in her eyes. Nick wanted both and couldn't have begun to say why. She was more than attractive, but prickly as a thornbush. He felt her hand go against his shoulder in a repulsing push.

He retreated. "I only wanted to see which author so engrossed you. He must be fascinating indeed."

"There is no name on the book, sir, yet I believe the author to be a woman." Closing it, she thrust it toward him and took her hand away almost before he'd taken it. He turned the book over in his hands.

"*Mansfield Park?* I've never heard of it. What's the story?"

"It's a tale of a poor relation."

Was there an emphasis in her words? Nick decided he was imagining things. "What is your reason for presuming the author is a woman?"

"Only a woman could see so much of another woman's life."

"Male authors write of such things. Maidens fighting for life and honor abound in novels written by men."

"There are other battles to be fought, Sir Nicholas. This author chooses to tell of smaller wars, fought at home and in the heart. She seems to speak of our inner lives. I don't know quite how to tell you. . . ."

"I shall have to read it." He liked the color and life that came into her face when she forgot herself in the pursuit of an interesting subject. "You are very interested in literature?"

"Yes." She drew back, both physically and mentally. He could feel her remembering that they were alone and that his previous behavior had been encroaching.

"I feel I should tell you that your father invited me to dine with him tonight."

"He did? When did you meet him?"

"At a public house. David Mochrie introduced us."

"Mr. Mochrie?" Her brows came together in a puzzled frown.

"Yes, we stopped in after meeting at your house. Your father was most pressing. May I come this evening?"

"My father's house is open to whomever he wishes to invite, naturally. I very much regret that I will not be present."

"Why won't you?"

"Really, Sir Nicholas . . ."

"Why not?"

"I have another invitation, of long standing. Every Thursday evening."

"With whom?"

She sighed again, her impatience growing plainer. "You are too inquisitive, sir. Why? Where? With whom? I am not accountable to you, nor to anyone save my father. I know why you take such an impertinent interest in me and I have no wish to further your scheme by answering your questions."

"Scheme? What scheme?"

She threw him a scornful glance and walked away. Though he was certain she knew nothing of the plot he and David had hatched, he followed her, telling himself he only wanted to be certain.

By the stairs, he caught her elbow. "Just a moment."

"Release me at once!" she demanded.

He threw his hand back, holding them both in the air as if surrendering. "I won't touch you again."

"Indeed you will not. Who do you believe you are? I

don't know you from Adam. You are trying to make a game of me and I will not have it!"

Cold, her face was regular, attractive enough, and pale. In a rage, she was magnificent. Her green eyes burned with a flame while her prideful stance turned her into Aphrodite. Her voice rang clear and bright.

He wondered if other men, knowing they could not win such a woman, had weighted her with cruel names to conceal their own cowardice. He was somewhat in awe of her himself. Yet he felt strongly that he could win her, given time to regain his equilibrium.

"I have distressed you," he said. "I'm sorry. But won't you tell me what you meant by 'scheme'?"

A lock of her bright hair had fallen into her eyes in her anger. She pushed it back. "I know perfectly well that you mean to charm me into allowing you to come and go as you please at our house."

"That would be delightful."

Her sneer was not quite so effective as her anger. "I'm sure you would find it so, having gulled the older sister into believing you come to call on her while indulging in flirtation with the younger. It has been tried before this by a man of greater address than you possess."

"Who would do such a despicable thing?" Nick asked, thinking that somewhere a man needed his backside kicked.

"That's rather the pot calling the kettle black, isn't it?"

"He must have hurt you," Nick said, ignoring his conscience.

For an instant, something bleak and lonely looked out of her eyes. "Not at all," she said, looking past him. "I knew he could not mean what he said to me."

Nick wanted to take back his vow. If ever a woman needed to be held, it was this queenly, passionate creature. Then she looked at him again and the full power of her dislike hit him.

"I am going to collect my sister from the milliner's and then visit the church, Sir Nicholas. I trust I will see you nowhere else today."

She dipped him a rather ironic curtsey and turned away. "Cat," he said without heat.

She turned back, her eyes narrowing. "I beg your pardon?"

A mew from the staircase answered her. "I didn't want you to step on the cat," Nick said.

Five

The parcel from Clarendon's arrived an hour after she returned home.

"What's that?" Mr. Ferris demanded. "Another gift for Blanche, eh? The minx."

"No, Father. It is addressed to me."

Mr. Ferris looked surprised, then smug. "First lilies, now parcels. Is there something you want to tell me, daughter? An admirer, eh?"

"No, sir, I have no one to tell you of." Rietta pulled on the string and broke the sealing wax. Three volumes, bound in brown cloth, were stacked inside the smooth paper. They were familiar to her before she picked one up.

"*Mansfield Park*?" Mr. Ferris asked, but it was not his voice she heard. "Never heard of it."

"No, sir. I begin to believe that it is not at all a well-known novel."

"A novel? Haven't I told you time and again not to muddle your head with a pack of lies? Novels only lead to unrestrained behavior in young girls—twaddle about love and romance! Marriage is a serious business."

"Yes, Father. I did not order these books. I cannot imagine what Mr. Clarendon can be about." She opened the small envelope but her father held out his hand for it before she could read it. She was taken aback by her own sense of reluctance to let go of the little piece of pasteboard within.

Rietta watched her father guardedly. To her surprise, she saw him smile and then chuckle as he read. "Well, my dear, you've got a string to your bow after all."

"Father?"

He dropped the card into her lap and pinched her chin. "Keep your secret, my dear, but not too long, eh?"

"I don't think I should keep them. I don't want to be indebted to anyone."

"Certainly you shall keep them! You don't want to insult the . . . mysterious benefactor." He gave his inane laugh. "That's good, isn't it? Maybe I should take up novel writing."

Aware that he studied her, she read the card.

> *So you may read* undisturbed
> —*N. K.*

That was too much to be hoped for. However, Rietta found herself smiling. The gift was thoughtful. Did he guess that her father would permit her to keep the books if they came from Sir Nicholas Kirwan? He could not have been in Mr. Ferris's company long before realizing her father worshipped rank. To him, a baronet would be as good as a prince.

"A gift to your taste, Rietta."

"Yes, Father. It's very kind of him. Yet surely a young woman shouldn't accept gifts from men."

"Such scruples! One shouldn't look a gift horse in the mouth. Look at Blanche. Gifts arriving day and night. She thanks the gentleman prettily and makes no commitment. It's a good thing, too, else I'd be bankrupt from keeping her in flowers. You sit down and write the gentleman a nice little note of appreciation."

"I shall do so at once."

"That recalls it to my mind. Sir Nicholas is coming to dine with us this evening. You will naturally put off your other engagement."

"I cannot do that, Father."

"What?"

"I'm sorry, sir. I must go tonight. Mrs. Athy has asked her brother to come on purpose to meet me."

"Such persons can be easily put off in favor of so distinguished a gentleman."

"I'm afraid it is my only opportunity to speak to her brother. He's away to America on the next ship."

"Then let him go."

"I'm certain Sir Nicholas will be able to dine with us all another night, Father. I will be going out this evening."

Mr. Ferris paced before the fireplace, flicking little fierce glances at her, his head sunk down between his shoulders like a vulture's. "It's my wish that you be here tonight."

"I hope always to be amenable to your wishes, Father, but I have a prior engagement. Sir Nicholas did not seem to mind when I told him I should be absent."

"You saw him today . . . after I invited him?"

"Yes," she said, her fingers stroking the gilted edges of the book. "I met him at Clarendon's."

"Alone?" The word should have sounded stern. For all his carelessness, Mr. Ferris had considerable regard for his daughters' reputations. Yet his tone was indulgent.

"We were alone only for a moment." They'd only been interrupted by the cat, but Rietta kept that from her father. He was acting most strangely.

"You must like him, daughter."

"Not very much."

"No, of course not. Well, we shall miss you at the table.

Write that note. It will have to serve to satisfy Sir Nicholas, robbed of your presence."

"Goodness, Father. It is not as though he were coming to see me, after all. Blanche will be company enough."

To her surprise, a smile showed her father's inhumanly regular teeth. "Very well, my dear. Perhaps you know the best of it. Absence, eh? Absence."

Some time later, Rietta sat before her glass, brushing out her hair. She played in her mind a pleasant scene in which she informed her father and sister that she, long despaired of, was engaged to be married to Sir Nicholas. Would Blanche scream and drum her feet on the floor? They'd probably have to revive her with brandy. As for her father, he might even elevate her to the rank of favorite child.

Rietta knew there would never be such a scene Sir Nicholas, in every physical respect her ideal, had much too masterful a disposition to ever make her a husband. Just from their brief acquaintance, she could tell that he would not care for a wife who had her own ideas and went her own way. A meek creature, who would make his will hers, would be more to his taste.

"Which is in no way my description," she told her reflection. "Pleasant to dream of, but there's no more to it than that."

"Talking to yourself, Rietta? Better be careful. They say that's how Mrs. Reedy began, and she wound up in the madhouse," Blanche said as she entered the room.

"Good evening, Blanche," Rietta said, beginning to braid her hair. "You should dress for dinner."

"Oh, there's more than enough time for that." Her sister drifted aimlessly about the room, brushing her fingertips over the bed coverlet, dragging a tassel across her cheek, flipping through the pages of a book. Rietta was glad she'd tucked the note into her wardrobe. She tried not to make too much of the fact that she'd chosen the drawer that contained her undergarments, simply reflecting that there it was most likely to remain undetected.

"I needn't do more than change my gown," Blanche said.

"You haven't heard, then?" Rietta said, pinning the braid up. "Father's invited Sir Nicholas to dine here."

"Dine here? Tonight?" She stopped drifting and put her hands to her face as though trying to hold on to a whirling top. "You're joking. He can't possibly eat here."

"Why not?"

"Aren't we having mutton?"

"Of course. Haricot mutton."

"You mean mutton stew? Oh, my God."

"Blanche, please don't take the name of the Lord in vain."

"If the Lord were here, he'd be swearing Himself."

"Blanche!"

"Oh, heavens! Why was I born into such a horrible, horrible family? Don't you understand even the simplest facts of life? When a man like Sir Nicholas comes to dine with you, you don't serve him whatever has been dredged up in the kitchen. You serve him the finest Galway has to offer."

"Oysters and Guinness?" She placed the last pin and gave her coiffure a pat. "It's the wrong time of year."

"Oh, my God!"

"Blanche, I've asked you not to swear."

"It's too much. On top of everything else, it's too much. At last there's a man worthy to be my husband and you must serve him haricot mutton the first time he dines with us."

"If you want things done differently, you must do the household ordering," Rietta said calmly, ignoring the sudden sense of depression that filled her upon hearing the words "my husband" in connection with Sir Nicholas and Blanche. "If not, you've no right to complain. Father likes haricot mutton."

"No right? No right? No right to see my future ruined through your stupidity?"

"That's enough," Rietta said sharply. She grabbed at the end of her disappearing temper. "I will not be at home this evening, so you must be Father's hostess. I'm sure you'll make a splendid job of it. Father tells me that Mr. Mochrie and Mr. Joyce will also be at table. The numbers will be uneven, but I'm sure you won't mind that."

"If you are suggesting that I like monopolizing men . . ."

"Monopolizing?" Rietta echoed. She'd been unaware that Blanche knew any words longer than three short syllables.

Blanche sniffed. "Mr. Joyce was most unkind to me when he met me at the milliner's. He accused me of flirtation. As if I would."

"You met Mr. Joyce at the milliner's? I thought you said before that you had met Mr. Greeves there."

"I did," Blanche said, preening herself in the mirror. "Only Mr. Mochrie didn't come, but as you say, he'll be at dinner."

"Blanche," Rietta began, rising. "You didn't let any of these men buy you anything?"

"Of course not," she said, shocked. She ruined the effect of her anger by giggling. "They offered, but I naturally refused."

"Thank mercy for that," Rietta sighed.

"Of course, someone did bring me a box of caramels that he bought especially for me, but there's no harm in that, surely."

"Mr. Joyce, I wager."

Blanche only hummed a light air as she rocked back and forth on her heels. She looked angelic, except for the smirk that twisted her rosy lips. "You lose," she said after a moment in which she plainly hoped Rietta was suffering tortures of unsatisfied curiosity.

"I trust you didn't eat them all before dinner."

"Oh, I couldn't resist being just the tiniest bit greedy. They were so good and he seemed to expect that I should. He was a dreadfully long time in getting them, too, so I had to show how much I appreciated his effort."

"Too bad," Rietta said, buttoning the grayish velvet pelisse that followed the lines of her dress. Though it was summer, the nights could still grow chilly after sundown.

"Yes, I had to try on ever so many hats while I was waiting for him, even ones that made me look completely hideous. There was one green straw that turned me bilious. And the clock kept striking the quarter hours till I was quite impatient. But Sir . . . he came eventually."

Rietta's fingers stilled on the last button. "So it was Sir Nicholas who brought you the caramels? Was he before or after the other two gentlemen?"

"After," Blanche said coyly. "It must have been a quarter to three before he came back with them. Even then, he had to rush away."

Rietta clearly recalled hearing the bell in St. Nicholas of Myra chiming three as she returned from walking down Quay Street to the bay. She had stood by the water for a little while until the unusual heat generated by her meeting with Sir Nicholas had faded. She had not wanted to meet Blanche while her cheeks were still flying storm signals and her hands still trembled with suppressed feeling. Yet even while she was attempting to cool down, he was fetching sweets for her sister.

"Men are base," she said coldly. "He was most likely rushing off to meet yet another woman—some other poor creature who has the misfortune to meet such a rake."

"Is Sir Nicholas a rake?" Blanche looked as though she entertained a daydream or two of her own. "It's always been my ambition to reform a villainous brute. I wonder if Sir Nicholas drinks?"

Rietta stared in wonder at her sister. "What have you been reading?"

"Reading? Nothing at all. Ooh, I wonder if he grows violent when he drinks. Wouldn't it be marvelous to bring a man like that to heel?"

"Kindly don't go through the world saying Sir Nicholas is a drunkard."

"But didn't you say he was?"

Nick hadn't been in the house ten minutes before he realized how intently Blanche watched him. Mr. Joyce had flown to her like a metal filing seeking a magnet, leaving Nick to the overpowering entertainment of Mr. Ferris. Yet even while she spoke to Mr. Joyce, Nick was aware of her gaze on him. Her lovely blue eyes widened with alarm when he accepted a glass of wine from his host's hand.

Nick turned to Mr. Ferris. "I'd hoped that your older daughter might change her mind and be here this evening."

"Not Rietta. She doesn't change her mind. Stubborn as flint." He seemed to recall suddenly to whom he spoke. He ducked his head ingratiatingly. "I'll not hide her faults from you. You won't be able to say I misrepresented her."

"I had already realized that one." Nick looked past his host, remembering her firm chin and steady eyes. "She told me she had a long-standing arrangement for Thursday nights. Where does she go?"

"She takes a basket to an old pensioner of her mother's. M'wife's old maid. A Mrs. Athy."

Blanche overheard. "Are you talking of that old woman Rietta goes to? Dreadful creature. She's as old as the hills." She snickered. "Smokes a pipe, too, if you please."

"How very charitable of your sister."

Blanche seemed to catch something disparaging in his tone. "I prefer charities closer to home. There's no need to walk outside the walls and into the Claddagh."

"She goes into the village by herself?"

"Every week. I've only been once—that was enough for me. They spoke nothing but Irish the whole time. I couldn't understand a word. And they expected me to eat herring!" She shivered throughout her frame in a wholly delightful way. Mr. Joyce's eyes seemed fated to fall from his head.

Mr. Joyce roused himself from contemplation of Blanche's figure. "The villagers are openly hostile to strangers wandering there. Especially, if you'll forgive my mentioning it, red-haired women."

"What's wrong with red-haired women?" Nick asked, thinking there had to be a word more descriptive than "red" for that shifting mass of gold and copper.

"The fishermen think red-haired women are bad luck. If they see one on their way in the morning, they turn around and go home. Or so they claim. It's a barbarous place, the Claddagh."

"I can't stop her," Mr. Ferris said with a resigned shrug. "She sees it as her duty. Besides which, Mrs. Athy is very well respected among the fisher folk. She'll see to it no harm comes to Rietta."

"Why, what harm could come to her, red-haired or not?" Nick asked. "I have been out of the country for some time, but it hardly seems possible that lawlessness should have taken such a grip."

"It's just those people over there have their own laws, their own ways. They even claim to have their own king," Mr. Ferris said with a chuckling contempt, adding, "It's a wonder the government allows it in these unsettled times. Come now, Sir Nicholas, you must have heard that at least, born and bred in the West."

"Yes, I know of it. My father was of the opinion that they were the original founders of Galway and when our lot came in, they were pushed back."

"Your lot?" Blanche asked brightly.

"The Kirwans are Norman," Mr. Joyce answered. "So are my people. We came here in 1140."

It was obvious to Nick that Blanche had no interest in anything that had happened more than a day or two before, if so long as that. "I wonder where Mr. Mochrie has gotten to? You did invite him, Father?"

"Yes, just as you asked."

Blanche pouted prettily when her father gave her game away. Mr. Joyce turned toward her with a half-wild expression. Nick had never seen the languid boy so active. She soon flattered him into a more compliant frame of mind that lasted even after David Mochrie arrived. Watching Blanche juggle her admirers was as good as a play. He declined to take a role himself, however, no matter how many encouraging glances he received.

After dinner, Blanche excused herself. Shortly after she'd left the room, the pensive strains of a harp song wound its way through the candle smoke. David and Mr. Joyce, daring each other with their eyes over the brandy glasses, excused themselves as one man and nearly tangled arms and legs in the doorway.

Mr. Ferris laughed low. "Like bees to a honey pot. It's not her fortune that wins her so many admirers. Why, when she was but fourteen a poet attempted to run off with her. I never dared send her to school for fear she'd turn all the masters' heads."

"I'm surprised you are willing she should be the wife of a squire. Such beauty deserves a title, at least."

Mr. Ferris winked at Nick. "You can't have 'em both, Sir Nicholas!" Perhaps Nick's distaste showed, for the man poured more wine in his glass and sat back. "Oh, she's had her opportunities to rise in the world," he said matter-of-factly. "When she went south to her aunt, there were a few lordlings who wanted her. But not legitimate—I'm not rich enough for that! Besides, she don't care to leave Galway and me."

Milton's lines about whether 'twas better to rule or to serve depending on where one was occurred to Nick. Better to be the prettiest girl in Galway than one of a hundred charming faces at a London assembly.

"She's a tender-hearted little thing. Wouldn't give me pain for all the world. Still, time she was married."

"I'm surprised, sir, that you cling to the tradition of marrying eldest before youngest. Surely with so many suitors, Blanche might marry tomorrow if you so choose."

Mr. Ferris poured himself more wine. He wasn't drunk, just loose enough to find confiding a pleasure and relief. "I'll tell you 'bout that. It's all due to the curse."

"The curse?"

"Right." He drank, seeming to feel that he'd said enough.

Nick hadn't seen anyone put away so much liquor without showing the effects of it since Gunner Barnes had wagered he could drink four bottles of the powerful local anisette liqueur which, as it turned out, was considerably less alcoholic than the stuff Mrs. Barnes had been making for years.

"What curse would that be, Mr. Ferris?" he asked, tipping the bottle over the older man's glass.

"I shouldn't pay any attention to it, I know. But m'father believed it. Wouldn't allow my sisters to marry out of order of their birth and neither shall I!"

"So the curse is on your family."

Mr. Ferris nodded as though the hinge of his neck no longer held. "Something to do with a girl from the hills who thought my great-great-grandfather should have married her instead of her sister.

"I don't believe it," Mr. Ferris added. "But I won't go against it. If you marry my Rietta, you shall have a thousand pounds with her and, at my death, half my estates, providing I do not marry again."

"And if you do?"

"If I do what?" His small, reddened eyes were blinking hard in order to focus.

"If you marry again?"

"Won't. Not after my . . . my Miranda. No one could ever take her place," he said and sniffed. "She was a queen among women, fairest of all the roses. Sweet, modest, and tip over tail in love with me. Ah, m'darlin', m'darlin'."

Nick recognized all the signs. He'd pulled the boots off more than one officer or cadet who'd underestimated his capacity for strong drink. Mr. Ferris had reached the maudlin stage, where it became necessary to mourn lost chances. He'd even known one subaltern to weep because he'd not yet met the love of his life and feared he never would. He'd been all of nineteen. Nick had dumped that one none too gently on his cot. The subaltern's plight had seemed minor indeed, compared with himself at twenty-seven with half a dozen love affairs behind him and yet no love to keep.

Nick stood up. "What time does Miss Ferris usually return from the Claddagh?"

"I don't know," Mr. Ferris said, dabbing at his eyes with the edge of the tablecloth. "Ten, sometimes. She's not often later than ten."

The stories and songs were over. The peat fire burned low in the earthen fireplace as Mrs. Athy saw out the last of her friends and neighbors. Rietta smiled at her hostess's brother, his head fallen to his shoulder, his buzzing breaths faint. The whiskey had loosened his tongue and sent him eventually to sleep, as his sister had predicted.

Mrs. Athy returned, picked up the kettle from the hearth, and gave it a questioning shake. A satisfactory slosh within rewarded her. "Another cup of tea, m'dearie?"

"Not for me, Mrs. Athy, thank you. I shall gurgle fearfully as I walk home even if I don't have another."

"As you brought it, 'tis only right you should have the drinkin' of it."

"Well, perhaps just a drop more. I shall have to be leaving soon."

"I'll rouse himself to see you home."

"Let him have his sleep. I know my way well enough by now."

Mrs. Athy sat down on her second best chair with a sigh. "Good *craic* the night. Did you hear anythin' new?"

"Yes, ma'am. The tale of Finn MacCool and the dragon was a fresh version of the one Will Darbes told me."

Mrs. Athy shook her graying head. " 'Tis still strange to me that anyone'd be wanting to write down our old tales. There's many here tonight who think you clean out of your senses and me with you. But so long as you bring this good tea and the whiskey for the men, they'll come to sing."

The older woman's eyes were gray as a stormy sea as they looked off into the shadowy corners of her one-room home. "But it is good to have them all about me and t'hear the good music and the laughter. 'Twould be lonely for me else with himself goin' off in the morning."

She shook herself all over, as though throwing off raindrops. Dressed in the traditional style of her village, with a heavy woolen skirt covered by a red apron, clogs on her feet, and a shawl about her shoulders, she seemed almost elemental, like Ireland itself made flesh. Though perhaps no more than forty, only fifteen years or so older than Rietta, she seemed aged, her face red from wind and cold, her eyes sad through loneliness and loss. Yet her heart had embraced the daughter of her former mistress when Rietta had come to her to record the tales she'd told two fascinated little girls years ago.

Blanche had outgrown them the moment she'd discovered men. Rietta never forgot the ancient stories of giants, cattle raids, and fair maidens wooed by warriors from the sea. She'd often dreamed of herself as one of the Children of Lir, turned into swans and forced to wander the earth for nine hundred years.

When she read that scholars had begun to collect the folktales of Germany and France, she decided that no country in the world had tales as rich as those of Ireland. Determined to be as exact as possible, she wrote letters to the men mentioned in the book she'd read.

Some ignored her; others wrote back. Only a few scoffed, seeing in her the continuation of the Ossian controversy. Several others were encouraging, especially when she convinced them that she had not invented any myths or languages as had the late Mr. MacPherson. She did not need to create an Irish Homer as he had done. There was enough invention in the minds of the Claddagh villagers to fill a hundred books.

"Forgive me, Miss Rietta, but you seem troubled tonight. Is anything amiss?"

"Oh, I'm just tired," Rietta began, turning away from confidences. Then she met Mrs. Athy's eyes and saw only concern and affection. "Truthfully? I'm confused in my mind. I don't know what to make of this person I met the other day."

"A man, is it?"

"Yes, it's a man. He's not like anyone I've ever met before. I don't understand him at all, but I keep thinking of him."

"Sounds promisin'. What's he like, then?"

"Irritating . . . and yet . . ." Rietta was too restless to sit still. She stood up and went to the fire. Holding her hands out to the warmth, she tried to find the words. "He seems to be everywhere I go. I half expected to see him here tonight."

"Is he followin' you?"

"No, I'm sure he isn't. Why would he?"

"You're a fine young thing. Why wouldn't he?" Mrs. Athy sat still enough, only her hands moving as she knitted a long scarf. "I mind when Mr. Athy first noticed me. I was more'n twenty and my mother'd given up hope I'd ever marry. Most folks thought me strange for working in the town, instead of staying home, but with m'dad gone we needed the money your sainted mother gave me. Then I started to see Mr. Athy everywhere I went. I couldn't take a step without tripping over him, 'less he was out workin' with his father."

The people of the village, nearly all of whom relied on the fishing fleet, rarely mentioned the sea directly. They seemed to feel it was too dangerous, as if to mention it would be to draw unwanted attention to themselves, attention the sea might repay with death.

"When did he ask you to marry him?" Rietta asked, glad to be off the subject of Sir Nicholas Kirwan.

"He called on my father two days after I first spoke to him. I mind what I said. 'Git off that crate, Robert Athy, and take it away to m'house.' He told me that before that, he wasn't certain I knew his name, for all we'd lived not ten houses apart in the Claddagh all our lives."

"And you were married soon after that."

"An' we were happy 'til he was took seven years later. An' so will you be, by 'n' by."

"I see no sign of it yet, ma'am."

"I do." She smiled like an oracle, remotely and wisely. "This man who you see everywhere—has he met Miss Blanche?"

"He met her first. He bought her candy today." Until she said it, she'd not realized how much that had rankled. "I think he may be using me to become better acquainted with her."

"D'you like the looks of him?"

Rietta smiled faintly. "You don't use subtlety."

"I don't hide in the bush, if that's what you mean."

"He's quite good looking," Rietta admitted, picturing

muscular legs and a straight jaw. "He's only just come home from the war in Europe."

"I ever had an eye to a soldier, for all I married a fisherman. They always look so clean."

"Yes, I suppose he does. He has such clear eyes. And yet . . . I don't know what to think of him."

"Don't be thinkin' hard of him, or of yourself. It's high time you married someone. You're not growing younger."

"I know," Rietta said. No one knew how she longed for a life of her own. "I can't marry yet. Not till Blanche chooses the right man. If I leave first, heaven knows what will become of her. She's not safe without me."

"She had ever a wandering eye, whether for the biggest piece of gingerbread or the prettiest flower. She'd make the whole world wait for her while she picked and then, most likely, she'd turn about and want the one somebody else had taken. You don't get a second chance to pick when it's husbands."

"I don't know if Blanche realizes that. I do hope that one day she'll fall in love, for all my father's views on the subject."

"She's in love, right enough. With her own sweet self."

Rietta shook her head. "I know she seems fickle and even cruel, but I can't help believing that if her heart were touched she would surprise us all. She must have unexpected depths of feeling, if only some man would discover the key."

Mrs. Athy knitted in silence for a moment. "An' were this miracle to be, what comes to you?"

"I've sometimes thought I should make a good wife for a clergyman. Parish work requires tact and courage to reconcile the different parties. Our own Mr. Middleton said that no one could have been more helpful to him during the Curtain War."

Mrs. Athy laughed deep in her throat, until she broke off with a coughing spell. "Quarreling like sea rovers over the color of the curtains in the vestry—fine way for ladies to act."

"Their blood was up. But there was no harm done."

"Thanks to you. Speaking of men, what about Mr. Middleton? He's a fine man, barring the wig."

"I have thought of him. Since Mrs. Middleton passed away, he has seemed lonely at times. Of course, he doesn't care for my father, but that wouldn't signify. Father . . ." But to say more would be disloyal.

"Ah." Mrs. Athy had no such scruples. Even when she'd been a very young maid in his house, timid away from her own people, she'd been insolent toward him. All her loyalty had been toward Mrs. Ferris and her daughters. "Your father'd not care if the Black Spy himself came to claim you."

"Well, a clergyman would be better than that," Rietta said with a smile. "My aunt, I daresay, knows dozens. They seem to swarm about watering places. If I ask her, she'll have me to stay with her at Leamington Spa. Yes, that's a possibility."

"Write her tomorrow, then. As you say, it should be easy to get your father's consent. Is he still seein' that whore what calls herself a lady?"

"Mrs. Vernon isn't that bad," Rietta said. "She's just like Blanche. A little careless, a little apt to spend more than she should."

"That's bad enough. She's buried two husbands; what does she want with a third?" She put down her knitting to rub the golden ring of clasped hands around her wedding finger. "One man is enough for happiness."

"I'm afraid neither Mrs. Vernon nor Blanche believes it. But I do." She came over to shake hands. "I must be going. I shall come again next week. Wish your brother a good voyage."

With her close-fitting bonnet and pelisse, the wind off the water couldn't chill her. Rietta walked at a goodly pace

over the bridge between the Claddagh and the walled city.
No one manned the walls, gleaming silver in the moonlight, but they were still standing in all but a few places
where new roads had been permitted to make a breech. Rietta never returned from her visits over the inlet between
bay and river without realizing how frightened the Norman
settlers must have been of the wild men of the Connaught
hills. History had visited Galway more than once, and each
time it had left its scars.

Though the shutters were up on the shops, there were
still quite a few people on the streets in the lower part of
the town, visiting friends or gathered in groups discussing
the latest news. Caught in her dreams, Rietta saw them as
figures from the past, despite their modern clothes. So
many footsteps had rung over these cobbles, from knights
in armor to fat merchants like her father. She did not want
to live in the past, for there she would have been sold in
marriage long ago without her consent, but it was a pleasant place to visit.

As she left the noise of happy people behind her, the
shades of the past gathered closer, some pleasant, others
not so kindly. The gleam of moonlight on a marriage stone,
a plaque marking the union of two families, reminded her
that even dynastic marriages could be successful. A dark
pool of rainwater, looking black under the shifting lamplight, seemed to reflect the image of the ferocious O'Fla-
hertys besieging the city. She hurried past a pub haunted
by the executioner of Charles the First even as she scoffed
at herself for the quickening of her pulse.

She paused on the edge of Eyre Square to catch her
breath after the walk up the steep street from the river. A
grand house at the edge of the common was ablaze with
lights. Faint music spilled out into the street.

The breeze wasn't so strong here and she opened three
buttons on her pelisse to cool down. A bird, disturbed by
the lights, rustled in the nearest tree, chirping softly as a

lullaby. Rietta listened, smiling, glad to have this moment alone.

"Good evening, Miss Ferris."

She knew who it was before she turned, but hearing Nicholas Kirwan's voice out of the night startled her far more than she could explain. "In the name of heaven, sir, what are you doing?"

Six

"Have you nothing better to do with yourself?" Rage made her voice tight. "You have some home somewhere, do you not? Go there and find yourself employment! Dogging young women's footsteps is not an profession that recommends itself."

"I'm sorry I startled you," Nicholas said, answering the feeling behind her words, though her dismissive tone raised his hackles. He won over his natural urge to throw her words in her teeth. "You were lost in thought."

"Yes, sir, I was. Being so contemplative, I resent having persons spring out at me in the night."

"I hardly sprang at you, Miss Ferris. It was more of a pounce."

Her hands clenched. "I will not be pounced upon like a plump mouse at the mercy of the cat."

In her closely buttoned brownish-gray pelisse, she looked like a particularly delicious creature. Nick wouldn't have blamed any tomcat for choosing to carry her off in order to enjoy toying with her in private.

"I dined with your father this evening."

"I'm aware of it." Her tone had cooled, yet her stance

was still stiff, her chin still raised. She looked past him as though he were not there.

"He said you often return home late from one of your evenings out. A woman shouldn't traverse the streets alone—not at night."

"It was kindly thought of," she said, but not with any sincerity. "I have never before now been troubled in any way."

Her meaning was plain. Nick smiled at her and knew he puzzled her by his agreeableness. "Nevertheless, I will walk with you as far as your door."

"I repeat, sir, that I do not require your assistance. Good evening."

"You can't stop me from walking behind you, Miss Ferris."

She ignored him magnificently. Her posture was rigid as she walked away. Her boots struck the pavement with sharp raps. He'd seen less uprightness from the Household Guards on parade. Only when he began to whistle a martial tune did her steps falter, but she caught herself at once. She gave him a glance over her shoulder that should have blasted him to bits, but he only grinned impudently. It occurred to him that he was enjoying himself, which he supposed was rather low of him. But watching her try to comprehend what he was doing entertained him more than anything else he'd known for years.

She stopped at the corner and rounded on him. "Thank you for your assistance, Sir Nicholas, but I am quite capable of walking home alone."

"It isn't proper."

"It's a good deal more proper than you following me about the streets. Now, if you'd be good enough to go. . . ."

"Whenever you're ready."

She sighed gustily. "You are the most impossible man."

He bowed. "Thank you."

"From the bottom of my heart, I pity the woman who marries you."

"But self-pity is so unappealing."

"Then I shall start at once to feel sorry for myself." Her retort was immediate. Only after a moment did she realize what he had meant. "You're mad."

"Not yet. Miss Ferris!"

Saying her name, he came quickly around to stop her from going any farther. She showed no fear, standing her ground as he came near. Then Nick understood her. She did not stand rigidly or look fierce because she disliked him. Quite the opposite. He'd lay odds that she'd been thinking of him half the day. Had he, all unknowingly, chosen the right way to go to work on her?

Nick put his hand on her shoulder and felt an unmistakable quiver run through her body. "You have no right to touch me," she said, but there was the least touch of uncertainty in her voice.

"Madmen take no notice of such things."

"You said you weren't mad."

"I am now."

His whisper touched her lips before his mouth. Rietta had no idea of his intention before he came so near. Not even Mr. Landers had gone so far as to kiss her anywhere, despite his perfect counterfeit of attraction.

Ordinarily, she would have thrown off Sir Nicholas's hand at once, but somehow it had moved to her throat, compelling her to lift her head at just the right angle. The touch of his fingers on the sensitive skin tickled slightly but it warmed her. She found it strangely exciting.

Then he kissed her, slowly. She told herself she would stand like a martyr, without giving way to undignified struggling. In a moment, he would surely stop, abashed and embarrassed by his presumption.

He did not.

He caressed her with his lips, moving them across hers,

awakening them to a new world of feeling. But the effect of his kiss was not on the surface of her mouth alone. It seemed to move inside her, filling her with the taste of the wine he'd drunk and the subtle fragrance of his skin. Trembling, she unthinkingly closed her eyes to block out everything but these physical sensations.

His arm went around her waist, pulling her tightly against his shockingly hard body. Her eyes flew open as she tossed her head back. She looked into his face and saw there the reflection of her own surprise.

She also saw that her hands had somehow crept to the strong shoulders beneath his coat and were clutching his shirtfront.

"My word!" she exclaimed and tried to push free. He was slow to respond to her demand, keeping his hold upon her.

"My God," he said as one stunned. "Rietta."

She read in his eyes and in the tightening of his arm that he intended to kiss her again. This did not horrify her nearly as much as it should have done. Appalled by her own lack of restraint, she made a great effort and set herself free.

"No, not again."

"Why not?"

"I don't like it."

"Didn't you?" His unhurried walk toward her, the way he reached out to run his hands up her arms, told her how utterly she'd given herself away.

"You'll never kiss me again, Sir Nicholas, that I promise you.

"Of course I will. When we are married, I will kiss you every day." His smile seemed to make a promise. "Definitely."

"Married? To me? You *are* insane. You've only met me twice."

"Four times."

"All right, then, four times. You can't wish to marry me."

"Not with enthusiasm. Not until now."

Rietta did not take the time to puzzle out his cryptic utterances. "You don't even like me."

He took her hand. She snatched it away and he laughed. "My dear Rietta, I grow more interested in you by the hour. Now be a good girl and permit me to give you my arm as far as your door."

"You are completely insufferable. If I were not convinced that you are also insane I should complain about you to the magistrate. As 'tis, no doubt you will soon be locked up and cease to trouble me." Followed by his laughter, she hurried up the street, knowing he was behind her but caring for nothing except the safety of her own room.

She didn't look behind her even as she dashed up the front steps. With shaking hands, she fumbled for her latchkey in the depths of her reticule and forced it into the lock. She heard his step—different from other men's—behind her and tried to hurry. His hand, warm and firm, came down over hers as he helped her turn the key.

"Rietta," he said in her ear. He was so close she could feel the heat of him all down her back. He said her name again and his voice was like a whisper she'd heard in a dream.

The door opened and she entered thankfully. When she tried to close it in his face, he held it open effortlessly. "You go too far," she said. "Let go, or I summon my father."

"I suppose I do exceed good taste when I want something very badly. It's a family trait."

"Master it," she advised, pushing harder.

He grunted but held the door. "I'll be bringing my mother to meet you."

"Save the poor lady the journey. I won't see you ever

again. As for your mad idea of marriage . . ." His hand slipped a little on the smooth-painted surface. Stepping back, she let the door swing toward her. He stumbled as the resistance gave way. Taking advantage of his lack of balance, Rietta slammed the door. "Forget it."

She heard him laugh and knew he stood outside with his hands flat against the door. "First round to you."

Rietta didn't answer him. She didn't want him to know that she hadn't run immediately upstairs. She didn't want him to know that she brushed her fingertips lightly over the wooden surface, just where she surmised his hands were. Madman or not, like it or not, Nick Kirwan was the first man who'd ever kissed her. The feelings he'd awakened would not soon be forced back into slumber. But she would triumph over them, she vowed.

After she judged enough time had passed, she pushed aside the narrow curtain and peeped through the sidelight. He'd gone down into the street. He stood there, gazing up at the house, his coat thrust back by his hands resting on his narrow hips. He seemed to be looking at each window in turn as though waiting for some signal. Had he planned to meet Blanche?

Then, as if informed by some unearthly power, he looked straight into her eyes. She saw the insufferable grin break out on his face and let the curtain fall, disgusted by her own curiosity.

Seizing the chamberstick that waited on the hall table, she hiked her skirt and trotted briskly up the stairs. A sliver of light still showed under her sister's door. Rietta's curiosity drove her to knock.

"Who's there?" Blanche called, her voice heavy.

"It's me." Rietta turned the handle and entered.

"Oh." Looking like a contented cat among her pillows, Blanche put her *Ladies' Magazine* on the bedside table. "How are your peasants?"

Rietta didn't even bother to sigh at her sister's incorrigible attitude. "It's the upper classes that trouble me."

"Has a renegade earl been making improper advances? What has he offered? A thousand pounds and a diamond necklace?"

"May I stay here for a few minutes? I don't want him to know which room is mine and he will if I take a candle in."

"Who? What are you talking about? Why are you looking out my window?" She threw aside the blue silken coverlet and crossed to Rietta's side. Craning her neck to see past her sister's shoulder, she followed Rietta's gaze. "I don't see anyone."

"He must have gone away."

"Who? If you don't tell me, I shall scream."

"Sir Nicholas."

"Sir Nicholas? Kirwan?"

"Yes. Is the town so full of men by that name?"

"Sir Nicholas was down in the street just now?" Blanche laughed. "You've nothing to fear, Rietta. I don't think he's swept away by your beauty."

"Is he so enamored of yours?" It was to be expected, and yet Rietta found the fact no less depressing. Then she remembered so vividly the touch and taste of Sir Nicholas's mouth upon hers. He had not, so far as she knew, kissed Blanche. She put her fingertips lightly to her lips.

Blanche tossed back her hair, preening. "He could hardly take his eyes from my face during dinner. I noticed, too, that he was more than a little short with Mr. Mochrie when he started paying court to me. Sir Nicholas didn't seem to like that very much, for all they're such old friends."

"You played them off one another, no doubt."

Blanche smiled, a gleeful goddess. "A man values a thing more if he thinks someone else wants it, too."

Though every natural feeling revolted at the idea of asking Blanche's advice, which was sure to be selfish, single-minded, and shocking, Rietta could think of no one more qualified to advise her.

"Blanche, what makes a man fall in love?"

Her sister ran her fingers through the fall of her honey hair. "Surely that's obvious to anyone with eyes. Are you thinking of finding a husband? It's about time. This nonsensical idea of Father's! Nobody cares how it affects me. I could have been married half a dozen times by now, if only he'd been reasonable."

"Hardly that," Rietta pointed out.

Blanche shrugged. "You know what I mean. Father's easy enough to manage on all points but this silly curse idea. He was explaining it to Sir Nicholas this evening and I was ready to sink through the floor. He sounded absolutely backward, like a rustic from the Islands."

"Father was telling Sir Nicholas? How did that subject arise?"

"I don't know. I think Sir Nicholas asked about Father's reasons for his silly rule about your marrying first."

But how, Rietta wondered, did he know enough to ask?

She saw that Blanche looked at her with an appraising glint in her clear eyes. "What is it?"

"If you are serious about finding a man, why not let me help you? A fresh coiffure, a little lip rouge, and a change of ribbons and you'd be much, much more alluring than you are at present."

"That's very generous, but I only asked one question. Purely rhetorical."

"Well, you might think about me instead of yourself. Do you think I like living with Father when I might have a nice, indulgent husband?"

"Blanche, are you in love with any of these men?"

"In love?" She tossed her blond head again. "I don't intend to fall in love with my husband. What a maudlin notion, and so very underbred."

"Our father is a merchant, Blanche, not the Duke of Killarney."

"A woman takes on the rank of her husband. Just offer me the chance and everyone will forget my lowly origins."

"What new bee has flown into your bonnet?"

Blanche sniffed regally. "I was just reading in that magazine about the Gunning sisters. They were Irish, with nothing to recommend them but their faces, and one of them married a duke. What's been done once can be done again."

"Napoleon failed to conquer England but you're going to?"

"Why not?"

"Go to bed, Blanche."

She waited until her sister had swung her little feet under the sheet, then Rietta pulled the covers up to lie snugly over Blanche. She bent and kissed the smooth white brow. "No more reading. Quiet your thoughts. Sleep well."

"You too, Rietta."

She followed her own advice but lay awake in her bed for a long time. She, who had never aspired higher than a stammering proposal from some clergyman had suddenly a beau of a higher rank than her own. Though she still could not suppose Sir Nicholas to be serious—in fact, she would have suspected that he might have had more wine with dinner than was wise if she had not known the quality of her father's refreshments.

Yet he'd promised to bring his mother to meet her, which argued a fair level of seriousness. What if he did mean it? Could she be so far infected with his insanity to even consider such an unequal match? It would be difficult enough with love on both sides, but all but impossible without it. No. At least with her thus far mythical clergyman, she could respect her husband. But what good did she know of Sir Nicholas?

Then she thought about how tightly he'd held her as his kiss possessed her. A cold shiver, both frightening and delightful, passed through her. She hugged herself, rubbing her hands on her upper arms. Letting her head fall back upon the pillow, she concentrated on that moment, which had seemed to last only one hurried second at the time, but which went on and on in her memory.

Nick rode home in the morning, a song on his lips despite his headache. Smoky rooms in staging inns never did agree with him. He'd hoped his travels were over, but with a woman to be wooed and won he foresaw more nights in Galway. He'd have to find better lodgings. Despite a bad night's sleep and the lingering effects of Mr. Ferris's cheap wine, Nick felt optimism swelling in his heart.

That kiss.

He'd gone to town as an experiment, to take a second look at Miss Rietta Ferris. He never meant to commit himself for any course of action, positive or negative. A mere reconnaissance, as he'd told David. If he'd learned nothing else in the army, he'd learned that previous knowledge of terrain and strength of the opposition could mean the difference between victory and defeat.

What had prompted him to kiss her? Even in the clear light of morning, Nick couldn't say for certain. A desire for mastery? An urge to make some return for her hard words? Overwhelming curiosity? A mixture of the three, in all likelihood.

He'd been ready with an apology if she had tried to slap him as he admittedly deserved. There had also been a compliment on the end of his tongue if she had been merely offended. The only reaction he'd not been prepared for had been the one she'd given him. Her response, sweet and fervid, had given him a completely unstudied craving to have more of her.

Nick didn't blame Rietta for running. She must have

been frightened by his bold escalation of their flirtation. She couldn't have known he was going to kiss her, for he hadn't known it himself. Then to give herself away so completely . . .

His body tightened as he remembered the brush of her hands over his shirtfront as she'd reached for him. Her slightly too full lips, pink as newly opened roses, had parted on a relinquishing sigh, but he'd had just enough sense left not to take advantage of her vulnerability. Nick couldn't help holding her so close; the instinct had been too powerful to deny.

Nick realized that Stamps had slowed to a dawdle. "Get up there," he said, urging the horse on. If the big shoulders could have shrugged they would have. "Yes, I know I'm woolgathering, but you needn't. Get on."

He'd given no thought to his wedding bed, not being certain he'd take on David's proposition. In the back of his mind had been some notion of a bedding based on a mutual understanding of their respective roles. Neither of them need make more of a fuss over the business than necessary. He had vaguely imagined that he would satisfy his wife, less through love than because of his pride in his abilities. His own pleasure would take care of itself. Let her be willing and he'd ask no more.

But now Nick began to feel a certain sense of anticipation. If he could rouse Rietta's passions, their marriage would be far easier. Everyone knew married couples lost interest in each other soon enough, but for those first heady months, passion would work like an ocean wave, smoothing away the rough edges and the jagged sticking points.

Rietta Ferris had passion enough; he'd swear to it. Once he had roused it, all other obstacles would be cleared. He trusted her for that. She was the sort of woman who defined an objective and headed toward it, allowing no other considerations to stand in her way. He'd known many men like that. Such people made excellent officers; he wondered whether it was a comfortable quality in a wife.

Pondering this point, he came over a rise and saw a man riding a white cob coming toward him. At first Nick's attention was focused on the horse, but as the man came nearer, Nick recognized him. "Arthur Daltrey, isn't it?"

"Yes?" The man drew rein, looking at Nick from under the brim of his shallow-crowned hat.

Nick was no judge of male beauty so he could not tell why the maidens all went mad for this farmer, but he liked the straight, clear look in his eyes. "I'm Nick Kirwan."

"Thought you might be. Your groom spent half yesterday tellin' me 'bout your horse. Fine, isn't he?"

Stamps obviously did not think the same of the farmer's cob, which could hardly stand still but would back and file while his master was speaking. Plainly determined to show what could be accomplished by a horse of intelligence, Stamps stood so still that he didn't even flick an ear to scare away a persistent fly.

"Everything is well with you?" Nick asked.

"Well enough. We've had too little rain, but then we farmers are never satisfied 'bout the weather."

"It has seemed unreasonably dry since I've come home."

"August," Daltrey said, as though that explained everything.

"Yes. Tell me, how does Badhaven suit you?"

"It's a fine property, indeed. I had my eye on it for several years. Steady there, Bobbs."

"I hope m'father fixed the roof before he sold it to you."

A rueful smile twitched the corner of Daltrey's mouth. "He didn't. Nor did he trouble to mention it, Sir Nicholas at the time. He was a hard man with a bargain, yer father.

It's a wonder t'me he didn't use his brains when he went gamblin' that way."

Nick stiffened. He did not like to hear criticism of his parent from a stranger. Then he recalled that if Amelia had her way, Daltrey would wind up his brother-in-law.

"My father had his faults, Daltrey. But he was my father."

"Indeed, I'd be feeling the same way were it me. Well, I'll be goin' my way, Sir Nicholas. G'day to you."

"And to you."

They rode apart, but Arthur Daltrey turned in his saddle and called, "It's good to be havin' you back. There's much to be done."

"Come to the house one day. I'd be interested in your opinions." Nick waved his riding crop and watched his sister's rumored lover ride away. Daltrey might not be high in rank, but Nick had been impressed despite himself by the man's air of self-sufficiency. Was it owning his own place that gave him the courage to talk freely with a landlord?

He wondered what Amelia saw in him, laughing at himself, for all brothers must wonder the same about their sisters' choices. No doubt when he brought his bride home, neither Emma nor Amelia would be able to see anything at all unusual or intriguing about Rietta.

When he arrived at Greenwood, he found his mother in the garden, in deep conference with the oldest Randolph boy. Nick kissed her cheek beneath the flopping brim of her old hat and acknowledged the boy's instinctive duck of the head.

"Oh, you're back," Lady Kirwan said. "How were your friends, dear?"

"Same as ever, Mother. Roger Hogan is his father's agent now and Ridley Pierce has been taken on as a partner at Mr. Hammond's solicitor's office."

"I always liked Ridley. I hope he outgrew that stammer?" She turned her smile on the boy. "Would you pardon us a moment, George?"

Once he'd drawn off to a respectful distance, Lady Kirwan crooked her finger for her son to bend low. "Did Ridley clear up all your questions about the estate?"

"Yes, Mother." He'd wanted to break it to her gently but there really wasn't a way to do that. "We're in as bad a condition as I feared."

To his surprise, she took the bad news like a trooper. She merely nodded as though his words confirmed what she'd surmised. "Then I shan't feel so bad about digging up the South Lawn."

"Digging up what?"

"The South Lawn," she said, waving her gloved hand.

"Why would you want to do that?"

"For vegetables, of course. Potatoes, parsnips, carrots . . . I'm not sure about beans. Dr. Markaby says they're most nutritious but I really can't make myself care for them."

"Who is Dr. Markaby?" Nick had never heard the name. Their family physician had always been Ridley Pierce's father.

For answer, Lady Kirwan went to the white-painted bench that commanded a delightful view of the South Lawn, stone walls, and the brook beyond. She brought back and put into Nick's hand a limp-boarded book in a particularly bilious shade of green,

DR. MARKABY'S IDEAL SYSTEM FOR TONIC HEALTH

crawled down the spine in florid letters of gold. Nick turned to the title page. Under the sprawling title was another:

A SCHEME TO PROMOTE
PERFECT PHYSICAL SUCCESS ON SIXPENCE

The frontispiece showed an engraving of a rather full-chinned fellow in an antique-style wig. Beneath it flew cupids bearing chastely draped banners declaring Dr. H. Markaby to be the hero of the age and the savior of mankind's collective stomach.

"Mother, what is this?"

"Our London bookseller is a convert to Dr. Markaby's system. He sent this book along with our last order. We haven't—er—paid for them yet."

"We will soon pay all our debts. But what has this book to do with the South Lawn?"

"Well, dearest, if you turn to the first page, you'll see that Dr. Markaby declares that if we all ate vegetables we should improve our health and our finances. So I thought perhaps if we began to grow our own vegetables we could save even more than buying them. While we're waiting, I suppose we could buy what we need. Dr. Markaby thinks a gross each of carrots, parsnips, and cabbage should do for a grown man for at least a month. There are receipts at the back."

"Mother . . ."

"Dr. Markaby says that the gross machine requires no more than a single spoonful of fat per day to maintain the vital grease. It doesn't really matter what kind, though perhaps bacon is best."

"Vital grease," Nick echoed, torn between laughter and disgust.

"You know. What keeps your joints bending?"

"Yes. But what is the 'gross machine'?"

Lady Kirwan's hand fluttered to her mouth. From behind it, she said very softly, "The body, dearest. He means the human body."

"I see. So you propose that we live on vegetables and a spoonful of bacon fat every day?"

"I thought perhaps we could beat up the fat in cakes,

dear. I can't think that Dr. Markaby thinks we should *eat* a spoonful in cold blood. I'm sure I couldn't manage that."

Now Nick did laugh and chuck his mother under the chin. Then he called to the boy. "George, is it?"

"Yessir."

"Here, George," he said, tossing the book over. "Drown it."

"Sir?"

"Toss it in the cistern—no, wait. It'd be indigestible. Throw it on the first fire you pass. And leave the South Lawn as 'tis."

"Yessir!"

"But, Nick . . ." His mother's forehead had relapsed into its usual fretful lines. "I'm sure it's a most beneficial scheme."

"Undoubtedly, Mother. But I'll stick to my beefsteaks and my ham. My health will remain in your capable hands, not those of some quack from London." He raised her hands to his lips, then pressed them against his cheek. "You're cold as the moon. I'm a dreadful son to let you stand so long out in the open. Come inside. I'll ring for some tea."

He insisted she put her feet up on the sofa and covered her with the soft yet heavy Norwich shawl she'd carried in the garden. "I'm sure we can do more," she said, "to save money. I don't believe we waste a very great deal but it does seem to run away rather."

"It has that habit. I've only met two men in my life who felt they had enough money for their needs. One was rich as Dives; the other never had two brass farthings to rub together."

"And you."

"I? You're too partial, Mother."

"No, I mean it. If it weren't for me and the girls, you'd go along quite happily within the straitened means your father left to you. It is we three who cause you to worry over money."

"Nonsense," he said, though in his heart he knew she was right. The income and securities his father hadn't gambled away would have been enough to keep a bachelor in comfort even in a great barracks of a house. It would not stretch to keep four, two of whom required dowries.

"Mother," he began, then had to wait, impatiently, while the maid brought in the tea and set it out. As soon as the door closed again, he said, "Mother, I've met someone."

"A young lady?" She looked at him brightly and said, "I thought you might have. It's the one you spoke of. Her carriage had broken down. Is it the younger daughter?"

"No, the elder."

"I don't think you mentioned her."

"I probably didn't."

"The younger one was very pretty, or so you said."

"Yes, Blanche is the most beautiful girl I think that I've ever seen. But Rietta . . ." He was aware of how closely his mother watched him and so let a hint of a smile show.

"Rietta? How unusual. I don't think I've heard that name in quite twenty years. I wanted to name Emma that, but your father would call her after an aunt. Awful woman. Used to smoke fat black cigars to keep the moths away from her draperies. Had a monkey, too."

"You'd think that would have been harder on the drapes than the moths. Anyway, Mother, Rietta is taller than Blanche and has red hair, not blond. Maybe she isn't quite as striking . . ."

"Isn't she, Nick? Then why are you interested in her? It isn't her money, is it?"

Seven

She answered her own question before he had time to do more than look astonished. "No, of course it isn't," Lady Kirwan said. "Forgive me for even saying such a thing. It's just that I've been so worried about money that I seem to see its shadow everywhere."

Nick poured her a little more tea. "It's troublesome, Mother, but we'll manage to support life without drastic measures. You're to give me a list of all the things you've sold, and to whom, so I may retrieve them."

"They weren't entailed things, Nick. They were either what I brought with me when I married your father, or things he'd given me."

"Nevertheless . . ."

Lady Kirwan stirred her cup. "I shouldn't want any of my children to marry for money. That's why I was married."

"You married Father for his money? Grandfather Darcy must have been mad. Or blind."

"No, dear. Your father married me for *my* money. Oh, don't look so shocked. Thirty years ago, a man was expected to make a prudent match. I'm not saying he wouldn't have done it if I hadn't been pretty . . . I was pretty, you know. Something in Amelia's style, if not quite so vivacious."

"I've seen your portrait."

She pursed her lips as though biting a gooseberry. "I never liked that one. I may have been plump, but I was never moon-faced!" She smiled when he did and then sighed. "We were all a little in love with Benjamin. He had such an air, such address, and he dressed exceedingly well. I remember one suit of spangled green velvet . . . I daresay you'd think it hideous, but we admired him very much."

"I'm glad I didn't live then," Nick said, smoothing the sleeve of his well-cut but otherwise unremarkable blue coat.

"You'd look handsome no matter what you wore. You've better shoulders than your father; his coats were always padded. Of course, I didn't know that then. It was quite a shock, I can tell you, the first time I saw him in shirtsleeves. By then, however, it was too late." She sipped her tea with a resigned air and asked him to cut some cake for her.

"You've never spoken of your marriage before."

"I suppose while your father was alive, it seemed disloyal. Naturally, I should not speak in this vein to your sisters. Girls have such a romantic dream of life. I know I did. By the time I woke up to the reality, I was already married and you were on the way."

"Surely Father never told you that he married you for money. He couldn't have admitted it."

"Not at first. He seemed so proud of me. I remember the tone of his voice when he introduced me as 'm'wife.'" Lady Kirwan laughed as she tried to imitate her late husband's gruff tones. "He paid me pretty compliments, never came home without some trinket or a bunch of flowers . . . I was the envy of all my friends for the first six months, but the focus of their pity later."

"What changed?" Nick laid his hand over his mother's.

"I'm not certain anything did change. It was simply that Benjamin couldn't keep up a pretense for very long. Sooner or later, the real man had to show his face. In that instance, bills began to pile up and dunning letters began arriving by every post. I'd never lived in debt and didn't really know how to manage under those circumstances. There'd been some delay in my bride portion due to a loss my father had suffered shortly before our marriage. Benjamin began throwing that up to me and eventually told me to my face why he'd married me. By then I had guessed, but hearing it from his own lips . . ."

She paused and seemed to be listening, her eyes half closed, to voices echoing out of the past. "He slammed out of the house and I didn't hear from him for three days. We were never the same after that."

Pulling free, she patted his hand, smiling. "You mustn't think I've been miserable all these years. I had you and then your sisters. He was always kind to me when I was increasing, though he didn't stay home very much after you. Sometimes Benjamin could be marvelously kind, but I was never central to his life after those first heady months."

Nick found it impossible to sit beside her another moment. His agitation required that he go to the window and stand, looking out, his back to his mother. "What of my sisters? What life do you see for them?"

"My one consolation," she said with great good humor, "in our reduced circumstances is that they need not fear being married for any reason beyond that of love. So long as they marry within their own sphere, my heart will never be troubled for them. My only worry is that you will act imprudently."

"Never fear, Mother. I shan't do that."

"This young woman—this Rietta—she is of good character?"

"She possesses great strength of character."

"Oh, dear."

"You mistake me. She isn't overbearing, though I believe she has yet to learn to compromise."

"She doesn't sound like the woman for you, my dear son. If you have learned to compromise, it is news to me."

"Yet if I were in love . . ." He returned to the table.

"Well, the Bible teaches us that with love, all things are possible. I don't know how far one can push that promise, however. You're not in love with Rietta Ferris, I take it?"

"Give me time, Mother. I only met the lady three days ago. I'll tell you plainly, though. I've never seen another woman who I would so readily make mine."

Lady Kirwan's face lit up as she passed Nick the macaroons. "I pray every night that you'll bring your bride to Greenwood while I am still here to see her."

"Come to Galway, Mother. You'll see her. I promised her that you'd soon call upon her."

"I suppose I must, then. It would never do to make a liar out of you."

If Lady Kirwan was surprised to find herself being driven into Galway before two days had passed, she concealed it admirably. It was otherwise with Amelia. "I really don't see why we must rush into an acquaintance with this young woman and her family."

"Because Nicholas wishes it, dear. I daresay we shall find her quite charming."

"I don't trust Nick's taste, Mother. She's probably dreadfully vulgar. After all, he's been in the army so long he's probably forgotten what a nice girl is like."

"Amelia!"

She slumped against the faded cushions in a most unladylike way. "He didn't even ask me if I wanted to go. Just ordered me into the carriage. Emma didn't have to go. It isn't as though I hadn't made plans for today."

"Mr. Daltrey will take no harm through waiting for you."

"I don't know what you mean. What, pray, has Mr. Daltrey to do with my plans for the afternoon?" Amelia asked, giving her mother a very blank look before turning her head to look out of the window. "I do hope we have some time to go to the shops. Emma needed to match some embroidery floss."

"We won't be buying anything today. Emma will have to learn to do plain sewing, not embroidery."

"It can do no harm to look."

"Yes, it can. We always buy some little thing that winds up costing a fortune, one way or another. We cannot afford such tricks now. Nicholas explained that we must track every farthing, not letting even one be wasted."

"Yes, Mother," Amelia said, repressed for the moment.

Nick swung down from Stamps's back to open the carriage door for them, waving to Barry to stay on the box. He felt unaccustomedly nervous. Though Mr. Ferris had made it plain that they would be welcome, Nick couldn't be sure of Rietta's reaction. Her father had expressed doubts about springing Lady Kirwan upon Rietta. She was a highhanded girl and might be rude to his mother. Shooting his cuffs, he told himself he'd know how to handle any such behavior.

"How do you do?" Rietta said, crossing the room to them, her smile warm and welcoming. She held out both hands, giving one to Lady Kirwan and one to Amelia. For Nick, she had a slight curtsey and a nod. Her eyes did not meet his for more than an instant.

"Lady Kirwan, may I present my sister, Blanche."

Blanche's curtsey was more graceful than her sister's

but her smile lacked Rietta's warmth. Nor did she speak clearly, muttering her greeting like a sulky schoolgirl.

Lady Kirwan seated herself on the settee at Rietta's invitation. Nick's resolution to keep Rietta within bounds evaporated, for it was plainly not needed. She was the gracious hostess to the life, inquiring into Lady Kirwan's interests. They found in two words that their shared passion was gardening.

"Living in town, of course, I haven't the scope to indulge in the garden of my dreams. But I know just how I should arrange things if I had the opportunity."

"Everything good must start with a dream," Lady Kirwan said. "You must tell me all about your garden."

"Oh, I'm afraid I change it all the time. It is my favorite thing to think of just before I go to sleep."

"I plan *my* garden just before I go to sleep myself. It's so soothing."

"Yes," Rietta said. Nick could tell now that her smile when they first arrived had been forced and false. The way she looked at his mother at this moment was different, gentle and true. "And it's much easier to reshape a bed or a path in ones' thoughts than in reality."

"Especially when one has only a single lad to help. Although I must say George Randolph listens much more attentively than his father ever did. Will Randolph had a head as hard as a stone. He'd never try anything new unless I wore him down."

"How exhausting!" She put her hands together in a suppliant's prayer. "One day, Lady Kirwan, perhaps you would be so kind to look over the little plans I have drawn. Purely fantastic, of course, but I so like things to be precise. The advice of someone with experience would be invaluable."

"I should be more than happy," said Lady Kirwan, looking up to meet Nick's eyes. He saw nothing but approval there. "Have you them here now?"

"They are in the library, but I don't like to impose upon you."

"Nonsense, my dear child. Let me see them."

Rietta excused herself. Nick sauntered to the door a moment after she went through it. With a glance, he saw that Amelia was being heartily bored by Blanche who had achieved some animation by a recital of all her social triumphs. His mother, catching his eye, gave him an encouraging nod that sent him through the doorway after Rietta.

He followed the sound of her voice. "No, she's not 'high in the instep' at all, Father. She's a very pleasantly spoken woman and I quite like the looks of her daughter. She looks as though she knows what it is to be a friend."

"All the same, I'll stay safe in here. I don't mind Sir Nick; he's a likely lad with a friendly gleam in his eye. But I'll have no dealings with titled ladies. They look down their noses at men like me."

At least, Nick thought in relief, he'd not suffered the usual fate of eavesdroppers. But then, he already knew Mr. Ferris liked him. It was Rietta's sentiments that were in doubt. It had been unexpectedly hard to meet her eyes. The way she contrived never to look at him directly had told him that their kiss still lay between them. He wondered how many times she'd found herself reliving that moment. He'd lost count of the number of times it had enlivened his thoughts.

"Very well, though I wish you would change your mind," Rietta said, and Nick peered around the doorframe to watch her kiss her father's cheek. Surely not the behavior of a shrew. . . .

"I've left Lady Kirwan and Miss Amelia with Blanche. It's important they should come to know her well, don't you think?"

"Eh? Whyfore? 'Tisn't she they've come to see."

"No, but as you will not come out . . ."

"Don't be so silly, child. 'Tis you Sir Nick has his eye on this time."

"So he says, but I do not believe it." She turned the bracelet on her wrist, keeping her eyes on that as she tried to express her feelings. "I cannot trust a man who, having seen Blanche, claims to prefer me. Such a man cannot exist. She is so very beautiful."

"So she is," Mr. Ferris said, sighing. Then he rallied. "Yet you are not so ill-favored that no man would look on you. Many men prefer a nice, mature woman to a heedless girl."

Nick thought that that could have been more felicitously phrased. Rietta was no matron, staid and soft, but a creature of passions and strong will.

"Besides which," Mr. Ferris added, laughing in his throat, "can you picture our Blanche knowing the first thing about being the wife of a landowner? You'd take to it like a duck takes to living in a pond. Have it all understood in a fortnight."

"As the point will not arise, Father, I don't think we need discuss it any further." She stirred the papers on Mr. Ferris's desk. "Did you answer the letter from Cathcart and Dean?"

"I read it over. It seems a capital notion on the face of it."

"Dig deeper," she said with a dry laugh. "It's their notion but your capital. I don't believe they'll find vast quantities of coal beneath the northern ice cap, and the cost of outfitting a research vessel is too great a burden for our present resources."

"You are too cautious, Rietta. Not every businessman is a hurly-burly fly-by-night sort of fellow. Take this gent here," he urged, stirring among his papers. "He's made a solid study of the existence of leprechauns and wants me to help back his work for the honor of Ireland. Now I can't refuse an appeal like that! Think of what it would mean to Ireland."

"It seems to me that the credit of our country abroad is quite low enough without dragging the wee people into it," Rietta said.

"Wist!" Mr. Ferris looked about his chair carefully, especially scrutinizing the corners and the mirrors. "It's terribly chancy to talk so with them so fresh from their winter rests."

"Yes, Father," Rietta said, her smile indulgent. "I'll tell Arabella to leave a cup of milk by the fire tonight for them."

Nick shrank back as she came out again into the hall. This time, however, he was careful not to startle her when he made his presence known. Nevertheless, it was only by a sudden clutch that she kept hold of the portfolio of papers in her hand. "Sir Nicholas! I thought you were still in the drawing room."

"My mother sent me after you."

"Did she? Why?"

"You were away so long."

"Pray assure her I rarely get lost in my own home."

"You don't? Then tell me—what's this room?" Nick asked, crossing behind her to open a door on the other side from the library.

"The dining room, as you well know since you have dined here recently," she said, peering past him perhaps to see what he found so interesting.

"Show me." He took her hand and drew her inside. He felt her unwillingness yet she followed him into the dim, stuffy room. The air was heavy with stale candle smoke through which the silver goblets and ewer on the sideboard gleamed as though with obscured moonlight. The room itself seemed to sleep, waiting for the clock to strike the dining hour when it might wake for a brief moment of conviviality before falling again into another twenty-four hours of slumber. It was not what Nick would have chosen for his proposal, given the wide world to choose from, yet it would serve.

"Sir Nicholas, I must go back. Your mother is waiting."

"Stay with me a moment and we'll go back together. She would rather wait to hear good news than none."

"What good news?" She had a sweet frown, three vertical lines between her straight brows. He knew already that this was her doubtful look.

"The best news. A marriage between two people she thinks well of. I can tell she admires you already." He stepped a little away from her so that he might read all of her.

Her puzzled frown increased. "You have hinted at this before; it is a game I do not like."

"No game. I will marry no one but you."

"Then you marry no one." She paced one step up and back, turning about in her agitation. She seemed to struggle to find enough breath to speak. "I–I don't know why you should make such a fool of me. These protestations do not move me because I do not believe them. Shall a man marry a woman whom he never saw in his born days less than a week since?"

"Yes, it happens all the time."

"Where does it? Arabia? China? The moon? For you are moon-mad if anybody ever was."

"I can't say about the moon. But in the other places, you would have been married long ago to a man you'd never seen before your wedding day."

"And you'd have half a hundred concubines. Well, go. They're waiting for you."

Nick laughed. "I've never heard a woman say that word before."

"What? Concubines? Solomon had quite a few, according to the Bible. And, by the way, Jacob labored seven years before he got a wife. Not a few days."

"As I recall, Jacob married the wrong sister. I won't have that wished upon me, even by you."

"Then go to Blanche and make your proposal. You have a title and she has a wish to be Lady Kirwan. It seems you are made for one another."

"Stop throwing Blanche at me, if you please. I confess I was much taken with her looks when first we met. She is a painter's dream and if I had a portrait of her I'd hang her in a place of pride."

"As I thought—" Rietta began, but Nick interrupted her.

"But paintings don't need to talk to be pleasant in the home, and women must do so. The first call I made at this house cured me of whatever infatuation I felt for her."

"You are in the minority, sir. My sister is very generally admired, even by those who know her well."

"For some reason, Rietta, you are more proud of Blanche's looks than of your own. Yet yours are nothing to be despised because they have a pleasant soul behind them. Your sister is a painted puppet whose looks have spoiled her humor. Let other men sit at her feet and play the dog, wagging their tails when she smiles and whimpering when she frowns. I won't."

She looked at him with her head slanted slightly to one side, the way a painter judges his own canvas. "No. I can see that. I apologize, Sir Nicholas, for thinking you were only attempting to flatter me to reach Blanche. Some other man tried this ploy once and . . . and hurt me rather when the truth was exposed."

The tinge of color increased in her cheeks at this admission. "You are wrong," she continued, blushing stronger still. "My soul is not pleasant. It is dark and angry. Sometimes I grow so filled with darkness that I must . . ." She tossed her head, lightening her too-somber mood. "Have you not heard that I am the most shrewish of women? That my father lives under the cat's foot? That I am a monster of unkindness toward my sweet younger sister?"

"Rietta . . . ," he said with too much warm understanding for her peace of mind. She pulled loose the hand that he'd somehow taken in possession.

"But these are not things with which to trouble you, sir. You have done me the honor, unmistakably, of proposing that you and I marry. I thank you from the depths of my heart but I must refuse you." She dipped a simple, respectful curtsey and started to leave.

He stepped between her and the door. His eyes were searching. "Tell me why not. I'm a clever man and can clear away many impediments."

Rietta laughed a little at his boast, countered by his anxious eyes. She had never had a proposal of marriage before. It left her feeling flustered and much too warm about the cheeks. She wanted to be certain that she did not hurt her hurried lover's feelings but she felt somehow that nothing less than the truth would do for Nick.

"I do not know you well enough, nor, were we the oldest of friends, I could still never be parted from my father and my sister. They need me. For the rest . . ." Rietta hesitated. If it was hard to put feelings into words, it was a thousand times harder to express a lack of emotion. English at times was an emotionally understaffed language. But not even lilting Irish had anything softer than a blunt, "You do not love me, Sir Nicholas."

She saw him struggle with the lie like a man with a fish bone in his throat. She saved him from it by saying, "Nor do I love you. Such a marriage—whatever happens in Arabia or China—could never flourish here."

She left him. Only she knew that to keep him from a lie, she'd told one herself. Could love happen in mere days? Rietta scoffed at the notion. She'd fallen for him in the first hour of their meeting.

Eight

Nick hadn't ridden a hundred yards from the Ferris's door before knowing that he had every reason to be grateful to Rietta for her no. He must have been mad to propose marriage to her, a woman who was all but a stranger. What had prompted so rash an act? If she'd accepted him, he would have found himself in a most insupportable position.

Riding on, with a glance back to be sure the carriage had successfully passed a brewery wagon, Nick asked himself why he'd chosen that moment to propose. He found the answer in the conversation he'd overheard her having with her father. His chivalry had been roused by the calm acceptance in her voice when she'd claimed that no man could love her having seen Blanche.

When Mr. Ferris had seconded that comment without a word of comfort, Nick had gone from chivalry to exasperation. How dare the man believe his daughter would only have value to a man so far as she was useful? Even should Rietta's temper prove as volatile as he'd been told, she had many qualities beyond those of a glorified steward. She had been sweetness itself to his mother and sister. She checked or smiled away Blanche's childish pouts and yawns. When the maidservant had entered with refreshments, she'd been kind while at the same time plainly expecting good service, unlike Blanche who had been both overfamiliar and contemptuous.

And when he'd kissed Rietta in the night . . . But such a memory had no place in his thoughts. There, too, he'd allowed a momentary impulse to overthrow his good sense. Nick sighed as he wondered if Rietta's answer today would have been different if he'd pulled her into his arms before he'd asked. It was a method that recommended itself on many levels. Then he remembered. He would never ask again because he was so very happy she'd said no.

They stopped at an inn halfway home to water the horses and give the ladies a chance to descend for a walk. "The carriage needs new cushions, Mother," Nick said, helping her step down. He noticed that she moved more stiffly than she had in the morning and regretted carrying her so far for so little result.

"They'll do for another year or two. Amelia, pray see if they have tea."

"Yes, Mother," Amelia said, then flashed an unladylike grin. "But I expect you to tell me what you said to Nick when I come back."

"If I wanted you to know, dearest, I would not send you on a bootless errand. Run along." To Nick, Lady Kirwan said, "Let me sit in the sunshine on that bench."

When she was settled on the rustic wooden seat, she lifted her face to the sun. Nick saw with a pang that the bright light showed so many more lines there than when he'd gone away. He picked up one of her hands and held it against his cheek a moment.

"She refused you?" Lady Kirwan asked softly.

"She did. It's all for the best."

"Why is it?"

Nick drew a heavy breath. "I'd not ask a woman to wed with me if she finds she cannot love me."

"She said she did not love you?"

"She refused me," Nick said, feeling that as it was answer enough for him, it ought to suffice for his mother.

"But she did not say so."

"Yes," he said, only realizing now that it had hurt him, even as he'd not felt the pain of a wound he'd once received until he'd seen the blood pouring from his side. "Yes, it was almost the last thing she did say to me. 'Nor do I love you,' she said."

"Had you told her that you didn't love her? 'Nor do I love you' sounds like an agreement to me. You weren't such a fool, my son?"

"I didn't lie to her."

"No, you wouldn't do that. I wonder if she would."

"Lie? I doubt it."

Lady Kirwan sat silently for a moment, her eyes closed against the sunshine. Not until it had gone behind a cloud, cooling the spot where they sat, did she speak. "I am an old woman and no doubt I misunderstand many things that I hear and see. Yet I remember a great deal and most of all I remember how I used to feel."

She tightened her hand around Nick's. "When I sat with Miss Ferris, she spoke to me but she was looking at you. I would swear in church that she loves you. There's a look in a woman's eyes when she gazes on the man she loves that cannot be mistook for any other expression. I swear she wore it when she looked on you."

"Wishful thinking, I'm afraid," Nick said, his whirling thoughts coming to rest on one point. "She refused me."

Amelia came out then, bearing a wooden salver carrying three sweating tankards. "Cider," she said, in answer to their suspicious glances. "It's fresh. The landlord declares his mother makes it."

"One can always trust a man's mother," Lady Kirwan

said, raising her tankard in a pledge and meeting Nick's eyes.

"Oh, it's not fair," Amelia said. "Won't someone tell me what's going on? Nick's not going to offer for that bubble-headed Blanche creature, is he?"

"You didn't like her?" Nick asked in accents of disbelief. "From this day forward you must be a stranger to me, Amelia, if you don't acknowledge her to be the most beautiful and sweetest of ladies."

Amelia looked at him with a tinge of fearfulness, then she saw the wink he threw their mother. "Ah, brother," she said in the throbbing tone of an actress in a French tragedy, "throw me not into the bitter snow merely because I tell you that Blanche is a spoiled, petulant baby."

Nick laughed, too. "But beautiful, you must admit that."

"Oh, yes. A pattern card of perfection and I'm jealous of her dressmaker. But if I thought you were planning to marry her, you wouldn't have to throw me into the snow; I'd leave of my own accord and take Mother and Emma with me."

"You don't think Emma would like her, either?"

"It's hard to tell with Emma. She might, but Blanche wouldn't like anybody who didn't wear trousers."

"Amelia!" Lady Kirwan said, half shocked, half laughing.

The girl looked a trifle embarrassed but added, "It's true. All she did was talk about clothes and conquests. I haven't many of either and want no more than I have, thank you very much."

"I haven't seen all your clothes," Nick said, "but I fancy I've seen your conquest."

"Oh?" The doubtful note came again into his sister's voice though her expression gave nothing away. Nick remembered that she did not know him well enough to predict his attitudes.

"Daltrey's handsome enough to turn any girl's head," Lady Kirwan said.

"Is he?" Amelia said. "I've never noticed his face particularly."

"Come now," Nick said.

She looked him full in the eyes. "If good looks were everything, Nick, you'd be marrying Blanche Ferris instead of Rietta. You looked past the beauty to find the goodness. Why not believe that Arthur's face means little to me beside the goodness of his heart and the intelligence of his mind?"

"I do believe it. I also believe," he said, loath to wipe the dawning smile from her lips but thinking it too cruel to leave her in hopes, "that a marriage with a former tenant would bring you nothing but sorrow."

"So it is to be rank for me? Who, Nick? What prince on which charger shall I choose for my husband? We've no money to dower me and Arthur will take me as I am."

"Hush, children," Lady Kirwan said. "An inn yard is no place to discuss such business. As for you, Amelia, kindly stop bandying young ladies' names in public. If you were a man, Nick would have to call you out for it."

Nick relaxed his shoulders. "I'm sorry, Amelia. Sorry for everything."

"'Tis Father that should be sorry, Nick. It's none of your doing. I'll call Barry from the taproom and we'll be on our way home."

In the carriage, Amelia leaned forward to ask in a low tone what her mother had thought of Miss Ferris.

"There's no need to whisper. Nick cannot hear you." She looked out the window at him, riding so straight and tall, and wondered why men, even the best of them, seemed to thrive on making quite simple things so unnecessarily complicated. "I thought Miss Ferris a most prettily behaved young lady. She will make Nick an excellent bride."

"I agree with you."

"Oh, then I know it's all right," Lady Kirwan said, showing a dimple in a cheek that should have been too thin to display such a thing.

Amelia rolled her eyes. "Anyway, at least he's not being such a ninny as to fall in love with the other one. Though, in justice, I have to say she is pretty, but I think Rietta shows more countenance."

"She has character."

"You only say that because she likes to garden."

"Love of gardening demonstrates that a person has patience and hopefulness and isn't afraid of difficulties. These are excellent character traits."

"Heavens, I shall have to learn to love it myself."

"They'll serve you well in whatever direction your life may take, Amelia. There is great comfort in raising a garden, almost as much as I have found in my children."

Amelia slipped across to sit beside her mother. Taking her hand, she stroked it affectionately. "I can't help loving Arthur, Mother. If you only knew him . . ."

"I should be happy to meet Mr. Daltrey, dearest. Just as I was happy to meet Miss Ferris. But a man may marry in a lower degree than himself. The woman is raised to his position. But when a woman takes a husband of lesser degree, she is degrading herself."

"I know it," Amelia said, her tone resigned. "I do know it. But to judge Arthur merely by his position is to miss his finest qualities. If love of gardening demonstrates nobility of nature, how much more noble must be a man who truly loves to farm?"

Lady Kirwan laughed softly. "Defeated by my own arguments. What a pity you cannot enter the law, my love."

As soon as they arrived at Greenwood, Lady Kirwan guessed there was something wrong. The house servants stood clustered together on the front steps, talking in whispers.

"What is it?" she demanded, throwing open the carriage door.

No one stepped forward until she'd made a second demand. Austin, the children's old nurse, dipped a curtsey, her old knees creaking audibly. "M'lady, it's Miss Emma."

"Emma? What about her? Where is she?"

"I dunno, m'lady. Nobody knows."

"What's wrong, Mother?" Nick said, swinging down from the saddle.

"I don't know." She glanced up at the windows. "I feel . . . Find Emma."

"She left a paper on her bed," piped little Lydy, Barry's niece. "Pinned to her piller."

"I'll go," Amelia said, jumping down. Even hampered by her skirts, she was still as fast as the coltish girl she'd been. She ran up and down again in seconds, though it seemed a long time to Lady Kirwan.

Amelia gave the note to her mother, but without her spectacles the page was a mere blur of blotted ink. She passed it to Nick, saying, "It's not . . . she hasn't done anything . . . ?"

She could hardly breathe while he read the letter. She was dimly aware that Austin rounded on the others, scolding them for their curiosity, ordering tea and whiskey, sending the youngest ones away before they could do more than whisper their conjectures of suicide, while allowing the older servants, members of the family all, to stay.

"It's all right, Mother. She's gone to say good-bye to Robbie Staines. I'll ride over and bring her back."

"Thank heaven," Lady Kirwan murmured, even as she sought her heart with her hand.

"Come in and have some tea, Mother," Amelia said. "Help me, Nick."

Together, they settled her on the sofa. Austin whispered something to him and he nodded. "What is it?" Lady Kirwan called.

"Nothing, Mother. A letter came for me."

"More trouble?"

"More nonsense."

"What did Emma really write, son? Give me my spectacles and the letter."

"I'll tell you. She says she's going away with Robbie, even without money, for she cannot let him go alone. But I'll stop her and bring her back. I promise. I'm not having Robbie Staines as a brother-in-law, even if it is only in America."

Late that evening, Mr. Ferris sat, half strangled by an overelaborate striped cravat and tall-pointed collar, in a drawing room far more lavishly appointed than his own. The walls and draperies were bright green satin, echoed in the cushion beneath him. A riot of half-read books, open boxes of candy minus the choicest morsels, and exotic flowers drooping for lack of water surrounded him. Until he'd blown out a few, the heat from several dozen candles had made him feel quite faint, the hot wax combining with the scents of flowers and her own perfume.

He heard a step outside and straightened up even more. The door opened. The owner of the house came slowly over the threshold, her skirts rustling with silk unseen. "Mr. Ferris," she said, her red lips parting in a smile that showed her tiny white teeth.

"Mrs. Vernon." His own voice fair shook with the pleasure of seeing her, his plump black-haired witch. She allowed him only one kiss on her cheek, which disappointed him. "Mrs. Vernon?"

"Oh, well, there." She kissed him on the mouth with an "mmm" of pleasure. "Now, no more. 'Deed, you hardly deserve that of me."

Sometimes she would play at being injured so that he could pet and pamper her into a more compliant mood, but there was nothing teasing in her glances tonight. She seemed almost sad, as she poked around in a box of chocolates with one finger. She chose one and bit into it, making the same humming sigh she'd given when she'd kissed him.

Mr. Ferris gazed at her adoringly. She was on the short side, perhaps not more than five foot one. The high-waisted fashions did not suit her rather waistless figure, but she wore them with such an air that one did not notice the deficiency. She emphasized a pair of full breasts to the point where they all but spilled over the top of the inadequate lace frill sewn to the front. Once, when she'd had a drop too much to drink, he'd put his head on her warm, soft breast and she'd not minded, stroking his temple with her cool fingers until the carriage reached her door.

Thinking of that evening, Mr. Ferris took Mrs. Vernon's hand and led her to sit beside him on the settee. "What's amiss, love? Servants give notice?"

"Oh, I don't mind that. There's always another maid to be had. I'd like a French one but things have grown so shockingly dear I'm sure I could never afford to pay her salary."

"If you'd only allow me. . . ."

"Now, we've done that and I'm not saying it again. I pay my own way so long as I'm a widowed woman. If I was your wife, it'd be a different tale."

"You know how I want that. It's all I do want. To spoil you." He kissed her hand. "To adore you." He kissed her wrist. "To make you happy." He kissed the bend of her elbow and would have continued higher if she hadn't pushed him away.

"So you say. My late husband—my first—used to say to me, 'If a man can't keep his word, Lucinda, there's only one thing to be done with him. Eschew his company.' He was a fearfully clever clock, my first."

"Now, now, Mrs. Vernon. Don't be hasty. I haven't told you my good news."

"Your lanky daughter's found a husband?"

"As good as wedded."

" 'As good as' is no good at all to the likes of you and me, Mr. Ferris. There's many a slip between the proposal and the wedding trip."

Mr. Ferris laughed at her wit. Mrs. Vernon only looked blank for she never had any idea of being funny and never understood why he sometimes laughed at the things she said.

"But you haven't heard it all. Rietta is certain to marry him. He's handsome and titled."

"Rich?"

"His father made some bad investments, but their land is in good heart."

"Title but no money. You watch yourself, Mr. Ferris, or you'll find him and his whole family hanging on your sleeve, begging for handouts. What Rietta needs is a fellow who'll stand on his own two feet and not come begging to his father-in-law whenever he needs sixpence."

"I doubt he will. Too much pride."

"Nobody's pride ever kept them from being clapped up for debt. He'll come to you quick enough, if I know men." Mrs. Vernon mulled her thoughts over. "And I'll lay you odds Rietta turns out quite the breeder. These spinsters take to making babies like a duck to water. I won't be having my husband providing for a passel of brats."

"Of course not, my love. Once Rietta's marriage portion is paid, they'll receive nothing else—not a penny piece, I swear—until I die."

"Oh, I hope it won't come to that!" Mrs. Vernon turned

her big golden eyes toward her guest and Mr. Ferris fancied he saw a little moisture gather there.

"Naturally, as my daughter, Rietta will receive part of my estate. But any wife I have at that time will of course receive her full rights."

"What a head you have for business, Mr. Ferris. I'm quite in awe."

"Rietta thinks nobody but herself ever understood a ledger. I'm so glad you are more discriminating."

"So tell me more about this gentleman who wants to marry our Rietta."

When he had, Mrs. Vernon said, "My! 'Tis a romance. When do you think the wedding may be?"

"She must accept him first."

"Tsk. My father didn't wait for such a thing with my first, nor did my second wait to ask m'father. The first time, they set it up between them that I was to marry and marry I did. In the second case, we set it up between us that we were to marry and we did it before the cat could lick her ear. I don't like these long, drawn-out affairs. I'd far rather marry in haste than stand about wishing I had."

"I want to marry quickly, too, but what can I do?"

"You say this fellow is handsome and titled? Depend upon it, the girl's already in love with him. _I_ would be. Why does he wait?"

"I don't know. I didn't ask him."

Mrs. Vernon was thinking, so he escaped a scolding for failure. "He's marrying Rietta for the money, of course," she said, following her own thoughts. "So how to bring him to scratch? More money."

"More money? But my sweet witch—"

"Double her portion. Send her with two thousand pounds, a hundred pounds a year for her clothes, and a proper remembrance at your death. If they're married before the end of the month, you'll add an extra fifty quid."

"My love, you can't bribe the gentleman into marriage."

"Of course we can. If he weren't penniless, he never would have made the offer. Such a managing girl, that one. But perhaps he hasn't realized it yet."

With the languid grace that had first attracted him, she rose and went to open the door to let him out. "You should go home and write to him with your improved terms. Send it by the coachman so that he receives it tomorrow. With luck, we'll see their wedding in a week and ours the fortnight after."

Nine

Perhaps it was the sea-coal fire that made the room so insupportable. Or Blanche's innumerable yawns as she paged through a novel, looking for the love scenes. Rietta's own newspaper had been tossed aside. She couldn't seem to rouse any interest in the progress of choosing delegates to the Peace Congress.

Perhaps the tournedos of beef they'd had for dinner had been off. That would explain the unsettled feeling in her middle. "Blanche? Do you feel well?"

"Of course," she said, shrugging. "Though I'm dreadfully sleepy. It's so dull here. I wish our aunt might invite me to come south, where at least there would be assemblies more than once a month."

"At least you cannot complain of having no partners worth standing up with."

"Oh, David Mochrie dances well enough, I allow you, but he spoils my rhythm with all the pretty speeches he makes. I cannot attend to my steps and to what he's telling me at one and the same time. Now, Mr. Joyce only gazes at me so I can dance uninterrupted."

She read a little in her book and sighed wistfully. "Listen to this. Lady Windrush has just permitted the duke to enter her bedroom."

"Blanche?"

"For breakfast," she said, smirking at her sister's folly. Lifting her book, she read aloud. " 'Attired in a costly black lace robe over a silken night rail, she sat before her dressing table mirror while her French maid arranged her hair in long ringlets. With her own diamond-beringed hands, she slid three or four sparkling bracelets onto her slender white wrists.' Wouldn't Father's eyes start if I wore that to breakfast?"

She sighed again, dreaming of herself attired like a sophisticated widow entertaining dissipated noblemen in her boudoir. Her sigh was echoed by Rietta, who knew of such a widow. She very much feared that Mrs. Vernon might wear even more "costly" and vulgar clothing with Mr. Ferris's complete approval.

Yet she couldn't help wondering whether Sir Nicholas wouldn't like to see a woman attired in black lace and silk. Wearing such things, wouldn't any woman be desirable? Mightn't a man forget that he'd not married for love, seeing his wife dressed so alluringly?

"Oh, I can't think why Arabella made the fire so hot," Rietta said, beginning to pace. "This room is stifling."

"Is it? Seems quite cozy. She said it looks as though it might actually rain later. I can hardly remember such a dry summer." She turned over another page. "Oh, spite. I thought he was going to kiss her but no. Just another bitter speech. I wonder if the duke is going to turn out to be the villain after all. He makes such a promising hero but he hasn't kissed her once. Or perhaps it's Lady Windrush who's the villain and the duke is going to marry Rose Devere."

"What are you talking of?"

"This book. Of course, it's only the first volume. I don't

mind reading aloud if you'd like to hear it. Mr. Greeves says I have a very soothing voice."

"Thank you, Blanche," Rietta said, touched by her sister's awareness of her restlessness. It wasn't often Blanche noticed anything not having to do with herself. "But I think I shall go for a walk."

"A walk? Now?"

"I often returned from Mrs. Athy's even later than this," Rietta said, smiling at Blanche.

"Yes, but that's when Father is at home. I shouldn't be left by myself at night. It isn't fair to me."

"You'll have Arabella." She should have known better than to assume Blanche had been motivated by fears for anyone's safety but her own.

"A maid is no protection."

"I'll ask Mr. Garrity to come and sit in the kitchen to support Arabella in case of housebreakers. He won't mind. I believe he's trying to fix his interest with her." Somewhat sharply, she added, "Love seems to be everywhere."

With a shawl wrapped about her head and shoulders peasant fashion, Rietta set out to walk, having changed her house shoes for thick boots. No sooner had she stepped outside, taking a deep breath of the warm yet fresh air, than the blue devils lifted from her spirits. Obviously, it had been the stuffy room that had oppressed her so.

She set off, walking up the rising street. The stars were being chased and swallowed up by racing clouds, yet on the ground there was little breeze. The moon shone bright behind her as it rose, sending Rietta walking over her own shadow. The scent of rain hung in the air like a remembered perfume.

Rietta knew she had been right to refuse Sir Nicholas's flattering offer. She hoped he had gone away without realizing how much she had been tempted. Not merely by the thought of marrying him, but by the life he'd shown her today. Lady Kirwan was sweet, mild, and gentle. The warmth that had glowed in her eyes when she'd looked upon her children had warmed Rietta, too. If she'd answered "yes" to Sir Nicholas, she would have had the right to call Lady Kirwan "Mother." Her own mother was little more than a memory of a sad smile and a weak voice, for she'd been ill from Blanche's birth until her own untimely death.

Amelia Kirwan could have been her younger sister, far more open-minded and far less self-absorbed than Blanche. She looked to be the sort of girl who would never be above being pleased. Upon parting today, she had not been content with a cool handshake but had kissed her cheek as well. Rietta could not recall the last spontaneous sign of affection she'd received from Blanche.

Well, perhaps it could not be expected. To Blanche she was an impediment to her future happiness. Which man would she choose were she free to leap before she looked?

Then there was Nick himself. She'd liked his smile from the first but now she understood the temper behind it. He stood back a little from life, as she did herself, content to observe and to comment. Love might be too much to ask of him. She could not blame him for withholding what she herself found so hard to express. After all, she had not confessed her true feelings to him for she could not have borne to see pity, or worse—laughter—in his eyes.

She increased her pace, as if hoping to outrun her thoughts. The street had leveled off somewhat and she saw another woman walking toward her, carrying two bandboxes. Rietta clutched her shawl more tightly about her and kept a watchful eye on the other woman in case she should prove to be someone she knew.

In all likelihood, she'd seen the last of the Kirwan family. Nick wasn't the sort to ask a girl twice. So farewell to them all. Good-bye to Nick, to Lady Kirwan, to Amelia, and even to the unseen and unknown Emma Kirwan.

"What?" the other woman asked as they passed. "Did you say 'Emma Kirwan'?"

Embarrassed, Rietta stopped stock-still. Had she been so zany as to say her farewells aloud? "I may have done," she said cautiously.

"Do I know you?"

"Are you Emma Kirwan?"

The girl gave a quavering sigh. "I am that unhappy creature."

The moonlight falling on her face washed away every vestige of color, leaving her haggard. However, it displayed with perfect clarity the dark bruise at the corner of her mouth.

"Are you hurt, Miss Kirwan?" Rietta asked, putting out her hand to support the girl's elbow. Tremors were shaking the girl's entire frame.

Emma started to cry. "I've been such a fool. . . ."

"We are all fools at one time or another," Rietta said with feeling. "I'm Rietta Ferris, a . . . friend of your brother's."

"Oh," Emma said, staring at her. "Are you really? Amelia said you'd be quite ugly—oh! I shouldn't have said that. Oh, I don't know what I'm doing or what is to become of me. I can't and I won't go home."

"Come to my house. It's just down the street. Does your brother know you are in Galway?"

"No, no one knows. That is—I left a note."

Emma Kirwan was shivering so much that Rietta could hardly imagine how she'd managed to walk even a few yards. There was, moreover, a slight savor of whiskey on the girl's breath, which seemed to impart a wobble to her steps. Rietta went from supporting her elbow to taking nearly her whole weight.

To add to the difficulty, Arabella's prediction of rain came true before they'd gone half the distance. By the time they'd reached the door, both girls were soaked to the skin and one of the bandboxes had developed a soggy bulge in the bottom. "I dropped it earlier," Emma explained.

Arabella exclaimed in horror when she answered the vehement ring Rietta twisted out of her own doorbell. "Miss Ferris? Sweet saints above, who's that with you?"

"Never mind the introductions, Arabella. Help me."

She left Emma Kirwan to the maid while she herself, in a perfect passion to get warm and dry, hurried out of her own sopping wet things and into a clean dressing gown. There was another sea-coal fire in her room and she did not find it too stuffy in the least.

In a quarter-hour, Arabella returned, bearing a pot of piping hot tea on a tray. "She'll do," she said to Rietta's inquiry about their unexpected guest. "I've tucked her up in bed with a hot brick to her feet. Seems to me you could do with a bit of that yourself, miss."

"This tea will cure my chill. Thank you, Arabella."

"I've given herself warm milk with a dot of vanilla in it. That'll settle her. When you ain't used to takin' a glass . . ."

"She *had* been drinking, then. I rather thought so."

Arabella tossed her head, the ribbons on her cap flying. "She's not the kind to drink, miss, nor to be brawling. I'd say he that gave her the glass, gave her the bruise."

"Tell Mr. Garrity I shall want him to take a note to Sir Nicholas Kirwan. Can he find the house?"

"Indeed. Hasn't your father given him directions this very night?"

"What? Is Father home so early?"

"That's why the chain was up, miss. He come in earlier than I've ever known him to return from the place he took himself off to tonight." She sniffed fastidiously. "But Garrity's not gone yet to take the master's letter. Takes a powerful lot more than Mr. Ferris's orders to move a man from my kitchen on a rainy night when there's rock cakes and tea."

"I trust, however, he'll move at *my* orders."

She couldn't ask Arabella why her father was writing to Nick for that would fall under the ban on gossiping with the servants. If Arabella had known, she would have volunteered the information already.

Emma Kirwan looked like a child in the plainest of Blanche's nightgowns, the only one she could spare out of the dozen or so she owned. The glass of milk sat untasted on the table, while the girl lay flat and straight as a rail under the covers, her eyes fixed on the ceiling, but not as though she drew pleasant pictures there. She did not look at Rietta, even when she sat on the edge of the bed.

"Pray believe me, Miss Kirwan, I have no desire to pry. Whatever you were doing, I'm sure you had sufficient reason for your actions."

"I thought I had," Emma replied in a deadened tone. "I thought I was in love, but now . . . I don't believe there is such a thing."

"Then the cause was a man?"

The lower lip trembled but the girl controlled it. She nodded. "I had such grand dreams. He said he shared them. Now I realize he was praying for the day he could leave me. He said . . . he said . . ."

"Don't think of it."

"He said I was a millstone around his neck. He said I was so earnest that I scared men away. He said he'd rather take a cold poultice to . . . He gave me a drink. I didn't like it."

"Did he strike you?"

The bloodless hand touched the corner of her mouth. "Yes," she whispered, then the tears came, breaking the unnatural composure that had brought her this far.

Rietta could not let the tears fall on a pillow when she had a perfectly useful shoulder. She rocked the girl who might have been her sister one day as she would have comforted her own blood sister, had Blanche ever known such strong emotions.

In between bouts of tears, Rietta heard enough to put her in command of the whole story. What little bits were left out, she had imagination enough to fill in for herself. This Robbie sounded like a thoroughly selfish creature who had found himself entangled with a wholly self-sacrificing woman. A receipt for disaster, whether he used her or discarded her.

In her opinion, Emma Kirwan was very well out of the affair even though he'd broken it off so cruelly. Every day would have brought tears and she had to admit that Emma had not the gift of being beautiful while she cried. A selfish man would use any means to escape from a woman who expected him to sacrifice anything at all for her. No marriage in which one partner did all the giving would be anything but hell on earth for both of them.

There was no use in trying to make Emma see that—not yet. She couldn't understand how her love and sacrifice could be rejected. "All I want to do is make him happy!" Emma said over and over.

At last, exhausted, she fell asleep. Rietta could go and change once more into dry clothes. She cast a longing glance toward her own bed but she had a letter to write and it was not, after all, to Nick.

> "*Dear Lady Kirwan—*
>
> *Quite by accident, I met your daughter Emma this evening. Finding her to be slightly indisposed, I prevailed upon her to return with me to my home. You would do me great honor by permitting her to remain with me tonight.*
>
> > *Yours, Rietta Ferris.*"

* * *

Lord Bellamy not only gave Nick his son's address in Galway, he accompanied him into the city, early though it was. "Never fear; he'll receive from me the thrashing his mother would never let me give him at home. Then I'll pack him off to America and not a soul will hear from me about your sister."

"Thank you, my lord."

"On the contrary, thank you. You have every right to call him out and I'd not blame you for it but . . . he is my son." He turned his high-nosed face to the dark window and Nick did not interrupt the older man's thoughts.

For himself, he had three letters that seemed to burn in his pocket.

His mother had sent young George after him last night with Rietta's note. He did not know as yet how his sister fell in with Rietta but he thanked Providence for it. If Emma had passed the whole night with young Robbie Staines there would be no salvaging her reputation save by marriage with the young wastrel. As it was, they could put it about that Emma had intended all along to stay with the Ferris family.

The letter from Mr. Ferris, offering him the moon would he but marry Rietta, would have found no place but the fire if it had not been for the third letter.

This bore the name of a famous, and fortunate, gambler. In the politest possible language, the gentleman expressed his condolences on the death of Sir Benjamin Kirwan and informed the heir that he held some half-dozen IOUs and would greatly appreciate immediate payment. The total sum was not large so far as such things went—a matter of four hundred pounds—but it might as well have been four million for all the likelihood of it being found.

Lord Bellamy dropped him and went on his way. Nick stood outside the Ferris home, looking up at the windows. It was awkward to meet the girl who had turned down his honorable proposal, especially on such terms of gratitude as these. What would have become of Emma if Rietta had not found her? Scenes of women and girls fleeing from one occupied city or another filled his memory. The luckiest took up with the first man they found. The less lucky took a series of lovers. The most wretched wound up on the streets, or following the army for pennies and crusts of bread. Such a life was understandable when war smashed all other options, but it was unbearable to think that his sister had almost fallen into such a fate through no greater agency that her own folly.

He saw Rietta come out of the house and stand on the exterior landing. She'd covered her head and shoulders with a cloudy green shawl that brought out the color in her eyes. Under it, she wore a loose white garment with a skirt pulled on over it. In a ballroom, she might not show to the best advantage but in the first pale light of dawn, she was so striking that he wished he knew how to paint so that he might capture her for always.

Nick went up to her, hat in hand. She came down the steps to stand with him beside the railing. "I came out as soon as I knew it was you, Sir Nicholas. Emma isn't awake just yet."

"Tell me at once how she is."

"Tired, heartsore, and most truly sorry."

"How could she be so foolish?" Nick said bitterly. Finding Rietta sympathetic, he added, "Robbie Staines is the worst kind of man, without compunction, without direction . . . even his own father cannot find excuses for him. Yet Emma—on fire with love—believes that for her he will change."

"She knows she has been a fool. I believe she feels that even more than the bruise he put upon her face."

"What! He struck her?" Unable to stand still, he took a pace up and down the gleaming pavement. "If I'd known that, I'd not let his father thrash him; I'd horsewhip him myself."

"Then it is as well you didn't know. Emma wouldn't want that kind of scandal."

"Emma, my dear Rietta, will be lucky if she isn't packed off to a convent after yesterday's work. She all but frightened Mother into a heart attack, running off like that. Of all the heartless, ignorant folly . . . and so I shall tell her."

"You're too angry to see her now. Why not let her stay here, with me, for a few days. No one will know that she did not come to Galway just for that purpose."

"Who are you to keep me from my sister?"

"I am her hostess," she said, looking him in the eyes. "Kindly don't raise your voice to me, Sir Nicholas. I shouldn't like to lose my temper."

"I suggest you don't. I am in no mood to humor your desire to rule."

"My what?"

"Come, Rietta," he said, in as reasonable a tone as he could counterfeit. "You have convinced half the town that you are a brawling, scolding female. You rule your father's household like a queen because no one there challenges you. Believe me, I am not so retiring."

She shook her head free of the encompassing shawl and her red hair, loose around her shoulders, floated in the cool morning breeze like a battle flag raised in challenge. Even though he was entirely exasperated by her, he couldn't help acknowledging that she looked magnificent, a Celtic princess of ancient days. Nick felt the thrill of incipient battle in his veins, for she was an adversary worth fighting against.

"I have come to see my sister and see her I shall."

"No, you shan't. She has been bullied quite enough."

"Bullied? Do you dare to class me with Robbie Staines?"

"And why not? Are you any better than he is? A decent man would give any woman time to recover her self-respect before charging in upon her to shout and stamp. But no, your anger will drive you to say and do things that will hurt her the more."

"I am not so brutal, Miss Ferris."

"Nor so kind, Sir Nicholas. If your mother were here, she'd say the same as I do." She looked about her and turned back to him, a sudden light of humorous embarrassment in her face. In a much lower tone, she said, "We are not alone."

Nick turned his head and saw a group of people, each with the tools of his or her trade in hand. A fishmonger with a basket of cod had the same expression as his fish, whereas the lamplighter, the milkmaid, and the rag-and-bottle man seemed to think they were at a play.

He took Rietta by her bare elbow and turned her toward her house. Silent laughter shook her. She stumbled. He held her up by main force. "Now may I come in?"

"Only until our audience disperses. Well, if I had not a reputation for shrewishness, I have it now."

Inside, in the dark quiet of the stairwell, Nick stood beside her as she peeped out through the sidelight. "They're still talking us over."

She glanced up at him with a smile that invited him to share her laughter, only to show surprise when she found him standing so near. He took his hand out of his pocket to reach up to smooth back her hanging hair, tangling his fingers in the soft, cool strands. She closed her eyes, but not as though afraid of him.

"You'll be able to leave in a moment," she said, giving herself a little shake as if forcing herself to stay awake.

"I like it here," Nick said. Her hair was like raw silk, shining despite being in a state of nature. He supposed it was against every rule to wish to kiss a girl who'd already turned him down, but he wanted to. Would her lips taste as sweet as he remembered?

"Rietta . . . ," He put a finger beneath her chin and tilted her face up. He looked into her eyes, waiting for, hoping for a protest. It was all that might save them now.

Then her gaze went past him and she jerked free.

"My father was up there," she said, puzzled. "Looking over the railing . . . I'm sure I saw him."

"Never mind him," Nick said and kissed her.

Ten

She should have been thrashing about, furiously trying to break loose, shouting for help. But Rietta didn't even murmur a protest—not because of his overmastering grip, but because she did not want to.

He kissed her the way a man dying of thirst drinks from a well he knows is poisoned, in desperate, violent consummation of need too long denied.

She could only grasp the front of his rough frieze coat and try to hang on as he took what he wanted from her.

Her head fell back, as he tasted the lobe of her ear and ran his hand along the sensitized length of her throat. "Rietta," he whispered, raggedly, then came again to take her mouth.

Rietta wasn't afraid, though she was shaking. She felt his need for her in his trembling hands, in the harsh rhythm of his breath. Yet more was working in her than the old instinct of response to another's need.

When he licked inside of her mouth, it was as if he'd lit a fuse that raced faster than a man could walk. She lifted into his kiss, answering his wordless demands with a muffled cry. She felt surprise run through him, causing his lips to harden as he drew back, but now it was she who held on to him with an unbreakable grip.

His shock wore off quickly.

Nick backed her into the wall with a thump that made the paintings rattle. He pulled her close, his weight supported on the hand splayed beside her head. His body was hard and urgent against hers, demanding things she could neither understand nor deny him. She felt his thigh press between her legs, dragging up her skirts, becoming the fulcrum of her existence.

"Why me?" she panted. "Why do you want me?"

His voice seemed to come from deep within his chest. "You make me forget the things I've seen. The things I've done."

Then he put his hands on her and she lost his words as her skin began to sing. Her shawl had already fallen to the floor, thrown out of the way. Now he ran his hands down her throat as he plundered her mouth, blindly finding the edge of her bodice. She'd only thrown on a simple skirt such as peasant girls wore over her dressing gown so she could run down to him before he awakened the household. The dressing gown tied with a sash at the side, no barrier at all to his questing hand.

Rietta's knees sagged as he pressed his palm over her bare breast. If he hadn't groaned with half-pained pleasure at that moment, she would have died of shame. As it was, she felt a strange kind of pride. Then his fingertips were circling and circling her nipple and she knew he could do anything he wanted with her.

Heat blossomed along every vein, all her will burning away in the fire he'd set ablaze in her body. He said her name over and over, his voice no more than a breath, but it was enough to fan the flames higher still. From her deepest instinct came the knowledge that he alone could save her from the burning.

"Oh, Nick!" she cried. "What have you done to me?"

"Ssh . . . sweetheart." He pressed his knee closer to her body. Not even the dress that screened her legs was protection. She met his movement halfway without realizing it.

Then, recognizing how completely wanton she'd become, she said desperately, "Please, stop this. I—I can't bear another moment."

He froze, his slickened mouth a hair's breadth from hers. She looked up into his passion-dark eyes and thought that the devil must have looked just like that when he'd been thrown out of Paradise. She wanted to unsay it, but it was too late.

Slowly, he pushed away to the full length of his arms and gazed down at her. Rietta hadn't been shy when he'd kissed her, but she couldn't meet his steady appraisal. She looked away, noticing that his arms shook with the strain of keeping off her. Her lips burned. She pressed the back of her hand to them but it didn't help.

"Of what church are you?" he asked.

She turned her head to stare at him. Of all the things he might have said . . . "If you are asking me where I will go for absolution . . ."

"No. I want to know where we will be married."

Bliss filled her heart. She looked into his eyes, a smile dawning on her lips, but it died, frozen to death, for there was nothing in his eyes to warm it save the brief, wasted heat of lust.

"We're not going to be married. I have already refused you once, Sir Nicholas. Don't make me do it again." She ducked under his arm but hadn't gone a step before he'd taken her elbows and pulled her back against him. She knew then without a doubt how much he desired her, but also knew that desire alone wasn't enough.

"I have your father's consent, you know."

"Then marry him."

He crossed his arms about her waist, locking their bodies together. She felt his lips against her temple. His hands were perilously close to her bosom. Rietta tried not to think about how she could drag his hand there again. How quickly she had learned to crave his touch.

She'd spent five passionate minutes locked in the arms of the man she loved. But those minutes had not changed the brutal truth. She loved; he did not. To marry under such circumstances was an even more appalling prospect than to be married for her father's money.

"Let me go," she said. "The house is stirring. I don't want you found here. Certainly not like this. We're going to be the subject of quite enough gossip as it is."

"I don't mind gossip. It can be very useful."

"Let me go." She heard a door slam up above. "In the name of heaven, will you let me go!"

He hesitated, only to release her at the same moment she tried her best to break free. Rietta stumbled forward. The instant she had her footing, she rounded on him. "Get out," she said, her tone no less peremptory for being whispered. "I will never marry you. If your sister were not here, I should have Mr. Garrity bar the door to you."

"As it is . . . when may I see Emma?"

"Come back at two. Don't expect to see me. Don't even try."

On the landing above, Blanche, her voice sleepily dovelike, called out, "Arabella? Where's my hot water?"

"Will you go?" Rietta said, pushing him toward the door.

He began to laugh, all the harder for Rietta's efforts to hush him. Suddenly, he sobered. "Yes. I'll go. But you haven't heard the last of this."

"Yes I have, for it's no more I'll listen."

Rietta closed the door behind him, purposefully turning the key so the brass lock snapped audibly. If only keeping him out of her heart was as easy.

Her body felt strangely heavy as she bent to pick up her

fallen shawl. Swirling it around her shoulders, she snuggled into it, suddenly cold without Nick's body covering hers. Why had he laughed at the end? Was it at the feebleness of her strength as she pushed him toward the door? Or was it directed at some joke she could not see?

Half under the shawl was a piece of white paper. She looked at it idly and saw a crimson crest at the top and read just enough to realize that the letter belonged to Nick. It must have fallen out his pocket during those wild moments when he'd seized her. She remembered his hands had been in his pockets just one instant before he'd reached out to pull her off balance. She laid it on the table that received visitor's cards, so he could collect it when he returned to see Emma.

If she married him . . . She felt a wild thrill run through her body to all the places he'd touched. He would attend diligently to the duties of a husband, of that she had no doubt. She'd always heard that a man came to despise a woman who permitted him liberties, but surely that emotion did not intrude upon the marriage bed? Perhaps passion growing into tenderness brought forth love, given time.

Rietta was tempted to give him that time. If she married him—she tamped down hard on that thrill—he might come to love her sooner or later. It was a gamble, a risk, for his feelings might never deepen. Against that chance, she would be staking her happiness for the rest of her life. To be married to a man who merely tolerated her would bring only years of heart-hungry misery. She'd be unable to show her feelings for fear of disgusting him, until they devoured her inwardly.

Also, she had to think of her father and of Blanche. How would they manage without her? Blanche could no more run a household than she could fly. She always put the servants' backs up with her arbitrary ways and her carelessness, her favoritism and her waywardness.

As for her father, he would have Mrs. Vernon to wife as soon as Rietta left the house. The thought of that woman in her mother's place was enough to terrify Rietta.

Any other woman would have made a preferable stepmother. Not a woman whose first husband had been a notorious rogue and whose second husband had been suspected of the first one's murder. Not a woman who had run madly through two respectable fortunes until not a tradesman in town would give her another penny worth of credit.

Yet she dressed fine as fivepence and never seemed to suffer any lack. No doubt word of her keeping a cup warm for Mr. Ferris nearly every night had reached everyone's ear by now. If Rietta married, leaving the way clear for Mrs. Vernon, Mr. Ferris would acquire both her debts and her extravagant ways in one fell swoop. The mills were doing very well, as were the family investments, but how long would that state of affairs continue if all were left in her father's hands? He'd never had much of a head for business and he'd have less yet after Mrs. Vernon was through turning it.

"Leprechaun schemes," she said aloud. "Good gad. What next?"

Later on, she would wonder whether she would have been wiser to listen to her father's warning. Perhaps the little giants had been listening to her scoffing at their existence and had chosen to punish her by way of proof.

That afternoon, Nick was admitted to his sister's bedroom. Emma sat up in bed. She unmistakably quailed when the pert maid introduced him. "Oh, Nick, I'm so, so sorry."

He bent to kiss her forehead. Her hair had been swept back in a bandeau, revealing a bruise on her forehead to match the one by her mouth. Both had been dusted over with powder in an attempt to conceal them, but it was useless. The purple marks under her eyes testified to how little she'd slept last night, and perhaps for days before that. Nick didn't know which made him angrier, the bruises or the signs that she'd been weeping for the man who'd beat her.

He tried to keep his voice gentle, but it came out like the growl of a bear. "Robbie Staines's father sends his regards and his congratulations at escaping from his son."

"Was Lord Bellamy very angry with Robbie? It wasn't his fault. I—I thought he wanted me to come with him, so I ran away. Robbie didn't know I meant to do it." She grasped at Nick's sleeve. "You didn't see Robbie, did you?"

"No, I came here early this morning but Rie—Miss Ferris didn't think it would be wise to disturb you."

"She's very good. She was so kind to me. Kinder than I deserve." She spoke mechanically. Only when speaking of Robbie did she seem to come alive. "I'm glad you didn't see him, Nick. I don't blame you for being angry, but hurting him wouldn't change this."

"I have hopes of seeing Mr. Staines later in the day," Nick said with a tight jaw. "He wasn't at home when I sent up my card earlier." He thought of how he'd thrown aside the greasy landlord at the boarding house and had gone upstairs, his riding crop in his fist. To his surprise, Robbie Staines was not cowering under the bed. He really was out. Remembering his promise to return and the bribe he'd given the landlord not to tell of his intention, he grinned. Emma, reading his look, gave a faint shriek.

"Oh, no, Nick. You mustn't. It wasn't his fault. He told me to go home, but I wouldn't. That's when . . ." She tenderly touched the side of her mouth.

"And the other?"

"What other?"

He found a hand mirror on the dressing table and gave it to her. She touched the lead-colored mark and winced. "I don't know. When I fell down?"

"When he knocked you down, you mean."

"He was angry."

"So am I. Now listen to me, Emma. Nobody knows what you did except the four of us."

"The four of us," she echoed.

"You and I, Lord Bellamy, and Mother."

"And Miss Ferris."

"And Miss Ferris. How much did you tell her?"

"I don't remember precisely. I was so agitated. I walked for miles, it seemed, and she was so kind."

"Well, Miss Ferris's knowledge or lack of it doesn't signify. It won't be long before she has as much interest in protecting my sisters' reputations as I have myself."

"What do you mean, Nick?"

Nick didn't satisfy her curiosity. "We will none of us speak of this again. Lord Bellamy will put his loathsome son on a boat for America and wipe his name out of the family Bible." Emma began to weep for him. "You and I will not speak of it, either, and as for Mother, you will tell her you are sorry to have caused her so much pain. Undoubtedly she will forgive you."

"Will you?"

He put his arm about her shoulders and gave her an abrupt squeeze. "Of course, you silly goose. Just don't do it again."

"Never. I promise." She sniffed and tried to force a smile. Nick thought he'd never seen one so badly feigned, not even on the face of some seventeen-year-old subaltern about to lead his troops under fire for the first time.

"Good girl. You'll spend one more night here just to add color to our story about your being invited by Miss Ferris. I'll come tomorrow to take you home."

"How is Mother? And Amelia?"

"Mother is well enough," he said, feeling that now was not the time to tell Emma about Lady Kirwan's recent heart palpitations. "Amelia was calling you twenty kinds of fool yesterday but no doubt the storm's over by now. She'll probably prove your staunchest defender."

"Yes, that's like her. Are you going?"

"I have strict instructions from Miss Ferris not to over-tire you. I don't dare disobey; she's even more outrageous than Amelia when she is angry."

"That doesn't sound like Miss Ferris. She never raised her voice yesterday and she stayed with me until I fell asleep."

"You must thank her."

"I will. Perhaps she'd like a new pair of slippers? I was embroidering a pair for Aunt Kate but they'd fit Miss Ferris, too."

"I'm certain she needs slippers. It is well thought of."

He left her to think of her indiscretion and, no doubt, to shed yet more tears over Robbie Staines. The waters he was to sail over must have been made of the tears he'd forced many women to weep. From what Lord Bellamy had said, even Staines's own mother was ready to put an ocean between herself and her son.

As Nick stepped into the hall, he looked about eagerly for a sight of Rietta. He caught no sign of her, not even a whiff of the clean-scented perfume she wore, a scent like the breeze on a high hill when the wildflowers hung in every hedge. Kissing her, it had filled his head like a drug, and he never would forget it. If he lived to be a hundred, one trace of that scent would, he felt, bring him back to feel her clinging to him as spirited and passionate as she'd been today.

Throughout the day, he'd relived those breathless moments, calling them up like a connoisseur to sample again and again. The memories only made him the hungrier to taste her mouth once more. She'd been inexpert at first, becoming more adept from instant to instant. The excitement of knowing that he'd been the first man ever to kiss her in such an intimate way fluttered under his skin. He'd been right when he'd guessed that her high passions were not confined to anger. How she'd pressed against him!

Nick knew he was no more in love with Rietta than she was with him. But their marriage bed need never be cold. He smiled confidently as he passed along the hall. His wife would never have cause to complain that he was not attentive in the bedchamber, or that he wasted his substance chasing strange women. Give him Rietta and he'd count all the others well lost.

But how to win her consent? He knew she was stubborn. Having once given no for an answer she had too much pride ever to change her mind. She'd persist in that no if the world crumbled and only she and he were left alive.

"Pst! Psssst!"

Nick had paused before a mirror to pass a critical eye over his shirt and coat. Having his sister alternately grip his sleeve and weep all down his lapels did not improve a coat that, at its best, was slightly past the mode. Hearing the summons, he looked around, surprised to hear it when he was apparently quite alone.

"Down here," the voice called, hoarse in its whispered attempt to be heard by Nick's ears alone.

Nick looked over the banister. David Mochrie beckoned to him.

David smuggled Nick past the cook, her back turned to haggle with the fishmonger for today's catch, down into the cellar. "Where are you taking me?" Nick said, whispering like the hero of a gothic novel.

"Secret conference. Just like Wellington would have done it."

Down in the moldy, dusty depth of the cellar, Mr. Ferris sat on an upturned keg, beating time on his instep with a loosely closed fist. "There you are, Sir Nicholas. We've been meaning to talk something over with you."

"I'm at your service, sir, of course."

"Well, that's what I want. Quick service. I'm tired of standing on and off waiting for you to marry my daughter. What's the difficulty?"

"Yes, old man," David added. "I'm not famous for the speed of my actions, but it seems to me that two weeks is plenty of time to propose to a girl."

"It's hardly been a week," Nick protested. "These things take a bit of time to do properly."

"Nonsense," Mr. Ferris scoffed. "Take a leaf out of David's book. Three days after he met my sweet Blanche, he shows up on my doorstep like a toadstool sprouting in the rain. Demands me girl with a gun to my head . . . near enough."

"You exaggerate, sir," David said.

"Near enough to it any road. I told him then, sir, that no younger daughter of mine shall marry while there's an elder available. But he didn't fancy my Rietta; too much strength of purpose. She'd have him organized, starch in his shirt, and plenty of stiffening in his spine before the poor man knew what he was about."

"No woman will mold me," David said, throwing his chest out. "Let a wife be obedient, I say. The man should do the teaching; the woman the learning."

Neither of them had mentioned her kindness, her warmth, her humor. Things which, even if they were aware of them, had no value to them. David's notion of a wife sounded like a dead bore—no wonder he was settling for Blanche.

"Rietta is a trifle masterful, perhaps," Nick admitted.

"A trifle?" David echoed with a laugh. "Well, perhaps you're man enough to take her."

"Oh, yes." Nick smiled with heartfelt confidence.

"Good, we're in agreement." Mr. Ferris rubbed his small hands together. "Now for the plan—David, m'boy, where's the plans we . . . ah, there they are."

He drew out a folder, tied at the side with green ribbons.

He laboriously picked at the hard knot the ribbons had become. "I always tie so carefully just so this sort of thing wouldn't happen."

"What plan, sir?" Nick asked. He didn't like this prowling about like a lovesick alley cat. Nor did he trust the others in this cellar cabal. Mr. Ferris seemed right in his element in the dim and dank room, and David was smiling like a drunken man given a pound for his off-key singing.

With a triumphant "ah," Mr. Ferris opened the folder. "This is the plan, my son . . . I mean, Sir Nicholas. When Rietta goes tomorrow night, the same as every Thursday, to that village of hovels at our gates, you follow her. She always goes afoot. I don't know why I keep Garrity on— he does nothing and eats like the giant he was billed as with the circus. If the girls hadn't made a regular pet of him . . ."

"Come back, Mr. Ferris," David said merrily. "You've gone too far ahead."

"'Tis clear enough. No need to make a piece of work over nothing. She'll be glad enough to marry once she understands the seriousness of her position."

"I don't understand," Nick said. "What are you talking of?"

David winked over Mr. Ferris's head. "Let me just go over that once more, Mr. Ferris. It's a trifle complicated. If I go over it with Nick, we'll both be understanding it clearly."

"There's nothing complicated about it," Mr. Ferris said sharply. "Stay straight on this road until you come to a fork. Take you the left. Over the rise and half a mile on, you'll come to a little town—hardly more than ten houses all told. The gentleman'll be waiting."

"What gentleman?"

Mr. Ferris rolled his eyes. "The one that's to marry you to Rietta, of course! You'll abduct her when she comes home from the Claddagh, carry her off, and marry her out of hand. You'll have my full consent."

Nick stared at them. They grinned back like a pair of monkeys. "Does Bedlam know you are out?" he asked. "Or did the madness come on you suddenly?"

"There's nothing mad about it," Mr. Ferris said blusteringly. " 'Tis a simple matter of business. Marry the girl and you'll never know a moment's worry over money—I swear it. Keep on as you are and I'll be dead before I can ever . . . ever hold my grandson in m'arms." Mr. Ferris's lower lip quivered. "I'm not growing younger as the days pass by. Soon I won't have the strength to enjoy such simple pleasures. 'Tis a dreadful thing to grow old, knowing that your line is fading."

"Stop it, sir. You're breaking my heart," David said, wiping his eyes ostentatiously with a flourished handkerchief.

"I can't marry Rietta against her will," Nick said. "It's impossible."

"Won't be against her will, m'boy." Mr. Ferris stood up, apparently just so he could dig a finger into Nick's ribs. "You mayn't be aware but I saw what the pair of you were up to down in the hall this morning. I'm not sayin' Rietta'll go willing, but it's a pound to cold pease porridge that she'll be willin' after the knot is tied good 'n' tight. She's never been one to pine after salmon in the sea if she's caught trout in her net."

"I'm sorry," Nick said. "It's impossible. I can't steal a wife."

"From what I hear," David put in, "stealing brides was quite the fashion not so long ago. My own grandmother was abducted from Limerick by an earl. Of course, he returned her, eventually."

Nick laughed but still shook his head at his friend. "It's out of the question."

The two other men looked long and hard at one another.

Finally, David shrugged and half turned away. "I don't approve, but I shan't argue."

Mr. Ferris pulled out a letter from his folder, strangely familiar. "Recognize this?" he asked, showing the top where a red crest was embossed.

"How did you come by that?"

"Found it. I read it, too."

"You had no right—but you knew that."

"I've my fair share of curiosity." Mr. Ferris tapped the letter against his thumbnail. "Have you the money to pay off this debt? I don't think you do. I have and I'll do it, over and above what I offered you today, if you'll marry Rietta this very day."

"You cannot buy me, Mr. Ferris. Nor can you blackmail me. Now give me my letter and I'll say good day."

"Don't be like that," Mr. Ferris said good-humoredly. "I'm making you a fair offer. All your little troubles will vanish as if by magic just by becoming m'son-in-law. Think of your father's debts. Think of your poor sisters. Nice girls, if the one upstairs is to be judged by, but even good men are hard to come by without a bit of clink in the stocking's foot, eh?"

Nick did think of these things. Emma's desperation had driven her to near-fatal folly. Amelia's love affair was no more likely to progress well. When their bruised hearts recovered, they would no doubt find other men to marry, and then dowries. . . . Furthermore, he thought of his mother, who had troubles enough without poverty adding to them.

But most of all, he thought of Rietta.

That there was something between them—if no more than physical attraction—could not be denied. His desire for her was like a humming in his ear, always present and impossible to be rid of. If he married her out of hand, he could silence it. Not immediately, for even if nothing more than her pride prevented him from coming to her bed, there could be a long delay before he was satisfied. But he was no closer to having her now, for she never would change her no to yes without a great deal of time passing. Time that he did not have.

But could she forgive having that choice taken from her?

"You seem to feel that there is some urgency to have Rietta wed soon. Why is that, when you've already waited this long?"

Mr. Ferris shuffled his feet and began to flatter him grossly. "I've never seen another man your equal, Sir Nicholas. David here vouches for your honesty, your sobriety, and your other good qualities. And, I'll not hide from you, your title makes you a most appealing prospect for a son-in-law. Besides which, Rietta likes you and that, let me tell you, is a first."

"That's true," David added. "Rietta had never cared twopence for any other man." He laughed. "Damn, if you aren't a conqueror of virgin territory!"

Nick shook his head, ignoring the crudity. "I can't do it. Not even my circumstances can excuse such cold-bloodedness."

A change passed over Mr. Ferris's face. Gone was the amiable, rather foolish tradesman. Instead, a kind of low cunning gleamed in his small eyes, while his forehead came down and his jaw moved forward pugnaciously. "There's nothing for it, then. I'll not have the girl in the house another day. I'll turn her out. Let her find a husband on the streets."

"Sir!" David protested, no doubt seeing his dream of Blanche moving farther away.

Nick waited to hear what else Mr. Ferris might say.

"Aye, let her take her airs and graces out of my house. I've done all I care to for her. There comes a time when a man needs his freedom from family ties."

"What about Blanche?" David asked.

"Let Greeves have her. He's got the chinks to stand her nonsense."

"What of the family curse?" Nick asked as a last resort.

"Yes . . . well, I'll risk it. Or better yet, I'll marry the chit off to the first good-for-nothing I meet tomorrow, whether Traveler, tinker, or tailor. Let Fate decide what becomes of her."

A wise man, Nick knew, would have gone on saying no to their very improper plan forever, walking away with a vow never to see Rietta again. But whatever wisdom he'd once possessed had been blown away with the cannon smoke at Waterloo. Whether Mr. Ferris meant his threat or not, it was impossible to think of Rietta living at his mercy for one more day.

"Very well. Tell me again where to go, and what of the license?"

"You have my consent and I have the license," Mr. Ferris said, his smile returning. Why had Nick never noticed how pointed and sharp the other man's teeth were? He rubbed his plump hands together. "The rest is up to you."

Eleven

Rietta stepped out of Mrs. Athy's cottage and into the cool sea-scented night, snatching a breath from the hands of the wind. The crescent moon shone down through the mist, like the glimpse of a lamp behind a window on a frosty night. There'd be rain before morning.

With a sigh, she turned away from the bridge that led back to the streets of Galway. Instead, she walked to the end of the quay to look out into the bay. Like ghosts, the fishing boats lay at anchor, their rust-colored sails furled until the dawn. She wished that she had nothing more to do than wait in a one-room cottage for her seafaring husband to come home.

She had been restless and uneasy all day. Try as she might to fix her thoughts elsewhere, they returned relentlessly to those moments when Nick had crushed her against him. The very memory was enough to make her blood sing crazily, but the thought of kissing him again made her head swim. His touch, his kiss, had awakened something in her, a new vitality that refused to return to serenity.

She'd invented and discarded a hundred methods for

seeing him again, whether sending a message by Emma, gone home this afternoon, or going to Greenwood herself tomorrow to take up Lady Kirwan's invitation. She told herself she had no intention of being seized upon in that fashion ever again, but her very bones ached with the need to have him touch her. He seemed to have no reluctance when it came to kissing her. Let them be alone again and Rietta knew the inevitable would happen.

She did not believe herself to be completely wanton. After all, she had twenty-some years of celibacy behind her. She'd never been tempted by desire before so she did not think she was entirely without moral restraint. Except when Nick was near. Then she seemed to lose the natural shyness of maidenhood with no more cajolery than the brush of his fingertips.

Rietta put her hands up to smooth back the neat bands of hair under the edge of her bonnet. Her gloves were soft against her forehead, soothing away her incipient headache. If she had only herself to consider, she'd cheerfully go with Nick, whether for matrimony or for whatever end he chose. But she had to think of her father and Blanche. They needed her and she would not abandon them even for Nicholas Kirwan, his title, or his strong hands that seemed to know of their own accord just where and how to touch her.

"Oh, for heaven's sake!" she said aloud, whipping off her bonnet and letting the sea wind cool her overheated face. A loose lock of hair streamed like a pennon as she turned to go home.

She'd spent years learning self-control. She'd repressed natural yearnings for a home and husband of her own. She'd convinced herself that she was valued for the good she could do. One caress from a man should not be permitted to blast that training into nothingness.

She'd expected to be wooed and won sensibly, calmly, and at a steady pace; not in this hurry-scurry fashion.

She'd not see Nick again; that would be safest. As for the pain she'd feel, she would apply what she'd learned from experience and show nothing of it. Eventually, the pain would lessen and she could be free of all except the faintest of tender scars.

If only she didn't have the feeling that too many of those scars would render her heart too painful to endure any more. Then she would turn into a cat-keeping old maid, bitter and resentful that her life had not kept its youthful promise.

"So be it," she said with a ghost of a laugh. "Better that than to be married to the wrong man."

The sound of a coach rattling over the cobblestones on the other side of the narrow channel between Galway proper and the Claddagh made Rietta look up from her pensive contemplation of a neat arrangement of coiled down falls of rope.

It was late for travelers, and most of the villagers wouldn't be riding in a fine carriage. Perhaps someone had fallen ill and needed a doctor from town. Should she offer her assistance? She was useful in a sickroom.

Rietta started walking quickly over the rough stones. The carriage had pulled to the side of the road, its lamps dark. Against the night, it was like an intaglio carved in onyx, a shadow on black velvet. Rietta slowed her pace, step by step, feeling a sudden sharp reluctance to pass the carriage. But there was only one way over the river's mouth and back to the safety of the streets of Galway. That way lay past the carriage.

Settling her bonnet on her head, holding her chin high, Rietta started past. Despite her attitude, she couldn't help stealing a glance, hoping her bonnet concealed the turn of her gaze.

The door swung open and Rietta stopped dead a few paces away. "Get in," said a well-known voice. "I came to meet you."

Rietta exhaled in relief. "Why don't you light the lamps? I didn't know what to think."

"See to it, Garrity."

"Yes, sir."

At ease now, Rietta came up to the carriage. "I'm glad you came tonight. Usually, I don't mind walking home alone but I've got the collywobbles or something. I almost don't dare look over my shoulder for fear of seeing what I should not."

"There is a touch o' chill in the air."

She put out her hand for assistance and mounted with his help. "Well, Father . . . ," she began, breaking off suddenly when she saw they were not alone. Two men were present, sitting silent as statues against the cushions. They each wore black domino cloaks, the hoods cast over their heads, creating impenetrable shadows in the folds.

"Father?"

The door had no sooner shut behind her than Garrity whipped up the horses. "What is all this?"

"I'm sorry," Mr. Ferris said. "But this is your wedding."

"My wedding?"

The coach lurched as it turned left, heading out along the coast road rather than right into town. Rietta fell against the hooded man beside her. She flinched from him when he would have put out a hand to save her.

"Father, have your wits gone begging? What do you mean, my wedding? I've no intention of being wed tonight or any other night."

"I've arranged it all," he said, smiling as though proud of his forethought. "The license is in my pocket, these are to be your witnesses. . . ."

"Their services will not be required."

She'd been afraid that one of these men would prove to be her bridegroom. If her father was mad enough to plan this wedding, he might be careless of his choice for her.

Rage was running hot in her blood, but behind it a cold thread of fear had begun to claim her. Fear and hopelessness. How could her own father abduct her?

"Take me home, sir."

"Your bridegroom will take you home tonight, my dear. I've thought of everything. Even your clothes are in the valises in the boot." Mr. Ferris chuckled and Rietta's heart turned to ice. "I don't know why I didn't think of this months ago."

As her anger ebbed, forced out by fear, Rietta looked at the three men in the carriage. The two hooded men had turned their faces away toward the window, attempting to give the illusion that they were not there. She could not expect assistance from them. They must have accepted her father's invitation knowing full well the bride was not willing.

As for Mr. Ferris, he had brought out a list from his pocket and was ticking off the items with a pencil. He would pause some times to lick the end, leaving black marks on lip and tongue.

"Who is my bridegroom?" Rietta asked, hating that her voice now held much less defiance. She tried to fan her wrath, but it was a dying ember. Sorrow swamped it. Rietta understood that her father did not value her. She was a nuisance, a block to his plans, something to be tossed away on the first reasonable man who offered.

"Where are we going?"

"To a small chapel where your bridegroom awaits."

"His name?"

He chuckled again teasingly. "I'll not tell you that! All I will say is, he's no stranger to you—I'd not do such a wicked thing. I think you'll be well pleased when you espy your bridegroom."

Rietta recoiled from the tone of smug satisfaction in her father's voice. She knew that tone. It was how he sounded when he felt he'd brought off a particularly smart piece of business—something that profited him at another's expense. She could usually explain to him the true cost; the loss of trust, of goodwill, of his reputation as an honest man; and convince him to make a more equitable arrangement.

But her heart failed her and she could not find the sensible, well-reasoned words that would change his supple mind. In a very soft voice, she said, "This is wicked, Father. Please . . ."

He only patted her hand and said, "We'll be there ere long."

She cast another glance at the two silent auditors of this painful scene. There were no sympathetic eyes there, and her pride forbade begging them brokenly for help.

For a mad instant, she weighed the notion of throwing open the door and flinging herself out. But Garrity had whipped up the horses when they'd reached more open country and they were racketing along at a fierce pace. Rietta absolved herself of cowardice. Anyone might be afraid of the broken bones, if nothing worse, that such a theatrical gesture might cause.

Besides, there was no need. No proper minister would perform a marriage when the bride was so patently unwilling. She'd demonstrate her unwillingness loud and long when necessary. Until then, let her father enjoy his moment of triumph.

She refused to think about any future farther away than her impending arrival at the church. She could never go back to living under her father's roof after he'd demonstrated how little fatherly feeling he had. Where could she go? She had no money by her. Begging a night's lodging from some peasant family would have to serve this night— or perhaps the minister's wife would offer her some kind of shelter.

After a long time, the carriage stopped. Mr. Ferris peered out the window, delight crinkling the corners of his eyes. "We're here," he said, as merrily as if they'd just arrived at a sunlit picnic spot. "I call that really excellent time. I shall have to see about raising Garrity's wages. Come, Rietta. Come, gentlemen."

The cold breeze whispered over the treeless ground. This was no village church where a quick marriage could be performed on the quiet. There was no kindly minister's wife come to see the bride married at such a strange hour of the night. There was only stone, austere, ancient, half ruined by the slighting touch of time.

Before her, a vast wall made from blocks of gray stone rose to a point at a vastly dizzying height. Only the delicate tracery around the great round window gave away the building's peaceful purpose. Otherwise, it borrowed the form and substance of a sturdy fortress against invaders. Even the base of the wall was slightly coved. In a castle, that meant the cannonballs of the opposing army would bound back upon them. What purpose could such have at a church?

It looked far more sturdy than it was. Through the window's tracery, Rietta could see stars shining with diamond-point beauty. Whatever roof this church once possessed had long since vanished into some lordling's pocket, sold for the value of the lead.

Tucking her arm firmly beneath his own, Mr. Ferris guided Rietta's stumbling steps through the graveyard stones that clustered thickly about the ruined church.

"What place is this?" she asked, desperate to delay him.

"An old abbey, destroyed in some battle or other. During Cromwell's occupation, I daresay. But it's a church for all that . . . still holy ground. This marriage will be legal all right."

"Not if I do not consent. And I shall not."

Mr. Ferris stopped between two crosses of antique design, each elaborately decorated with sinuous visions of life and death, entwined for all eternity.

"Now, listen, my girl. You've had it all your own way too long. Why, strike me if you don't think you run *me*."

"You prefer the management of Mrs. Vernon," Rietta said bitingly. "Father, she'll run through your money in a month."

"What's that matter? I'm not going to die to oblige her like her last two husbands—not but what they died with smiles on their faces. You'll have your marriage portion, as will Blanche. What I do with the rest is no concern of yours."

He started forward again, but Rietta literally dug in her heels, taking a firm grasp on a headstone. The carved image of a grinning skull impressed itself into her palm. "Father . . . ," she began, desperate to change his mind.

"Come along, girl."

"No, I won't do it. You can't force me!"

"Damn you, Rietta!" He struck her sharply across the back of her hand, breaking her grip.

Her eyes closed over hot tears. It was not the blow but the curse that had called them there. What did anything matter now? No one loved her; she'd only been fooling herself in thinking that her family did.

Suddenly so weary she could hardly move, Rietta made no further protest. She entered the ruined church, hardly noticing the cold rain that had begun to fall. She could only tell her tears by their heat.

She stood where she was pushed to stand, her shoulders feeling weighed down as if by carrying turf. Dully, she watched her father—could she still call him that?—showing a piece of paper to a man muffled in a monk's robe, a man so withered with years that he might as well have been a founding member of this ancient abbey. She saw gold pass from Mr. Ferris's hand to the clawlike and dirty fingers of the old monk. Everything, it seemed, had a price. She wondered vaguely how much a funeral would be.

The two hooded and cloaked witnesses signed the paper. Rietta saw that one bore upon his littlest finger a golden ring she'd seen a hundred times in the drawing room at Prospect Hill. Mr. Greeves, then, was a party to this game. No doubt he now saw his way that much clearer toward Blanche's hand.

She heard her father demand, "Where's the happy man?" followed by a request that the second man speak up.

The hooded man tossed back the muffling cloth. David Mochrie said, "He'll be here. He's not fool enough to throw away the bargain of a lifetime."

Rietta turned away from the appraising glint in his eyes when he looked on her. She felt the faintest stirrings of outrage that he should look at her so familiarly, as though she were lightly clad for his pleasure.

A clatter came as a second carriage arrived. Rietta started toward it as if in a dream she'd once had of running soundlessly and uselessly through an enormous yellow custard. Was it succor? Oh, let it be some kindly old woman on her way home, or a sober matron! She'd settle for an elderly grandparent or a gallant youth—anyone but these loathsomely complacent familiar faces.

A huge figure stepped out from among the shadows. Garrity stopped her with an arm like a tree trunk. "Now, then, it's all for the best. . . ."

"Garrity, please, take me away from here. I've always been your friend."

"Yes, Miss Ferris, but 'tis your father what pays my wages."

"What are you doing there, my man?" demanded a voice that awoke an echo of hope in Rietta's heart. "Let Miss Ferris go at once."

"She'll run if I do," Garrity said, his hamlike hands holding on to Rietta's upper arms with both gentleness and might.

"I said, let go." Nick came up, looking both tall and

wide in a greatcoat with many capes at the shoulders. "Don't make me knock you down, Garrity."

The big coachman laughed. "I wish I may see it!"

"You wouldn't see it; it would merely be done, leaving you holding a beefsteak to your jaw. Shall we try it?" Nick said, coming nearer.

Garrity released her so quickly that she all but fell. Nick was beside her in one stride, it seemed. She clutched his sleeve. "Please, take me away from here. You don't know what—"

"Poor sweet." A welcome note of compassionate friendliness sounded in his tone. "It will soon be over."

Rietta cringed away as though from an upraised hand. "Not you. Not you."

"No one but me, Rietta. I'm sorry it had to be this way."

He'd brought her flowers, white roses in a silver filigree holder. She held them in nerveless fingers, too worn out with disillusionment even to tremble. It was easier to stare at the roses than to think. A spider's web glinted among the petals.

The monk or priest had a very few brown and broken teeth, a deaf right ear, an inclination to mumble, and commanded a breathtaking grasp of the native Irish tongue. The entire marriage ceremony was conducted in a language half dead from repression and wholly incomprehensible to the woman most closely concerned. The old man poked Rietta with an impossibly desiccated finger while he said, as though to an idiot child, "Ah do . . . Ah do."

She repeated the agreement as though it were as meaningless as the rest of the ceremony. But then she chanced to look up during Nick's vows to find his eyes fixed on her with so intent and unvarying a look that she blushed, though she would have sworn a moment sooner that her blood was far too chilled by this strange wedding to summon up more than a slight pulse.

Then the monk looked at Nick.

Nick took a firmer grasp of Rietta's unresponsive hand. He spoke the vows in Irish, each dancing syllable a poem in itself. The monk grinned with all his remaining teeth, nodding in approbation as each word came correct. Rietta had said nothing beyond her bare acceptance. Nick wanted her to smile at him as she well knew how.

He wished with all his heart that this ceremony could have been different. He wanted to see Rietta arrayed like a queen in white silk and silver lace. After agreeing, he'd labored to convince Mr. Ferris that putting it off a few weeks could make no material difference to the outcome, but the smaller man wouldn't hear of it. He kept saying something about "the cup and the lip," but which part Nick was expected to take wasn't clear.

So he said his vows as ardently as possible in this cold crypt of ancient belief and tried to catch Rietta's eye. But she seemed hardly able to keep her eyes open. Had Mr. Ferris made sure of her docility by dosing her with something?

Then it was over, with a placing of a ring on her finger and the hurried mumbling of another interminable prayer. He hadn't even kissed her. Nick could have sworn he saw the whole ring of heaven go reeling across the sky as time passed before the monk gave his final blessing.

Then, at last, he had his bride tucked into the carriage. He refused to shake anyone's hand, not even David's, though he accepted with thanks the old monk's wedding gift of a bottle of illicit whiskey and his wishes for many children.

Then he swung onto the box and whipped up his horses.

Twelve

Nick gave a pull to the ribbons and walked his horses onto a half moon of rough-cropped grass. A bench of stone slabs invited wayfarers to stop and admire the willows overhanging the small yet swiftly running stream. Though not seen at its best by night, the sound was soothing to overwrought nerves. The light rain had stopped, and the moon shone its face through a few dramatically piled clouds, golden at their edges.

He tied off the reins and swung down to peek into the carriage window. "Will you come out, Rietta?"

For a moment, there was only silence. Then a stirring of skirts and her face, white as the moon's, swam toward him from the dim interior. Her eyes looked blind in the moonlight, for it reflected only her tears.

Nick held out his hand and she groped for it. On the turf, she walked away from him, hiding her face while she dug in the reticule that still hung from her arm. Her handkerchief flashed white. When she sniffed, his heart was wrung. "Ah, don't be crying now, love. . . ."

"I'm not," she said, blowing her nose like the blast of

an elfin trumpet. "It's silly to cry over what can't be helped. Utterly silly."

He reached into the carriage and brought out a basket he'd foreseen might be needed. Taking it to the bench, he invited Rietta to come forward. "Even if you're not hungry, you'll take a glass of wine, I hope?"

"I could do with a glass of something," she admitted.

"My father had this laid down on the day I was born," Nick said. The pop of a champagne cork startled her.

"To serve at your wedding breakfast, no doubt." Her tone held a forced brightness that made Nick feel like the lowest thing that crawled.

"Exactly." He poured a glass and put it into her hand. "I'll not offer you a toast," he said. "Not yet."

"No, we've nothing whatever to celebrate."

"I hope you won't continue to feel that way, Rietta."

"What a charming spot this is, Sir Nicholas. Is the river very deep at this point?"

"Not deep enough to drown in."

"That's too bad. A spot deep enough to drown in would be marvelously apt at this moment."

"On the contrary, I would find it of no use at all." He wiped the dew off the bench with a napkin and encouraged her to sit down. "My grandfather set this bench here, fifty years ago or more. He proposed to my grandmother here."

"Are we on your land already?" she asked as politely as a guest making conversation at a rather dull party.

"Yes, all this belongs to Greenwood. The family castle was on the far side of the stream once upon a time. The river widened, the castle fell down, the river narrowed again, and here we are. The bench is made from stone recovered from the river."

"Your family didn't rebuild your castle?"

"There was no need. The days of stealing cattle from our neighbors were long over and a castle was no protection against Cromwell's guns. So we moved up over the hill and built Greenwood—a few times over."

"Your home is nearby, then?"

"Half a mile away. You can see the lights around the next turn."

"And yet you break our journey here?"

"We need to talk before we go home."

"I suppose we must." Her glass glinted as she tilted it to drink the last few drops.

"More?" Nick asked.

She hesitated before refusing. "I shall face my ordeal without Dutch courage."

"So bad as that?"

"Why did you do it?" she demanded as though the words were torn from her. "Why? You must have known I was unwilling. If you had refused . . ."

"Your father made it impossible to refuse."

"My father," she said brokenly, turning away. "I can never forgive him for this."

She spoke so sadly, as though her inability to forgive was more her pain than her father's, that Nick couldn't resist leaning down to put his arm about her, to comfort her as though she were a child. But Rietta shrugged off his touch.

"Rietta, if there'd been another way . . . he threatened to throw you onto the street or to marry you to the first man he met. What could I do but marry you to save you from that?"

"You are too kind, sir," she said, her body rising along with her voice. "Shall I express the depth of my gratitude? I cannot. I have none to give you."

"I don't want gratitude, Rietta."

"It never occurred to you, I suppose, to offer me sanctuary in your home. Or, say, fifty pounds to take myself to my aunt in England?"

"I didn't know you had an aunt in England. But no, it didn't occur to me."

"Why not?"

"You know why not. Surely if anything is clear, it is that. I want you." He didn't take so much as a single step toward her, although every impulse in his body was urging him to do so.

"So it wasn't entirely from altruistic motives that you have married me this night."

Nick shook his head. "I begin to wonder if there was any unselfishness in my soul at all."

"Perhaps there was. A little." She held up her hand. "No. Don't touch me."

"I wasn't. I won't. No matter how much I want to."

She began to pace restlessly, her dress sweeping over the wet grass. Nick guessed that she felt as trapped as a lioness in a menagerie cage, confined through no fault of her own, and now people were poking sticks at her through the bars. "I suppose there is no doubt that ours is a legal marriage."

"Your father's consent is all that was required. And, forgive me, Rietta, you did take the vows of your own free will."

"Did I? My father made the same threats to me as he did to you. Marriage by menaces. I am so . . ." her voice trailed off as she covered her face with her hands.

Nick longed to take her in his arms and kiss away her tears, but he did not feel he had the right. She'd been overpowered by male authority enough for one day. Even the tenderest of coercion would be an insult from which their marriage might never recover.

"Marriage," he said aloud. "Our marriage."

The words warmed him in a way that was new and strange. Nick suddenly realized that, whatever else happened, he need never fear being alone with his ghosts. Rietta would be his wife, in name only for a time, in full flower later on. For their lifetimes to come, this tie would be between them, a halter sometimes, a lifeline at others.

"What about it?" she asked.

"My mother mustn't know the full tale of our deeds tonight. The thought that her children should marry for anything but love is repugnant to her."

"She is a very kind woman."

"Yes. And not in the best of health, I'm afraid. Life with my father was not conducive to a happy or secure outlook on life. I'd do anything to spare her pain."

"What tale can we tell, though, to explain my sudden arrival at Greenwood and in such a condition?" Rietta seemed to become aware that her hair was imperfectly stuffed beneath her bonnet and took off the confining headgear with an impatient jerk of the ribbons.

She shook her hair free, combing through the tangles with the fingers of one hand. Nick's mouth went dry and he took a hasty gulp of champagne. The bubbles went the wrong way, making him choke, but it wasn't the alcohol that made him feel so dizzy. With hair neatly coiled on the top of her head, her eyes mild and intelligent, neat in her dress and movements, Rietta had attracted him both physically and emotionally. A quiet, uncomplicated girl made a precise antidote to the horrors of war.

Now she appeared to him like a wild water spirit, her hair blowing free like a spume of sea mist thrown up on the rocks. Naked emotion shown in her eyes, moving him as her fortitude had not. She was disheveled, exhausted, and infinitely dear, all the more so when he knew tomorrow she would appear as controlled and engaging as before. Only he had this glimpse of the other side of her. Nick found himself wishing jealously to keep this image of Rietta all to himself.

"I suppose we might tell your mother that we have eloped," she said.

"Eloped? That might work. But why have we done this rash thing?"

"My father's objections?"

"She won't believe he could have any. She thinks I'm perfect."

"There's no accounting for a parent's partiality. I would have staked my life that my father thought I was . . . valuable."

Nick had to cross his arms, tucking his hands away securely to keep from embracing her, so bleak and miserable did she sound.

"We'll tell Mother that I rescued you from him," he said bracingly. "She'll like that; it sounds romantic. Your father was pressuring you into an uncongenial marriage, say with James Greeves."

"Yes," she said, sniffing but attempting with great courage to join in the game of make-believe. "That's a stock device from plays—the older man who wants to marry youth."

"It never fails to intrigue the audience. At least, not this audience. Mother's very fond of gothic novels. It's a pity we can't make Greeves some sort of Italian count with his own castle, preferably with an oubliette under the floor. She'd be happier with a few exotic trimmings."

"My father has dealings with Egyptian cotton merchants. We could claim that Father has sold me to one such, a sheik perhaps, to pay a lading bill or something."

"A distasteful suitor will serve without dragging in the Egyptian cotton market. So, you have an elderly suitor, preferred by your father, and then—what? I suppose you toyed with the notion, only to find me more to your taste?"

"No, I resisted tooth and nail, determined never to agree to a marriage of such inequality. Then when I met you . . ."

"You met your beau ideal?" he said, grinning.

"Hardly that. We don't want to have to pretend to be . . . to be fond of each other."

"I am fond of you, Rietta. I cannot imagine another woman for whom I'd have so willingly run my head into this noose."

"But you do not love me."

He would have gladly damned himself for a swifter tongue, one that would not hesitate over a firm "yes." As it was, he could neither lie ardently, nor would a flat negative serve to answer her. Nick did not believe that he loved Rietta, but he certainly loved no one else.

"If you try to counterfeit love," Rietta said, not waiting, "your mother will know that you do not mean it."

"I haven't been in love since I was seventeen." Nick strove to recapture their easy banter. "Would you like to hear about her?"

"In truth? No."

"Pity. I make quite an affecting tale of my lost beloved." He made some show of sighing sentimentally. "It comes in most useful at times."

"When you wish to be out of an entanglement?" Her voice sounded a trifle choked. In the uncertain moonlight, he couldn't tell if it was with laughter or tears.

"Exactly. How well you understand me."

"Have there been many women in your life? Not that I care," she added hurriedly.

"It depends on what you mean by 'many,' I suppose. I haven't been a saint, Rietta."

"I did not expect you to have been one, Sir Nicholas."

"That won't do. You'll have to call me Nick."

She turned her shoulder to him. It was all he could do not to reach out to draw one of her silky strands of hair through his fingers, but he'd promised not to touch her.

Walking around her, Nick captured her gaze when it wanted, butterfly-like, to land everywhere but on him. "You must call me Nick, Rietta, or they'll wonder why."

"Are we married, Sir Nicholas?" she asked desperately. "Are we, in truth?"

"In truth, Rietta, we are."

She nodded like someone hearing the official word of a crushing defeat. As if too exhausted for the moment to even negotiate a surrender, she hardly seemed able to stand. "Very well, Nick. Tell your mother what fiction you will and I'll agree."

Tears came to Lady Kirwan's eyes as she embraced her new daughter. "You're going to think me a foolish old woman, but the moment I saw you I knew you were right for Nick."

"I'm sure you must find the nature of our marriage to be peculiar, to say the least."

"*I* think it's romantic," Amelia said firmly.

"Very romantic," Emma echoed, but with a sigh.

They'd all come down in various states of undress when Nick had shouted their names up the stairway. For a moment they'd stood on the landing, staring in amazement at Rietta. She'd felt her cheeks burn as she instinctively moved closer to Nick. Then, without giving either of them a chance to explain her presence, his sisters and mother had hastened down the steps to greet her. Rietta had been almost overcome by the warmth of their welcome.

Only after they'd seen her seated by the fire, a cup of tea and plate of biscuits at her elbow, loving hands having taking her bonnet and pelisse and given her a towel for her damp hair, did they spare an instant to hear Nick out. But at the words "we're married," all further explanation had to wait for exclamations of joy and warm embraces all around. Even Emma, who was dressed as though in deepest mourning, clapped her hands in glee.

"Married! What could be more wonderful?"

A flood of questions followed their first pleasure. Nick answered them all, leaving Rietta to recover her equilibrium. She'd never expected such a reception. Where were the disdainful glances, the doubtful questions, the repulsing gestures? If they knew the truth, Lady Kirwan and her daughters would retreat from their friendly attitude. Any woman would, upon realizing her adored son had been trapped into marriage. Wouldn't Lady Kirwan assume that Rietta had been involved in her father's plot?

She'd seen upon their first meeting that Nick was the center of Lady Kirwan's universe. If he was in the room, she had no eyes for anyone else. Looking at him now, Rietta realized that she'd never seen him be himself before. He looked relaxed, his mouth ready to smile at Amelia's forthrightness, while he gave Emma a reassuring squeeze of the hand when an incautious word reminded the girl of her false lover. When he turned to his mother, his eyes betrayed much tenderness.

Rietta closed her eyes and leaned her head back, trying to recall exactly how his expression appeared when he looked at her. Did his smile warm his eyes? Or was it only the heat of lust glimmering there? She sighed sadly.

"The poor dear," Lady Kirwan said. "Quite worn out. Take her upstairs and then leave her to us, Nick."

On a sensation of floating, Rietta opened her eyes. Nick had only to turn his head a fraction of an inch to look into her face, for he was carrying her. He must have felt her tense. "You fell asleep," he said softly. "My mother told me to carry you up to bed."

"No. . . ," she whispered in a panic.

"Never fear. I have my orders and they are quite precise. I carry you. I place you on the bed. I leave. That's what you want, isn't it?"

"That's right. But I can walk very well."

"Don't squirm so; I may drop you."

"Please put me down."

"I can't. About the only thing of value that I learned in the army was to follow orders blindly." A moment later, he said, "Whoops!" as she dropped a bit lower. "It would help if you'd put your arms about my neck to take some of the strain."

She quickly did as he asked, though it brought them into even closer contact. Her breast rested against his shoulder, while she could have buried her hot face in the side of his neck. Instead, she stared straight ahead, as nearly as possible ignoring the man who carried her.

"That's better," he said.

"For whom?"

She felt a chuckle shake his chest. A moment later, they entered a candlelit room on the next level. Rietta hardly had a chance to glance around before he placed her gently in the center of a curtained bed. He bent over her, his hand flat on the mattress. Rietta blinked up at him, motionless as a bird that fears a cat prowling nearby.

Nick swept the loosened hair back from her forehead. "Sleep well."

Perhaps he would have kissed her then; Rietta saw the desire darkening his eyes as he began to bend lower still. The door swung as his sisters came in, chattering. Nick straightened and went to help Amelia with Rietta's carpet-bag. Rietta didn't know if she was glad to be spared or sorry not to be taken into his arms.

For she had no doubt at all that if Nick tried to seduce her, he would not find her difficult to persuade. It was for this reason that Rietta was determined to keep him at arm's length. She would not give in to her own desire until she could be absolutely certain that he loved her, rather than merely wanted her.

Thirteen

When the knock sounded at her door, Rietta pushed aside the tray, the tiny circle of soup at the bottom trembling. She stole a moment to push her hair behind her ears and pink her cheeks with a pinch. "Come in."

Lady Kirwan peeked around the edge of the door. Rietta smiled at her, trying not to feel disappointed that it was not Nick. He'd left her to his sisters' care and she'd not seen him since.

She could not complain of the room they'd given her. Though the wall covering had faded to an uneven sky blue, it had been of the best quality once. The same was true of the silk hangings around the tall-frame bed and the curtains. She walked on a worn yet highly decorative carpet, probably French, and the furniture gleamed with years of polishing. Yet a faint, musty smell told how long the room had been vacant and darker squares of wallpaper showed where pictures had hung once but no longer.

"Do you have everything you want, Rietta?" Lady Kirwan asked, coming into the room.

"Thank you, my lady, I do. Emma and Amelia have made me most comfortable. My lady . . ."

"You must learn to call me Mother," Lady Kirwan said gently. "You needn't if you don't wish to, of course, but as your own mother is no more, I hope you will come to look on me as a substitute." She smiled so warmly that Rietta found it difficult not to tell her the unvarnished truth. But Nick's feelings on the subject of disturbing his mother's happiness had been quite clear.

"I want to apologize for appearing out of the night in this hole-and-corner fashion. You must think it very remarkable. . . ."

"Nick wouldn't be Nick if he brought home his bride in some commonplace manner. He has always been one for the grand gesture."

"Nick?" She supposed marrying her could count as a dramatic act of chivalry, were it not that he'd made his motive plain. Rietta felt a warm flush under her skin at the remembrance of how he'd looked when he had told her he wanted her. She could have saved the effort of pinching her cheeks if just the thought of him could make her blush.

Lady Kirwan laughed, a dry sound like a rustle of leaves. Her eyes were bright in their nests of crisp wrinkles. "Forgive me. I don't believe you know him yet, however much you may love him."

"There hasn't been a great deal of time to grow our acquaintance," Rietta admitted.

"Nick has always been ready to throw his heart into any adventure that offers. It hasn't always been easy being his mother—oh, my heart was in my mouth a thousand times a day when he was a little one. His nurse would tell me such tales—goodness, it's a wonder to me he ever lived to grow up."

"You'll have to tell me all your stories, my lady . . . Mother." She felt she could grow quickly used to calling her that. Much easier, in fact, than calling Nick by his given name.

"I'll avail myself of that invitation, my dear. Not just

now, however. You need your rest." She turned away from the dressing table, a hairbrush in her hand. "May I help you?"

"Oh, no."

"I should like to. My own girls rarely permit me to pamper them anymore. They are too busy worrying about me."

The long strokes of the brush through her hair was very relaxing. Lady Kirwan hummed an old lullaby as she worked. Rietta knew the words well, from those far-off days when Mrs. Athy had served the Ferris family.

"What a lovely shade of red! Like the old chalices our medieval monks hid away from the Viking sea robbers. I do hope your children inherit it. All the black hair in my husband's family makes them look so gloomy. I actually looked forward to Sir Benjamin's hair turning gray."

"I notice Nick has a little gray in his hair. Did your husband change so early?"

Lady Kirwan's brush strokes paused for an instant. "Not that I recall. There. That's done."

Rietta glanced across the room to the dressing table mirror. There were dried flower swags draped over the mirror so that her face peered back at her like the image of a nymph glimpsed at the bottom of a pool in springtime. Her hair lay sleekly around her shoulders, as smooth and shining as glass. Lady Kirwan passed her hands over either side of Rietta's head. "Just like red-gold," she said. "Charming. I have a piece of green silk laid by in a trunk. It should make a delightful scarf for you."

Rietta caught one of Lady Kirwan's dry hands and held it against her cheek. "I don't know why you are so kind to me."

"Because my son loves you," Lady Kirwan answered as if it were the most natural thing in the world. She patted Rietta's face. "And because I think you can help him."

"Help him?" Rietta was interested. She couldn't imagine how Nick could possibly need anyone's help. From the first time she'd seen him, flirting with Blanche, he'd seemed strong and determined. His smile had been supremely confident, echoed in the way he stood with his hands on his hips, surveying her sister and his surroundings like a man completely at ease with command.

Apologizing for her bad manners, Rietta stood up and offered Lady Kirwan her chair.

"He'd think me very foolish if he could hear me, but I cannot get it from my head that Nick has changed since he came home," Lady Kirwan said.

"Are you concerned about his health?"

"Not his bodily health. I don't wish to alarm you, my dear, but he hasn't been himself. I blame myself. I should have given him a clearer picture of the state of our finances. I'm afraid it was a shock."

A knock interrupted her. Rietta saw Lady Kirwan smile at her with warm sympathy and realized she'd sat up like a dog hearing her master's voice.

"That will be the girl come to take away your tray," Lady Kirwan said softly. "You'll find the servants at Greenwood have all been taught to knock before entering. It's eccentric of me, I know. In my father's house, you see, they would come in soundlessly and I never cared for the lack of privacy."

"I never thought about it, but I'm certain you are right. Come in!"

The maid was young and thin, and her cap wobbled on top of her head. She all but tripped over the rug, her clear blue eyes fixed on Rietta's face. Lady Kirwan smiled. "This is Sarah Boole—such a help."

"How do you do, Sarah?"

"My lady," the maid said, bobbing an uneven curtsey. She wore heavy boots beneath her black skirt. "I come for the tray, my lady."

Rietta suddenly realized that the maid was addressing

her—she now was a Lady Kirwan as well. She honestly had not considered that change in circumstance until this very instant. Bitterly, she wished that her father could be here to experience the height of his hopes.

"Bring some tea. The chamomile," Lady Kirwan said. "I use it to sleep," she confessed in an aside.

She waited until the door had closed behind Sarah before continuing. "I suppose a mother shouldn't have a favorite among her children. I adore my girls—they have been my reward for continuing in the face of all my difficulties."

Rietta reached out to press the other woman's hand. There was such unyielding resolution in her tone that Rietta couldn't help wondering whether Lady Kirwan had ever been tempted to make away with herself, only to reject the notion as being more cowardly than immoral.

"But Nick . . . ," Rietta prompted, and saw a tender smile dawn on Lady Kirwan's wan lips.

"Nick was always my favorite—there, I admit it. I can admit it to you, for if he were not your favorite you never would have married him."

Rietta shifted, her mental discomfort at continuing to build this lie manifesting itself as a physical inability to relax. "I'd never met another man whom I'd be willing to marry."

"I knew it as soon as I met you. You're right for Nick. Ever since he came home on leave the last time, I knew something was wrong. He looked so tired."

"Army life?"

"Yes, I suppose. The conditions in the army—especially on the Peninsula—were appalling, by all I ever read. My husband used to storm up and down whenever he received a newspaper. Benjamin had quite the talent for inventive swearing." She paused as though in an enjoyable reverie, though what could be pleasurable about invective, Rietta did not know.

"Yet I don't think it was bad food and ill housing that made the change in Nick. He spoke less, laughed less, and seemed so . . . so lonely. That's it. He seemed terribly lonely here, and I'm sure he never was before. True, Greenwood is rather an isolated house—I do so hope you won't find it dull."

"Do you?"

"Find Greenwood dull? Certainly not. I have my gardens, though I cannot do all I could wish. My health . . . well, it's indifferent and no one has ever been able to say why. Thin blood, perhaps. My parents were cousins and until Benjamin married me I doubt we had many outsiders marry into the family. I was an O'Shamson, you know."

"If you find enough to occupy yourself, Lady . . . Mother," Rietta smiled shyly. "I'm certain I will have no trouble."

"And once you have children, you'll never have another dull moment, if any of them turn out like Nick. Amelia, too, has high spirits. I'm afraid Emma takes after me."

Rietta had not thought so far ahead as tomorrow, let alone to a distant future complete with imaginary children. She knew something of where children came from. The notion of creating a family with Nick should have left her confused and embarrassed. Instead, she felt quite at home with the idea and could almost picture her eldest. The mix of Nick's dark coloring with her own red hair and pale skin should make for handsome children.

Then a second knock sounded at the door.

"That will be Sarah," Lady Kirwan said. "She's not usually so quick."

Lady Kirwan instantly assumed it was Sarah returned with the tea tray, but Rietta knew better. There was no mistaking Nick's rapping for any shy and country-reared maid's.

She hoped that her face didn't glow the way Lady Kirwan's did when she saw him. She hoped, but it was a vain hope. She knew she was giving him a welcoming smile that promised too much that she, newly married under protest, could not give her husband. Rietta wished that she had needlework or a cup of tea to focus her attention upon so she might hide her eyes.

"Talking secrets?" Nick asked with a teasing grin. "Emma and Amelia have gone to bed."

"So should I," Lady Kirwan said, slowly rising from her chair. "I've quite lost track of the time, talking with my enchanting new daughter. Thank you, Nick, for giving her to me."

Outrageously, Nick winked at Rietta over his mother's head as she embraced him. "I took your taste into account, Mother, before I chose."

"I'm sure that's not true, but I thank you kindly for the thought. Good night, Rietta."

"Good night, Mother," Rietta said, rising. She tilted her chin in response to Nick's startled glance, hoping he'd realize that he did not pipe *all* the tunes they danced to.

Nick held the door for his mother and closed it behind her. He turned, pressing his back against the panels. He passed a lingering glance over her and she felt a strange quivering deep inside her heart. Slowly he began to walk toward her, avoiding chairs and bibelot-laden tables by a seeming instinct, for he never took his eyes from hers. "And now, Rietta . . . and now."

She stood her ground, though every instinct told her to back away cautiously, as any creature would while being stalked by a hungry predator. "Nick. Remember what we agreed."

"If I go to my room now, Mother will notice and wonder why. I'll have to stay until she's asleep. She always reads her Bible for half an hour before she puts out her candle. What shall we do together for the next half hour, hmm?"

"Play chess?"

"I'm not interested in games."

He was so close now that Rietta had to tip her head back to see his eyes. Lowering his head, he brushed his lips over her cheek, nuzzling her neck, breathing in her fragrance and sighing on a humming sound. "You smell good."

"Do I?"

"The flowers of Spain grow in the dust and their perfume is almost enough to make an artillery man drunk. But they're nothing compared to you, Rietta. You're a rose, sweet and golden."

He was bound to kiss her. She could hear it in the sudden huskiness of his voice, see it in the gleam of his half-closed eyes. If only she didn't feel such an overwhelming compulsion to give in, to let him take what liberties he pleased. But to permit her baser feelings to crush her better sense would strip her of all her self-respect. She'd been imposed upon enough today; she'd not add to her burdens by giving herself to a husband who did not love her as she felt she deserved.

"No," she said and meant it.

Nick stopped instantly. He didn't move away, but he didn't attempt to press his advantage. Rietta's hands were flat against his chest. They were small hands, but he was a man who could be stopped by even less strength than she had.

"I'm not to kiss you?" he asked and noticed, distracted, that she was breathing faster than she had a moment ago.

"No. Not until I say you might."

"So the hen will rule the roost at Greenwood, my Lady Kirwan? Well, it should be used to that state of affairs by now. Pardon me." He smoothed a stray lock of her hair. "I may touch you casually, I suppose? Just in passing, no harm meant."

"I don't think you should." Her arms hadn't relaxed yet from their outthrust tension.

Nick backed away, crossing his arms over his chest and

eyeing her. In contrast to the magnificently female lines of her body, her face was set with such stern resolve that he could only think of the colored saints of carved wood he'd seen in Spain and Portugal. Many of them had similar expressions of utter determination, for no soft words or pleasant sensations could sway them from their martyrdom.

Not that Rietta would sacrifice herself to preserve her virginity, he hoped. He'd much rather have a willing wife. As he thought that, it struck him that she might never be willing.

"Very well, Rietta. It will be as you wish. You need time to accustom yourself to all this."

She let out a breath she seemed to have been holding a long time. "Yes. I feel like I've been picked up by a whirlwind and dropped into another world."

"I only wish my world had more to offer you. We should discuss many things that you will need to know, but not tonight, I think."

Her smile warmed him, making him feel less of a brute. After all she'd been through, he really had no business even being in her room. Certainly, making advances to her was the act of an unfeeling cad. Sitting in his room earlier, he'd told himself not to trouble her, only to find himself powerless before the compulsion to visit her, to prove with the evidence of his eyes and hands that she was indeed his bride.

"Who's that?" he asked, glad of the interrupting knock. A third party would make it easier yet to control his needs.

"Only the maid. Your mother sent for tea."

"Mother's tea. You'll find she has a tea or tisane for every ill from a headache to . . . to gangrene."

Nick stood by the fire while Sarah Boole brought in the tray. He kicked at the ill-burning log both to let the air in and to change the pictures he saw in the depths of the embers. He heard Rietta speak to the girl.

"Thank you, Sarah. Pass my thanks to the others."

"Yes, m'lady. Thank you, m'lady." She curtsied her way to the door. On the threshold, she took courage. "May the Lord keep ye in His hand, m'lady, and never close His fist too tight upon ye."

"May I see you gray and combing your grandchildren's hair, Sarah.

The girl grinned, showing the wide space between her two front teeth. Her bright eyes flicked between the man and the woman, then she giggled, cast her apron over her face, and ran from the room.

"You've made her great in the eyes of her fellows," Nick said, sitting down.

"Have I?"

"She's the first one to see you, but she won't be the last."

"I'll pay a call in the servant's hall tomorrow, if you don't think your mother would find it impertinent."

"She'll most likely take you there herself. She can't wait to show you off." He leaned forward to cover her hand with his own, then remembering her strictures, took a cup of tea instead. After a sip, he made a face.

"You'd prefer whiskey, no doubt."

"I'm not a drinking man. At least not often. A man hopes that drink will destroy the thoughts he cannot bear; in truth, it only ruins the strength he needs to bear them."

"Have you many thoughts that you cannot bear?"

Fourteen

Nick sat back, seemingly at ease, but Rietta had seen the slight tremor in his hand until he'd lowered it to his knee. Now she noticed that he gripped tight, his fingers pressing into the cloth of his breeches. Yet his other hand was as steady as could be as he lifted the cup to his lips.

"You've been talking to my mother," he said with a laugh so nearly believable that anyone else would have thought all was well.

"Yes. She's troubled in her mind about you."

"She's a good mother, but she should realize that we're not children anymore."

"Perhaps, to a good mother, her children are always children. Perhaps worrying about them becomes a habit impossible to break."

Sipping from her own teacup, she watched him over the brim. She didn't doubt that Lady Kirwan had reason for concern, but never having met Nick before his return from Europe, she herself could not judge how much he'd changed. Except for the trembling hand, which he seemed to have under control, she could discern nothing amiss.

"Does she have cause?" she asked. "I'm not idly curious, you understand."

"Yes, I see that you'd rather not have married some man of unpredictable moods, prey to gloomy ruminations upon mortality."

Rietta smiled warmly at him. "No woman minds a philosophical man, so long as he doesn't pursue it when there are more vital issues at hand."

"Like?"

"Oh, I don't know. Musing on theology while the supper burns."

"I'm not much of a cook. My friends used to tell me they'd rather have a Spanish muleteer cook supper than me."

"You had no servants?"

"Batmen, Rietta, we call them batmen. Oh, yes, I had MacMurray—a short, plump fellow from the Lowlands of Scotland. Whoever went short in the regiment, it wouldn't be MacMurray. Once, I remember, he found us rabbits on a night so wet and dark the bivouac fires looked like volcanoes of mud. The Spaniards couldn't find their own stew pans, let alone anything to put in 'em, but MacMurray came back with a brace of rabbits—scrawny enough, but the first meat we'd seen in a week. Cashman said those rabbits saved his life. . . ."

He stood up abruptly, almost turning over his chair. He caught it, set it upright, and threw her a swift sideways glance as though wondering if she'd noticed his perturbation. "I'll say good night."

"Good night, Nick."

"If you need anything in the night," he said, after clearing his throat, "knock on my door."

"Which is your room?"

He paused, out of all proportion to the question. Then he stepped to what she'd thought was a closed window curtain. Drawing back the swath of blue silk, he looped the heavily tassled tie over a wall hook. Underneath the curtain was a six-paneled door that matched the door to the corridor.

"This is mine," Nick said. "Our rooms connect."

"Do they, now."

"Naturally, my mother and sisters assumed . . . they made the natural assumption. You needn't worry, Rietta. The door has a lock—on this side."

"Must I ask you for the key?" Rietta asked, holding out her hand.

Nick tossed his head toward a delicate ladies' desk against the same wall. "It's in the top left drawer. You'll have to get it out to let me through. And if I may have the loan of a candle? They weren't expecting me to use the room tonight."

"Won't the servants wonder if you use it?"

"Let them. They'll talk about us anyway."

The key was long and gilded, with a faded blue ribbon tied through the scrollwork at the top. Nick slipped it easily enough into the lock but, though he tried until the veins stood out on his twisted hand, he could not turn it. "Rusted through," he said, stepping back.

"Perhaps it needs oil."

"No doubt. It's been a long time since these rooms were occupied. Mother left this one when she became a widow."

"I didn't put her out? I wondered."

"She always planned to leave it when I married anyway. Of course, I have my father's old room, but the bed's too soft. . . . Listen to me run on. I forgot for a moment that you've no interest in my bed. Here, take the key and put it away and bury all my hopes of you coming through that door with it."

"Good night, Nick," Rietta said, controlling her lips with effort. They so wanted to smile. "You'll have to risk the hall."

"Good night," he said again, but didn't move toward either door. "I wonder if I may ask a favor, Rietta?"

"Of course."

"May I . . . ?" He opened his arms stiffly, awkwardly, as if afraid of a rebuff.

Rietta walked into his embrace. His arms closed about her, warm and strong. Nick made no advance. He merely held her tightly, his cheek resting atop her head. Her own arms were looped lightly about his waist, his warmth seeping through to her. She had not realized how completely chilled she was until he wrapped her up in his strength. Rietta closed her eyes, savoring the moment.

They stood like that, their separate rhythms of breath mingling into one even pace, until the clock chimed softly. As though it awoke them from a spell, they stirred and parted in the same instant. Rietta felt him drop a kiss upon her hair before she opened her eyes to find herself alone. One candle was missing from a branch of three on the dressing table.

Rietta had never known the pleasure of a simple, spontaneous embrace. Her father was not demonstrative with his children and her sister accepted the affection of others but offered little generosity in return. Was Nick's the action of a generous man, giving comfort and warmth without expecting any recompense? She knew what she could give him in return.

Nick's arms around her had seemed to send a heavenly shaft of light flooding through her body. To be cherished like that was all she'd ever wanted. Rietta promised herself that she would prove to be worthy of Nick's affection. She vowed that she would be an absolute saint. Not another word of recrimination for his actions tonight would ever pass her lips. After all, he had saved her from the fearsome fate that her father had threatened. The manner of her wooing may not have been all a girl dreams of, but at least she'd met Nick before she'd been forced into marriage.

Whether it was exhaustion, chamomile tea, or simply a desire to escape into the relatively simpler world of dreams, Rietta fell asleep almost before her head touched the pillow. When she awoke, it was to a sensation that no time at all had passed.

She lay on the bed, quite cold, the bedclothes tumbled and tossed so that hardly a corner covered her. Contrary to all training and habit, Rietta had only removed her gown and corset before falling asleep. She'd always despised sleeping in her petticoat, and thought it the epitome of vulgar laziness. This one time, she hoped that circumstances would plead for her before whatever judge punished lazybones. She would have changed had she not literally run out of strength and energy by the time she'd unlaced her gown and washed her face.

At first, she attempted to pull the smooth linen sheet over her shoulder and retreat again into sleep. Yet it was not bodily discomfort that had awakened her. Something else had done that—a sound on the farthest shore of consciousness.

A faint white light washed through the curtains. Rietta sat up, rubbing her forehead in an attempt to clear her head. She shuffled her feet across the carpet as she crossed to open the curtain. Was it dawn?

Rietta blinked stupidly at the darkness beyond the window. Had she slept all day and into the following night? Or, horrible thought, had she hardly been asleep any time at all?

The moon had to be riding the sky above the house, for there was milk-pale light everywhere, deepening the shadows to impenetrable depths but highlighting trees and the undulating ground. Rietta thought the view in daylight from this window must be remarkable both for beauty and tranquillity. The colors of the flowers were all asleep under that bleaching light, but the beds looked well-filled and healthy.

Rietta yawned and indulged in an ill-mannered scratch
of her neck. She'd take a moment to change into something more seemly and then the world could just try to
wake her. She started to untie her petticoat, then became
aware of a strange sound.

All the time she'd been gazing like a moonstruck ninny
out of the window, this sound had been with her. Perhaps
her neck had itched because of rising hackles.

It was a voice, murmuring on and on, as ceaseless and
as senseless as the waves tumbling onto shore. Was it
Emma, dreaming of her false-hearted lover? Lady Kirwan,
as troubled in sleep as in her waking?

Rietta didn't yet know enough about Amelia to hazard
a guess over her secret sorrow. Advancing to the hall door,
Rietta pulled it open as silently as possible and stood listening. Somewhere a clock was ticking, monotonous and
reassuring. A skritching in the wainscoting told her that at
least one mouse was keeping its tiny nose to the grind-
stone. But she didn't hear the faint rumble of an indeci-
pherable voice.

She drew back into her room and instantly dismissed
the idea of ghosts. Nick would have told her if Greenwood
was haunted. But the prickly feeling on the back of her
neck wouldn't leave her.

Then she could have slapped her forehead. Of course.
The sound came from Nick's room. Once she realized it,
she recognized his voice—the rhythms, the depth, the
thousand and one tones that expressed feeling. But who
was he talking to so late? His mother, perhaps, come to see
why her son had returned to his own room instead of lying
close to his bride of a few hours.

Rietta raised her hand but thought better of knocking.
Her feelings toward Nick had whipsawed too much already. The intimacy of calling him through a matrimonial
door might increase his already matrimonial ideas.

Instead, Rietta turned her ear toward the door. She

didn't press against the keyhole or fetch the water glass from her bedside to amplify the sounds. She simply listened, her concern her excuse.

At first, she heard only a continuation of the confused murmuring. Then a long silence—so long that she straightened up with a kink in her back. Just as she was about to give up, she heard a shout.

"No! Not that way, you bloody fool!"

His voice fell off again. A man being tortured, fighting to defy his tormentors with silence, must make those same muffled gasps and cries. Only a few words were understandable and those wretched pleas wrenched Rietta's heart. "No . . . oh, God. Go back. Please. Please go back."

Snatching up a silken shawl from the foot of the bed, Rietta swirled it about her shoulders. Barefoot and swift, she passed from her room to Nick's without so much as a glance about her to see if anyone was watching. The house lay as if under a spell of silent enchantment.

Rietta pushed open Nick's door and stole in. His curtains were wide open, the maddening moonlight pouring in like a cataract of quicksilver. Nick lay as though on a gridiron, the crosspieces of his window frames quartering the moonlight with shadows. His coverlet, pillows, and nightcap had all slithered to the floor.

Slipping closer, Rietta whispered, "Nick?"

He muttered in sleep, a grumbling sound like a thunderstorm threatening on the horizon. He was sprawled out, every limb pointing to a different compass heading. The moonlight was so brilliant, she could see the sheen of sweat on his forehead and the restlessness of his eyes beneath their lids.

"Nick," she said again, reaching for his hand. His skin felt as hot as a coal snatched from the fire. A delirious notion of sliding into bed beside him possessed her. What would it be like to share so much heat?

"Come back," he pleaded, like a lost thing. His eyes

opened. His gaze rolled aimlessly past her face, past the window. "Where are they? They've all ridden away."

"Who has?" Rietta wondered aloud, her voice as soft as the wind brushing its fingers over the window.

"Fox. Allenby. Ribera. They've all ridden away. They should have waited for me." He shivered and crossed his arms, drawing into himself. Rietta swept up the coverlet and put it over him. She wasn't certain if he was awake or answering her out of some dream. If so, it might prove dangerous to wake him while he was so deeply enmeshed in the toils of a nightmare.

"Where have they gone?" Rietta asked, still bending low.

"Cashman?" he said. "Tompkins?"

He sat up suddenly. Rietta fell back, clutching her shawl to her breast. Though the room was flooded with light, he didn't notice her. He stared toward the exposed windows, pushing the fingers of one hand through his tousled hair.

She heard him draw a great deep breath, on and on as though he were coming up from the bottom of a river and needed the air to live. Then he sighed and rubbed his face. "I—I'm home. Thank God."

Nick fell back, his arms thrown wide. He no longer looked as if he were tied to a rack. His pose bespoke the luxury of waking from a dream into the comfort of a bed that moments ago had been the scene of mental horror.

The moment she moved, even though she felt sure she was silent, he rolled on his side and looked at her. "Your bed isn't comfortable?" he asked. "Or perhaps you're hungry?"

"No. I'm not."

"Too bad. I'm as empty as a gallon jug after a wake. If I had an accomplice in crime, I'd go poaching in the kitchen."

Rietta considered questioning him about his nightmare, but his sharp, bright tone warned her off. It would have been easier to deal with him had he demanded angrily to know how she dared to come into his bedroom. She suddenly realized that he might leap to a natural conclusion—that she'd changed her mind about consummating their unusual marriage.

He swung his legs out of bed. Rietta turned her head away, but she'd already taken notice of his smoothly muscled thighs. "I'll escort you back to your room, if you're quite sure you're not hungry."

The dressing gown's medieval lines suited the thin lines of his face, making him look like a scholar. But the glint in his eyes as he came nearer was that of a man who had studied sensual arts not sanctioned by church or law. "Unless you'd rather stay here, Rietta. You're more than welcome to at least half the bed."

Rietta retreated toward the door. She might entertain the idea of joining him there but she couldn't escape the feeling that it would be wrong. "I—I am a little peckish, come to think of it."

"Very well. I'll show you the way."

He carried the candle through the dark hallways. The black shadows swirled around them like blind ghosts as they walked. Remembering that her hair was loose, Rietta bundled the mass up into a more seemly knot, twisting it so that it would stay.

Nick paused before a portrait and held up the chamberstick. "This is my grandfather, Sir Artemus."

"There's a man behind that beard?"

"The family theorizes that the law was interested in the old gentleman and that he grew the beard to baffle identification."

"I'm sure it must have. His own mother would have been hard-pressed to know him," Rietta said, peering at the few inches of skin visible behind a veritable hedge of hair. "What do you suspect him of having done?"

"Murder. They say he had terrible nightmares. . . ."

Rietta schooled her features to reflect nothing but mild interest as the candlelight fell on her face. "You have his eyes, I think."

"Possibly. Anyway, he's the romantic fellow who built the bench we stopped at earlier in the evening."

"Oh, then I'm certain he's completely innocent of any wrongdoing. A man with such romantic gifts in his soul . . ."

"Romantic notions have led men into desperate enterprises before now, Rietta."

"Such as?"

He walked on. "Explorers must have romantic souls. Who'd seek a new world without one?"

"True. The Crusaders must have been rather romantic, don't you think?"

"Perhaps they started out that way, but I imagine the realities of the Holy Land must have quickly ended their illusions."

"Did you have any relations in the Crusades?"

"Not that I know of. Our family tends to stay at home. Except me."

"And Emma. She tried to find a new world, didn't she?"

"Did I thank you for taking her in?"

"Your mother did."

"Well, perhaps there's some wanderlust in our family nowadays. But in the past, we've always kept to our own fireside." His voice dropped. "I intend to honor that tradition henceforth."

"I can see why. I've never been in a house I like better than Greenwood, although . . ." Her voice trailed off.

"You can see that it needs some money spent on it," Nick said, finishing her sentence for her.

"I wasn't going to say anything of the sort, Nick. I was going to say that I can't wait to see it by daylight."

Nick took her elbow to steer her behind the staircase. "The servants' quarters are downstairs. We'll have to go quietly. Cook grows irritable if she doesn't have enough sleep. She cooks like an angel when she's rested, and burns things like the devil if she's not."

"Then I'll go quiet as a snowflake."

But when Nick pushed open the door it was to find the cook wide awake. "And this is a fine time o' night," she began before she saw who it was. "Master Nick!" she gasped, rising to her feet from behind the broad table. "And yer ladyship!"

"Good morning," Nick said genially. "You're up late."

The cook's pale cheeks flushed pink, the color flooding up into the roots of her white hair, braided into a thick coil that hung halfway down her back. Like Rietta, she wore a flowered shawl around her shoulders, though over a brown, stuff dress. "There's much work to be done," she said. "Your lady mother's inviting half the country to come meet your bride. Good luck to you, my lady."

"Thank you, Mrs. . . . ?"

"Cook, my lady."

"I can't call you—"

Nick saved her. "Mrs. Cook has been working here since I was a boy. She knows all my favorites."

"I shall have to speak to you about him," Rietta said. "I'm sure he was no better than a pirate."

"We're hungry as pirates," Nick said. "Can you help us?"

The cook's warm brown eyes flicked between them. "You'll be hungry, sure enough," she said, and the understanding in her voice and the sly touch of her finger to her nose made Rietta turn pink.

"Come down to raid my kitchen, have you? And if I'd not been here, half tomorrow's victuals would have been gone come the morning, I'll warrant." The plump lady cast a calculating glance at the windows. "All right. Sit ye down and I'll cook eggs for you. But you eat 'em up quick as lightning for I'll not have you sitting in my kitchen 'til cock crow."

Nick pulled back a chair for Rietta and indicated with as much studied grace as could be found in a ballroom that she should sit down. Rietta swept him a curtsey and took her seat with dignity.

"Isn't it terribly late for you, Mrs. Cook?" she asked. "I hope you are not unwell."

"Not a bit of it, your ladyship—barring a mite o'pain in my joints from time to time. It's my knees, creaking like the handle of a pump, so they do."

Rietta saw with an inner smile how Nick sat back, well out of the way, as she and Mrs. Cook were instantly plunged into a discussion of goose grease versus some patent remedy. It wasn't long before Mrs. Cook had brought out a bottle of her special mixture, a bright yellow liquid that gurgled thickly when poured. Rietta rubbed a little into the back of her left hand and blinked back tears. "Good heavens! It's liquid fire."

Quick as winking, Nick snatched his handkerchief from his pocket, dunked it in a pitcher of water standing on the drain board, and draped it over the back of his wife's hand. She threw him a glance that had more gratitude in it than any she'd shown so far. He'd moved so quickly, with so little wasted motion, that she'd hardly seen him act until the soaking cloth was comforting her hand.

"How . . . how can you stand it?" Rietta asked hoarsely.

"It's the burning that gets the good of it well into the skin," Mrs. Cook replied with pride.

"I'll make you up some of my mother's preparation. She enjoyed messing about with herbs and such."

"My lady's the same. But I'll swear by Dr. Mountjoy's horse rub t'my dying day. Eat your eggs."

"Please sit with us," Rietta said.

After a token protest, Mrs. Cook did so, but she perched her voluptuous figure on the very edge of her chair.

Though Rietta had only just met Mrs. Cook, she did not seem the sort of woman to be so nervous. Yet she would start at every noise, whether the tick of a fork against a plate or the shuffle of Nick's feet under the table. When Rietta accidentally dropped her knife to the floor, she thought Mrs. Cook was going to have a convulsion. She'd leap about in her seat and start chattering on any subject that came to mind. Then she'd wind down after the manner of a musical box until the next slight noise.

Rietta could not ask Nick if this was his cook's usual behavior, but they exchanged an eyebrow-raising silent conversation that seemed to indicate it was not. What, then, had her so on the jump?

About the time Rietta swallowed the last forkful of an excellent eggs Benedict, she found out.

The door from the outside swung open. Mrs. Cook leapt to her feet with, "Ah, look at the time! And me so tired, Sir Nick, as would—"

The door swung to much faster than it had opened, but Nick was even quicker over the ground this time than before. He tore the knob out of the other person's fingers and pushed it wide open.

Amelia stood there, her chin tilted in what should have been mature defiance but looked more like the pose of a martyr. "I'm surprised to see you, Nick."

Fifteen

"*Not nearly so* surprised, I'll be bound, as I am to see you. What the devil's the meaning of this, Amelia?"

"You're a fine one to demand explanations from me. You haven't been making any yourself, now have you?"

"Don't change the subject. This isn't about me. What are you doing coming home at this hour of the morning? Where have you been? And who, may a brother dare ask, have you been there with?"

Rietta had enough experience to recognize all the signs of a huge family quarrel approaching at the speed of a summer thunderstorm. But it was not yet her place to make peace. She stood up. "I'll be retiring now."

"Stay, if you please, Rietta. You've more knowledge of sisters than I have. Where do you think she's been?"

"Looking at the moonlight?" Rietta offered.

Nick didn't listen to this feeble answer at which even Amelia stared at her disbelievingly. He stormed on. "Lying to Mother. Convincing Mrs. Cook to wait up for you. Sneaking out of the house at all hours of the night . . ."

"Actually, she was sneaking in," Rietta said. "I doubt

Mrs. Cook needed much convincing, as I'm sure she's known you all since your cradles."

"That I have, and if I ever thought I'd live t'see the day when Master Nick acts so high and mighty over a little kissin' in the moonlight with a man who, for all he hasn't a grand name, has a fine future."

"Not if I catch him, he won't. He'll have no future at all," Nick responded. "May I remind all of you that it is past three o'clock in the morning? No girl sneaks home at three o'clock in the morning because of anything so innocent as stolen kisses."

"That's horrid of you," Amelia said, stamping her foot. "We didn't do anything . . . anything wrong. He's not the kind to take advantage—no matter how I want him to."

"What? God, Amelia, if Mother could hear you now her heart would stop like a broken clock."

"Then lower your voice so she won't come in. Anyway, why should I deny the truth? If I'm not sleeping in his arms at this moment, it's through no fault of my own."

For all Amelia's shamelessness, Rietta felt a pang of reluctant respect for her new sister. She had prided herself on her honesty—looking facts in the face had always been a cardinal virtue in her eyes. But she would not have had the spirit to admit openly that she wanted the love of a man.

Thus far, Nick had kissed her twice. She'd not been able to resist him, but now she wondered whether that was his doing or her own. She thought she loved him. Certainly seeing him helpless in a nightmare, her thought had been how best to aid him in her capacity as a loving woman. Yet even then, she'd been visited by a fantastic desire to crawl into the bed beside him. Were desire and compassion so closely linked that one could lead to the other? She was beginning to believe that love was much more complicated than she'd ever guessed.

"What's his name?" Nick demanded, rounding on his sister. "It's Arthur Daltrey, isn't it?"

He stood above her, a potentially threatening figure, though Rietta had noticed that he hadn't so much as shaken his fist at his sister. His finger, yes; he'd shaken that an inch in front of her nose. But Rietta doubted that Amelia was much intimidated by her brother's raised voice or powerful shoulders. There was too much pride in her face as she tossed her head and refused to answer.

"If I hurry, I can be at his farm before he's taken his first leg out of his breeches. He'll learn that no man despoils a Kirwan and lives."

"No, Nick," Amelia gasped, shaken out of her martyred silence by this threat. She stumbled forward to grasp at his arm. "No, it's not Arthur. It's . . . it's another man."

"You're a poor liar, m'dear." He looked over her head. "Mrs. Cook, I'll trouble you to find my sword. I brought it home with me and haven't seen it since."

"No!" Tears filled Amelia's widened eyes, thickening her voice. "You can't . . . you mustn't . . ."

Rietta came and put her arm about her new sister-in-law's shaking shoulders. "No, he won't. No soldier could attack an unarmed farmer."

She looked up into Nick's face, sure she'd see him wink. What she saw turned her cold as floating ice. His sea-blue eyes seemed to have gone black as he stared out the open kitchen door into the night beyond. Then he caught his breath and his clenched fists relaxed. "No," he said. "No soldier could do that, not in a time of peace."

Rietta caught his eye. Nodding toward Amelia, she put as much meaning as possible into her expression.

"Go to bed, Amelia," he said with rough kindness. "We'll talk about this in the morning, after we've all had the counsel of sleep. But you must understand that I will call upon Mr. Daltrey come tomorrow. As your brother and head of the household, I must demand an accounting from him of this night's work. The family's honor depends upon it."

Rietta stopped Amelia from speaking. "Don't say any more now. You'll only say something you'll regret. Come. If you'll show me the way to your room, I'll help you off with your things."

Nick had stayed behind in the kitchen to have a censorious word with Mrs. Cook. Rietta only hoped he hadn't scolded her so much that they'd find themselves without her at breakfast. She didn't imagine that he'd follow his own advice and go at once to bed following this scene, so she wasn't surprised to see him when she came down the hall.

"Amelia's almost asleep," Rietta said.

"Is she?"

"What will you do?"

"What I said. I'll pay a call on Daltrey."

"From what she told me, they're truly in love."

"Poured out all her girlish secrets, did she? Did she happen to mention that Daltrey used to be one of our tenants? How can I agree to a marriage between my sister and such a man?"

"I wouldn't have thought it mattered. After all, haven't you married a tradesman's daughter, and not of your own free will at that?"

"Against my will? Perhaps. But not against my inclination."

He was leaning against the frame of the door, eyeing her. Pushing himself upright, he took his hands out of his dressing gown pockets and reached out to grasp her wrist. Against the pull he exerted, she had only her words for defense.

"You said you'd not touch me." She spoke pantingly, which robbed her words of much of their force.

"You changed that when you touched me in my bed."

"You were asleep!"

"Rietta, my dear girl, your touch would rouse a dead

man." She could read his intentions in his eyes. They weren't dark or cold now; they sparkled with a wicked fire.

He stopped pulling her toward him one instant before she would have gone to his arms on her own. He smiled. "You'd not stop your humble, grateful husband from kissing your hand, would you?"

"Just my hand?"

He laughed at the confusion and disappointment in her voice. Rietta blushed.

Slowly, Nick raised her hand to his lips, his gaze focused on her eyes. Rietta couldn't look away let alone set herself free. She watched, fascinated, as he brushed the lightest of kisses over the thin, tender skin on the back of her hand.

"There," she said, relieved that his teasing breach of her rule was no more shattering than that. "Now . . ."

"Now." He pressed a kiss, harder yet, to each of her knuckles and then to each fingertip. His breath stirred her skin as he turned her hand over to make love to the sensitive palm and the ticklish webs between each finger. She couldn't think of anything but knew a tense curiosity as to where his fancy would take his talented lips next.

Rietta regretted giving him a far too intimate knowledge of her sighs and shuddering breaths but she found it impossible to keep silent as he drew cool patterns on her skin with his tongue. And when he gently bit the swelling at the base of her thumb, she cried out, her knees weak, losing the last of her restraint.

"I told you I only wanted to kiss your hand, my lady," he said. Perhaps he'd wanted to sound hatefully superior, but his voice gave him away. It shook with desire.

Rietta knew later that what happened next had nothing to do with her good resolutions or even her confusion over her future. She only knew that she had to ride this eager need as far as it would go.

"Nick . . ." Leaving her exquisitely awakened hand in

his, she untied her shawl with the other, letting it fall to the floor. Her low-cut chemise revealed the whiteness of her bosom. She breathed in deeply, making the mounds rise, and saw the fire in his eyes burst into an inferno that devoured all rational thought.

Stepping over the threshold, she reached out to caress his face, the roughness of his skin, in want of a shave, surprising her. But her hand welcomed the contrast between the velvet warmth of his mouth and the harsh scrape of his beard.

Rietta closed her eyes, her mouth opening in mute invitation, as she rose against his body. He stopped her and held her snug against his chest, his arm hard around her waist. "Say yes, Rietta."

"Yes," she whispered, so close to his mouth that the formation of words brought their lips into contact.

"Yes, Rietta. You are going to be mine."

"I won't be owned," she gasped.

"It's too late for that now."

He kissed her, not with the branding possession she'd obviously been steeling herself to meet, but with a soft, gently persuasive nibbling over her tender lower lip. Her hands on his shoulders tightened, holding on to his dressing gown. What did she feel? There was heat in her; he'd be willing to swear to it. No woman could be so passionate in an embrace without being the answer to a lonely man's prayers.

When Rietta touched his face with floating hands, Nick brought her hard against him, letting her discover the full knowledge of what he wanted from her. She gasped, and he took advantage of her open mouth with a lightning thrust of his tongue. Rietta's hands fell to his shoulders.

He licked her neck, biting the spot before she could react. She rewarded him with a soft, wondering cry that went through him like lightning. He cherished the sound and plotted how best to cause it to break forth again.

"It's too late," he said again, his lips against the rising swell of her white bosom. "I'm possessed by you. You've been haunting me since that first day and now I'm going to have you."

"You've been possessed by me?" she asked, and he could hear her disbelief. "But Blanche was there."

"Yes, I looked at her. But I never wanted her. I wouldn't have rescued her had your father plotted against her as he had against you. Not for anything she could offer."

"But I . . . oh. Oh, my," she said sharply as he traced a line from the base of her throat to the tip of her breast. He untied the gather tie of her chemise and slipped his hand inside.

From the first, she'd been strangely attracted to his lean, powerful hands. The thought of his hands on her body had been overwhelming; the reality was all the more stunning. They were hot against her skin. Her breasts tightened, the tips responding to his touch, and he closed his eyes and made a low hum of satisfaction in his throat.

He kissed her again, his tongue sliding slickly, hotly, over zones of sensitivity she'd never imagined. Rietta found herself moving against him wantonly, making primitive sounds, calling his name urgently.

Suddenly he took her face between his hands. Staring down into her eyes, Nick forced Rietta to look at him. "When I'm deep inside you, you'll say you are mine. You'll know it with every move I make and you'll know it when you spend yourself helplessly in my arms."

The words were forbidden, dark, indecent. Why then did she long to hear more, while, at the same time, wishing he'd kiss her and kiss her until neither of them could speak?

She pressed her hands over his, dragging them down over her skin until she brought them to the resilient weight of her breasts. Even this blatant act left her agonizingly unsatisfied.

"What is this feeling?" she asked breathlessly. "It's like aching hunger and violent thirst together. But the hunger is devouring me. The thirst makes my whole body burn, not just my mouth. Please, Nick . . ." She pressed up against him, seeking his mouth, kissing his chin, his cheek, the join of jaw and neck.

Nick groaned—a sound like nothing she'd ever heard from him. Was his damnable good control slipping at last? Her own was long since gone, leaving not a trace.

His fingers sank under the line of her chemise, pushing down thin linen. When her breasts were exposed, Rietta didn't care about modesty anymore. It seemed so unnecessary. This moment had been inevitable from the first. Even if her father hadn't interfered, she would have given herself to Nick at the first opportunity. Destiny had brought them together; let destiny have its way.

He stroked her skin with a feather-light delicacy, building with maddening slowness toward the rosy point. Rietta looked down at herself, seeing his hand moving over the whiteness of her skin. She could not force him to go faster, to give her some ease from the uncontrollable fire he'd lit. She looked up to find him watching her. She saw such passion flare in his brilliant eyes that she was humbled by a sense of her own power.

Still meeting her eyes, as if daring her to object, Nick bent to take the pink tip of her breast into his mouth. Rietta threw her head back as the heat washed over her in long, rolling breakers that picked her up and carried her away.

She felt the impact as he pressed her back against the wall, his so-hot mouth moving on her breast while his broad thigh lifted between hers, carrying her petticoat skirt with it. The brush of the hair on his thigh aroused her wherever it passed. When she was straddling it, she stilled the instinctive and repetitive motions of her hips.

"Something's happening to me," she said on a gasp.

"Yes, I know. Let it," Nick said, and even in her dazed state she recognized the tone of male satisfaction and superiority. She wanted to reprimand him for taking that tone but then he started to rub his thigh back and forth in the same rhythm she'd unconsciously adopted while flexing her hips. A sense of expectancy, as if she were waiting for a marvelous gift she had only to find to possess for always, filled her. "Come on, Rietta—I promise you'll like it. Let me show you."

She clung to his shoulders, quivering, shaking her head, trying to speak. "Please. . . ."

"No," he said, slowly lowering his leg. "It's not enough. Come to bed."

Nick moved back to arm's length and began taking off his dressing gown. He tossed it toward the bed but it fell short, floating in billows to the floor.

Rietta lolled against the wall, needing its support for her suddenly boneless body. She knew a wiser woman would take this chance to steal away, virtue intact. But she couldn't bring herself even to close her eyes as Nick continued to disrobe.

As deliberately as though he were alone, Nick pushed the buttons through the cuffs of his nightshirt. He left them hanging and eased other buttons through the buttonholes at the throat. When he reached down to pull the shirt off, Rietta moved at last, reaching out to close Nick's bedchamber door behind her. The key was in the brass lock plate. Rietta turned it with a clear snap of the tumblers.

The curtains were still wide open and in the pearly light of the approaching dawn, Rietta saw him without the misrepresentation of clothes. Hair spread over his chest right where a woman's hands might go. Thinking of the arousing abrading of his thigh between hers, Rietta trembled at the idea of brushing against his naked chest with her breasts. His belly was flat, as muscular as his arms and legs. In addition to muscles, his limbs and torso showed something else in common. Scars, some pale, some twisted, reflected the dawn.

"My God," she said. "Where were you wounded?"

Nick chuckled. "Now is not the time to talk of the past. Come here, Rietta."

She'd had a willful blindness when it came to looking below his waist. She'd noticed his hard thighs, honed by months in the saddle, but nothing else had registered. Now it did. She was appalled, curious, and strangely thrilled.

"Don't be afraid."

He kissed her so tenderly, one hand beneath her chin, that she forgot everything but the touch of his lips. She felt the coolness of the morning air about her legs as he loosened the drawstring of her petticoat and it fell away. The chemise followed a moment later.

Nick eased back to look at what he'd uncovered. "Jaysus," he said reverently. "Oh, Rietta, what a woman you are. Concave, convex, hills and hollows, so smooth and so strong . . ."

Then his hands—oh, his hands—slid over her, expressing his appreciation for all the things he'd mentioned. There wasn't even one moment for shame to sneak in. She lifted and swayed in response to the fancy of his wandering hands. Enjoyable as it was to be so caressed, nothing felt quite as thrilling as when he'd used his thigh so wickedly in the doorway. Could she dare ask him to do that again?

He seemed to understand without being asked. He stroked down the front of her body until he reached the center of all her yearning. Rietta gasped and tried to turn away, suddenly knowing that this had all been a huge mistake. How could she have fallen so far, so swiftly? To be naked in the arms of a man she'd not even known existed a month ago . . .

"Don't be ashamed," he whispered, his breath a warm sigh in her ear. He teased her earlobe with his teeth, stopping only to whisper ragged poetry until she pressed her scarlet face into his shoulder.

Then Nick splayed one hand over her lower back and held her still while he did something so shocking with his other hand that Rietta couldn't comprehend the details. She only knew that the fire that had begun with his first kiss was suddenly burning in every atom of her flesh. She called upon heaven as Nick moved his fingers in such a way that her prudent mind fled, leaving the field to her unscrupulous body. It cared nothing for her worries about the future, content to be the recipient of the pleasures of the present. The sweet tension built until she couldn't keep it inside for another instant.

Rietta shouted his name, all three syllables. Nick felt a rush of pride unlike anything he'd known before. Her face was transformed from a passably attractive woman's into that of a goddess in the throes of spiritual ecstasy. It passed with that pinnacle of emotion, yet Nick was still in awe of her.

She could no longer stand, and the bed, he realized, was much too far away. Nick took her down to the floor, lying back to protect her delicate body from the harsh carpet.

"Is this wise?" she asked. "I can't hurt you?"

"No! Well, not if I'm careful . . ."

Then he touched again between her thighs, giving her more time, more experience. When she arched in climax, he held her legs open. His first attempt went awry, and he ground his teeth in frustrated apology, meeting her eyes. He read apprehension there and considerable determination. Nick almost could have laughed, for he knew her well enough to realize that fear would not hold her back.

She rose up, her knees on either side of his hips. Nick held very steady, in an agony of suspense, while she positioned herself, rubbing lightly over his stomach and groin, tearing a groan from his throat. She paused inquisitively and it was all he could do not to grab her, roll her under him, and do all that he'd dreamed of.

Then, finally, everything began to go right. He was safely where he wanted to be, brushing away his lady's tears while she moved experimentally, trying to accustom herself to this so natural, so unnatural act. Then Nick put his valor to the test. He held on, fighting his understandable urge to find his own pleasure, until Rietta began to be more at ease.

All his good intentions were shattered when she leaned down over him, breasts like ripe fruit, to kiss him as he'd shown her. The sight, the taste, the fragrance of this woman, coupled with the excitement shining in her beautiful eyes just for him, wiped out his self-control like a tidal wave sweeping him off his feet. Even as he shuddered in a long release, he was wondering how he could make up to her for his inconsideration.

She sat across him, staring down with a peculiar expression on her face. She looked like a wild bird, wondering if it were safe to investigate a seed. "Are you all right now?"

"All right?"

"You didn't breathe for the longest time."

"You take my breath away, Rietta." He reached up into the mass of her hair to stroke her soft cheeks, to drag a finger across the contour of her lips and be rewarded by a gentle clench of secret chambers.

"Did you like it?" he asked, daring his masculine pride.

"Oh." She closed her eyes and let her head fall back, loose and easy. Her long hair swished down her back, but Nick had eyes only for her upthrust breasts and the smooth slide of his hands over the perfect contours of her figure.

"If an ancient Greek sculptor saw you like this," he said, considering the matter before he spoke, "he would have bitten his chisel in two and thrown the bits to Poseidon."

To his delight, she preened. He guessed there'd been little enough praise of her in her father's household. Yet what he'd told her had been no less than the truth. Blanche would have been a dream come true to a man newly returned home from the uniquely men's idea of a good time—namely, fighting a war. Yet no man with eyes to see past her beauty into her shallow soul would look twice at Blanche if Rietta stood nearby. Nick vowed then and there that not a day would pass without him finding something pleasant to say to her.

Her eyes shy, she moved away from him to sit cross-legged on the carpet, her body curving protectively inward. Though her modesty was not displeasing to him, Nick wanted to put her at ease. "Are you thirsty?"

"No, thank you."

"Hungry?"

Her long hair swished as she shook her head. "Mrs. Cook's eggs were enough for now, thank you. But don't worry. I shan't stay long."

Nick suddenly couldn't bear her being so coolly polite. He ran his hand over her shining back, her start of surprise communicating itself to her. "You may stay, Rietta, till the sun and the moon dance their way into the sea if it pleases you. You are my wife; that's eternal."

"I suppose it must be, or I never should have walked in here tonight."

With his hand on her shoulder, Nick made her face him. "You wanted this?"

She closed her eyes. "I must have done. I cannot lie and say 'it's all your doing,' can I?"

"No, you mustn't lie to me. Naked, like this, on the floor, like this, all we have is our honesty." He stroked the back of his fingers down her cheek. "I couldn't resist you when you were just another woman. My powers of self-denial are utterly gone now that you are mine."

He kissed her again, feeling deep in his soul that he had made a vow more solemn than those of the marriage tie he'd contracted. This was the first true kiss of their marriage and every one that followed it would be a continuation of his promise to keep and cherish forever. He could not tell if what he felt was love—that word carried too many burdens—but, in his case as he well knew, responsibility was far more binding a tie than adoration.

"Nick?" she murmured. "I was wondering . . ."

"Hmmm?" One of her hands rested on his waist. He placed his own over it and guided it lower.

"Oh! Oh, my."

He sucked in breath through his teeth. "Gently. Smoothly. God, yes. . . ."

A few moments went by before he prompted her. "You wondered something."

"Did I? Oh, yes. Could we move to the bed? This floor is rather hard on my knees."

He laughed, not loudly, for he was in no case to shake with laughter. "Whatever you desire, my lady," he said.

He moved her hands away and stood up. She remained, kneeling at his feet, gazing up at him with that air of hesitant curiosity that charmed and confounded him. "You're very handsome," she said. With slim fingers, she reached out to curve around him again.

Nick woke up hours later, his wife asleep beside him, her long, red hair flowing over his shoulders and stomach like curling silken ribbons. At some point, he realized, he'd dragged a coverlet off the bed to swirl over them, while his dressing gown made an admirable pillow. Really, he thought, floors aren't that uncomfortable. I wonder if we ever *will* make it to the bed? He grinned and closed his eyes once more.

Then he realized what had awakened him. Someone was knocking softly at the bedroom door.

Sixteen

Rietta awoke to the sound of a voice and blazing sunlight. In an effort to evade both, she rolled over and pulled the coverlet over her head. The light was filtered to a softer glow, but the voice went on.

"Yes, I'm coming," Nick said. She remembered his door having a peculiar chirping creak. She heard it now as it opened. "Thank you, Sarah."

"Gentleman to see you, Sir Nick." That was the young maid—What was her name?

"A gentleman, Sarah? Who?"

Rietta peeped out of a gap in the coverlet, her eyes blinking against the light. She saw Nick's back, draped with a sheet held negligently against his hip. His back was marked by scars, the worst one ragged and star-shaped, high on his left shoulder, but she only noticed them in passing. She studied instead the play of muscles under his shoulders and the dimples above his firm backside. Then she noticed that some of the marks on his back were straight lines, so new they were still red. Her hands seemed to pulse with the realization that she'd left those with her raking nails.

The maid gave a giggle. "He says he's yer father-in-law."

"Does he?" Rietta saw him turn and appraise the formless lump which was all he could see, she hoped, of her. Nonetheless, she shut her eyes tightly just in case their gleam caught his attention. "Kindly tell Mr. Ferris that I shall be with him shortly. Offer him some tea or whatever is suitable for the hour. What time is it, anyway?"

"Her ladyship took luncheon an hour ago, Sir Nick. She said we weren't t'be bothering you. 'He'll ring when he's hungry,' she says."

"I'm hungry, Sarah. Tell Cook."

"What should I ask for?" Sarah said, obviously thrown off her balance by this unusual hour for eating. "Luncheon or breakfast?"

"I'm not certain what my lady would like. Send up a variety."

Nick closed the door. Rietta felt his footsteps rattle the floor as he walked toward her. Though part of her longed to throw off the coverlet, exposing her body once again to his amazing touch, another, slightly more embarrassed, part demanded time. She needed to assess all that had happened and what it meant to her future.

The instant passed. Nick walked away. She dared to open her eyes once more. She saw him, the sheet restored to the bed, standing before the window. In his hands he held a brightly flowered bundle which she recognized, after a few moments' squinting study, as the shawl she'd dropped outside his door last night. The maid must have given it to him.

Now he stood smiling down at it, like a man pleasantly puzzled. Rietta wondered if he, too, might not appreciate some time to be amazed at all that had happened. She'd steal these moments to gaze on her husband as much as she liked. Remembering what astounding pleasure he'd given her, she sighed luxuriously.

He tossed the shawl on the bed and proceeded to dress. His movements were marked by neatness and a rapidity that was quite efficient. He shaved, dressed, and pulled on his boots without the aid of a servant. So far as Rietta could tell, he never made an unnecessary motion and she knew he didn't make a single sound. If it hadn't been for the vibration of his feet and later the tap of his boots, she would have believed herself to be alone.

When he had tied his cravat and adjusted the single pin in the folds, he came and knelt beside their impromptu bed. He ran his hand lightly over the contours of her hidden body and Rietta deeply regretted not having thrown off that cover when she'd had the chance.

"Rietta? Rietta? Are you awake, my dear?"

"Just barely."

"I must go downstairs now to see a man about something. I won't be long. Sarah will bring you breakfast. If you need anything else, just ask her."

"See a man?" Her voice was thick enough without her having to feign anything. She threw back the coverlet, wanting to see what he looked like when he lied. "Mr. Daltrey?"

"No, not him. This is someone utterly unimportant but he'll make a nuisance of himself if I don't see him at least once. Never mind." He smiled at her and she hated him for the smug complacency she saw there. "Maybe you'd better move to the bed. Shall I carry you?"

"No. I don't want to muss you."

"You would, too." He leaned down and kissed her, in a way that made it quite clear that he was pleased with himself. Then he paused before kissing her again in a way that showed how very pleased he was with her. Rietta, despite everything, longed to wind herself around him like a purring cat.

"What have you done to me?" she asked in despair.

His brows twitched together at her tone, yet he could

still smile. "Let me get rid of this old fool and I'll come back to refresh your memory. Rietta . . ." He shook his head. "It'll take all day to tell. When I come back . . ."

Even so, he lingered a moment more just gazing down at her. He made Rietta nervous when that possessive gleam showed in his eyes, but it was a nervousness that had more to do with anticipated pleasure than fear.

When the door had closed behind him, Rietta sat up. Then she groaned as her back, especially her lower back, protested against the sudden movement. It reminded her of the way she'd felt the morning after she'd first learned to ride a horse. The experiences were not that dissimilar, now that she thought about it.

Rietta learned that even depravity did not mean a loss of the ability to blush.

A hot bath had relieved the ache after her riding lessons but there was no time for that remedy now. She must find out what her father wanted with Nick. She doubted he wanted to know how the honeymoon progressed. For all he cared, Nick had murdered her in the night and put her body in a room with those of his other eight wives.

Attired in a man's dressing gown five sizes too big, and a dusty shawl, Rietta crept back to her own room, praying fervently that she wouldn't meet anyone. Ignoring the twinges that plagued her with sudden motion, Rietta hurried into a simple dress that buttoned down the front from breast to hem.

Her hair was a tangled knot. Dressing gowns did not make good pillows! She scraped the mass ruthlessly off her face with a comb and bundled the rest into a lopsided snood. With her stocking garters tied, feet scuffed into shoes, and a little perfume rubbed in behind her ears, Rietta ran downstairs, determined to find her father and her husband.

She found her new mother-in-law instead. Lady Kirwan stood bent at the waist beside a pair of large wooden doors, her entire attitude that of an eavesdropper. She saw Rietta and a darker color came into her cheeks. But she held a finger to her lips, enjoining silence, and held out her hand in invitation.

Rietta glanced around, saw they were alone, and glided noiselessly to Lady Kirwan's side. The older woman squeezed her hand and whispered, the merest breath of sound, "Nick and your father—"

"I know. Ssh."

"Quite a touching ceremony, I thought it," said her father. "I was touched, all right. That mad monk wanted another twenty pounds on top of what I'd already paid him. There's no charity left in this hard world."

"Quite the philosopher," Nick said, though Rietta hardly recognized his voice for it had turned cold and sneering. "Come to the point, Ferris. I've no time to waste on oily pleasantries."

"Nor have I, come to consider it. A man in my position has many calls on his time."

Rietta could imagine her father preening himself like a fat cock on a dunghill. He'd achieved everything he wanted in one master stroke—married a daughter to a titled son-in-law, become the sole voice of authority in his house and business, and bound to him the woman of his tawdry dreams. The fact that his daughter would never forgive him didn't even weigh in the scales

"Come away, Lady Kirwan," Rietta said in nearly a normal tone. She couldn't bear it, listening to her father beside a woman who must be sick at the revelation of the sort of man who'd raised her new daughter-in-law. "Let's not listen any further. . . ."

"Ssh . . ." Lady Kirwan took the big brass knob in her bony hand and pushed so that the opening widened slightly. Now Rietta could both hear and see, though only in flashes as the two men circled around each other like panthers sharing the same cage.

"I like to do my business in a timely fashion," Mr. Ferris said. There came a muffled clink that had something strangely aggressive about it.

Rietta knew what it was without looking, for she'd seen her father do it before. It was his trick, the mannerism he used at parties or meetings, to increase his prestige without involving any actual work. He kept a bag of shiny golden sovereigns handy so that he could lob them onto a convenient surface if there was any doubt of his wealth. "There." His tone was a marvelous combination of pride, greed, and haste. "As promised, the first of your little bags, each containing a hundred pounds in gold."

"I don't want your money," Nick said. For an instant, Rietta's heart jumped high. The he added, "However, I have no choice."

"Indeed, sir, you've none. Oh, this morning I sent off a draft on my bank to that fellow in London who is dunning you for your father's debt."

Lady Kirwan squeezed Rietta's hand tightly.

"That's very good of you," Nick said, his tone still rigidly proper.

"The rest I'll deposit to your account—the full two thousand. This little bag will serve for your wife's clothes. I promised you that, I believe. Tell me, have you my letter handy?"

"What letter?"

"The one that laid out the terms, of course. I want to give it to my lawyer. You know how lawyers are, Sir Nicholas. Want everything laid out—quid pro quo and such. Didn't you receive it?" Mr. Ferris bit his lip anxiously.

"Your letter? Yes, a letter came. What did I do with it?"

Rietta freed herself from Lady Kirwan's grasp. Her head held high, without an instant's hesitation, she entered Nick's library. Nick rummaged in the open drawer of a well-worn desk that had gracefully curving legs. Mr. Ferris, who had obviously not been asked to be seated, stood ill at ease in the corner. They were both startled by her sudden appearance.

"Of course he's read it," she announced. "The terms were generous, quite surprisingly generous."

"Rietta. . . ," Nick said, recovering. "It's not the way it looks."

"No?" She turned to her father. "You must be thirsty, Father. A glass of wine?"

A tantalus stood on a side table. She poured him out a glass, her fingers caressing the beautifully cut old crystal even as she wondered whether throwing the decanter at him would be too dramatic for daytime. She forced a smile as she gave him the glass.

"I thought I'd find you still spitting fire at me," Mr. Ferris said merrily enough, yet with some wariness in his eyes. Perhaps her wish to bombard him with the decanter had been more blatant in her posture than she'd believed.

"Why should I be angry? You did me a great favor by trapping this man into marrying me."

"I knew you'd come to see it my way. I know how to provide for my girls."

Rietta ignored that. "And I think I shall be more contented here at Greenwood than ever in my life. Certainly more than I ever was at . . . well, I don't wish to hurt your feelings. Have you found the letter, Nick?" she asked, walking to his side, leaving Mr. Ferris looking as if his wine were corked.

"Here it is," Nick replied.

Rietta caught his hand before he could flourish the letter. With a simple gesture, she broke the wax seal before Mr. Ferris could see that his letter had never been read. The fact that it was still sealed was a point in Nick's favor, but Rietta was too angry to give it fair weight. Besides, they'd probably been discussing the arrangements long before Mr. Ferris had set pen to paper.

"Write it out, Nick," she said. "So my father can take the copy to Mr. Bright."

"I'd rather have the original," Mr. Ferris put in.

"Naturally you would, Father, but we'll keep it. Original documents are so often the key to the writer's true mind. You taught me that, didn't you?"

Mr. Ferris opened his mouth but nothing came out. Not one to waste such things, he drank his wine instead of speaking.

Rietta picked up the letter as Nick sat down. "Two thousand pounds on the marriage, a hundred a year for my clothes and incidentals, and half your estate at your death. Very generous, Father. How very desperate you must have been to get me off your hands. And am I to understand that you have paid a debt of honor as well?"

"Young people need to start life with a clean slate, I say." He drew out his handkerchief and mopped his forehead.

"Indeed," Rietta said, eyeing her husband. "The cleaner the better."

She dropped the letter on the desk. Crossing the room, she sat down across from her father on one of two leather armchairs. The room was entirely masculine, filled with old books, well-polished furniture with smooth lines, and dark rugs. But like everything else she'd seen thus far at Greenwood, the library showed its age. Helping Nick restore his family fortune would not have troubled her, for it was a wife's duty to hold household. But to have been convinced that he married her for *her* good, to save her from a vile fate, and then to learn the truth was both maddening and cruel. Especially after last night . . .

"How is Blanche?" Rietta asked politely.

"Well enough. She sends her love and hopes it won't be long before you permit her to visit."

"She's welcome at any time, of course. You needn't come with her—if you'd rather not.

From behind her came the sound of a pen scratching over paper. "I trust Mrs. Vernon is well?" Rietta said.

Her father shifted in his chair. "Aye, she is. Asked after you.

"You've seen her today?"

"Yesterday evening, after you . . . after I came home." Her father seemed to be attempting by sheer willpower to drive Nick's pen to move more quickly.

Rietta forced herself to continue her patter of politeness, though the desire to shriek at him to leave tore at her throat in an attempt to escape. "Was there much rain last night? I'm afraid I didn't notice."

"The drought's broken, it seems. The potatoes will be there this winter."

"That will mean fewer starved people in the cities."

"That reminds me, Rietta," said Mr. Ferris, leaning forward. "A letter came this morning from Mr. Pradd—a matter of a boatload of indigo. His price seems reasonable enough. Do we want it?"

Nick slid his chair back. "I can't have my wife troubling her head about business, Mr. Ferris. I don't approve of women meddling in matters that do not concern them." He held out his copied letter. "Here you are. I'll expect to hear from your man of affairs shortly."

"Er, yes. I'll tell him."

Rietta stood up. Mr. Ferris had no choice but to rise as well. Nick came around to take her arm and together they escorted her father out of the room. Rietta permitted Nick to pretend to be a loving husband. No doubt this was the last time either of them would wish to carry on such a pretense.

At the door, his hat on, Mr. Ferris tried again. "Well, good day t'you both. It's a fine property, Sir Nicholas, a fine property."

He turned to his daughter. "It's not so bad, is it, Rietta? Fine house, pleasant-spoken young man with everything handsome about him, barring a little lack of the ready. But you're so thrifty and wise, 'twon't be long before you're beforehand with the world. I didn't do such a very terrible thing to you—now confess it."

"Good day, Father. I'm sure we'll be giving a dinner party soon. I shall let you know when it is."

She turned away as if by accident when he tried to kiss her cheek. Mr. Ferris was handed into his coach by Garrity, who did not look at her. As the big coachman mounted to the box, Mr. Ferris said, "About that indigo . . ."

"Drive on," Nick called.

Nick stood and watched the coach drive away. Even plumes of road dust were kinder to his eyes than the sight of Rietta's fury or tears. But when he looked at her at last it was to see something even more horrible. When she raised her eyes to his face, he saw that they were completely empty of all feeling. She gave him a pleasant smile, as one stranger to another. "If you'll excuse me, Sir Nicholas, I believe I should like something to eat."

"Rietta, please," he said when he caught her hand in the middle of the entry.

She slipped her hand free without saying a word about it, yet making it clear that he wasn't to touch her. "I think the first order of business should be to acquire two or three more house servants. I notice you don't have a valet—you really should."

"I don't want one. He'd be terribly in the way."

"A good one should know how to tend you without vexing you. We should hire a butler as well. I know it's difficult to find one in this part of the country—West countrymen just don't like to be house servants—but we shall manage somehow. Your mother deserves the aid a really good butler can give her. I believe she has been doing far too much for her state of health. Is the breakfast room through here?"

"Yes. Rietta, let me explain."

"There's nothing to discuss, Sir Nicholas. You must be ravenous, unless talking with my father has destroyed your appetite."

Nick stood alone in the hall, eager to talk to a woman who wouldn't listen to him. He didn't know whether she was whistling in the dark, talking just to hear herself, or truly so furious with him that to discuss anything but trivial subjects would lead to inevitable bloodshed. For the first time, he thought that life facing Napoleon's armies had been more peaceful than he'd realized.

From behind him, he heard his mother's voice. "Nick? May I speak with you a moment?"

Seventeen

When Nick rode out to seek Arthur Daltrey, his intention was not to rail at the man for his possible seduction of Amelia. All he hoped for was five minutes' conversation with a sensible person of his own sex. He'd had enough of women to last him quite some time.

Badhaven Farm had never been one of Nick's favorites. He thought the setting, in the fold of a valley, unhealthy, and the house had smelled of dust and chickens the one time he'd been in it. In going over the accounts, he'd seen that the property had actually cost more to keep than it ever brought in. If his father had been forced by his circumstances to sell some land, he could have sold pieces much nearer his son's heart than Badhaven.

He wondered why Arthur had been fool enough to buy it. Of course, it had belonged to his grandmother at one time. Perhaps its proximity to Greenwood and Amelia also swayed his judgment.

Drawing Stamps to a halt, Nick leaned forward onto the horse's neck to stare at Daltrey's property. Stamps's ears twitched back as his master whistled softly.

The half-tumbled cottage was now twice the height it

had been, the thatched roof tight and still crisply yellow.
Stones had been replaced along every foot of the gray
walls that crisscrossed the land. Nick's own fingers ached
in sympathy at the thought of all the work repairing a fence
required, not to mention the price of strained backs and
smashed fingers. Chickens scratched in the side yard and
from somewhere near at hand pigs grunted contentedly in
their sty.

The house presented a tidy and prosperous appearance,
one any woman would be proud to name as her own; but
the thought of his own sister having to raise chickens,
pigs, and children here was enough to turn Nick's stomach. However, Amelia had cried at the merest hint that
taking up the hand-to-mouth existence of a common Irish
farmer's wife would not suit her. She swore that love
could overcome the worst differences of class and educa-
tion.

Nick shouted once to let the people inside know he'd
come. Then he swung down out of the saddle and led
Stamps through the gate. "Hello?"

"Haud your horses; I'm coming."

Nick smiled at the lady who came hobbling out holding a blackthorn stick no less twisted than her back.
Even had she been able to stand straight, she would
hardly have come to Nick's elbow. She needed to come
very close to Nick to see who her visitor was, but one
glance sufficed. "You're Sir Nicholas Kirwan, aren't
you?"

"I am, ma'am. Whom do I have the honor of addressing?"

His courtliness set her off in a fit, though he couldn't
tell whether it was laughter or coughing that shook her frail
body. "Ol' Widow Daltrey, that's who I am. I remember
you, a proper little gentleman, you were, with your 'please,
ma'am' and 'thank you, kindly.' And you with a leg pouring blood all over my floor."

"You were the woman who helped me?"

"Yes, you ninny. Remember me, do you?" She seemed pleased.

"I was very grateful to you. So was my mother." His first horse, not usually nervous, had reared up at the sudden appearance of three wild boys who'd come charging over the wall, screaming like panthers in the course of some game or other. Nick had come down, landing on a sharp knife of broken stone. It had ripped his thigh, his first scar, though at the time he'd been more concerned with the tear in his breeches and the wrath of his nanny. He couldn't have been more than seven. This old woman had bound it for him, scolding fondly all the while. He could hardly believe she was still alive, twenty years later.

"How is your good mother?" Mrs. Daltrey asked. "She came t'bring me a basket in thanks the next day. A light-footed creature she was."

"She's very well. Thank you for asking."

She chuckled, a thin, ropy sound. "I'd know you for a Kirwan anywhere. They always have the simplest, yet neatest manner o' speaking. Sir Benjamin never passed my door without takin' a drop of wine and a piece of honey-soaked bread, whether he wanted it or no. I told 'em to be like you."

"Who?"

"My grandsons. Arthur, Windam, and Guy. I said to 'em, 'You couldn't choose a better 'un.' "

"I'll wager they hated me after that. I always despised the very boys held up as a model to me."

"P'haps, p'haps. Windam and Guy, they've gone away. Guy's in Dublin, mending the streets. Windam's married, an' living in the Connaught—if you can call it livin', with rocks in the fields bigger than the cows!" She threw a glance of scorn toward the West, where the sun had begun to drop in anticipation of night.

"And Arthur stayed with you."

"Aye. He's the pick of 'em all. Look at the fine house he's built me. Livin' like the lady of the manor, an' me a horse trader's daughter who grew up in the back of a caravan."

"Is Arthur at home, ma'am?"

"He'll be home to take supper soon enough. Won't you come in t'wait for him?"

Thus it was that Rietta and Amelia found Nick seated by his sister's lover's fireside, a cup of dark tea and a slice of crumbling rich cake balanced on his knee, when they arrived half an hour later.

Rietta had not intended to accompany Amelia. Her intention had been to stay with Lady Kirwan, who, upon finding that her son had married for money, walked about with such a sad, white face that Rietta was frightened. Somehow, though furious with Nick, her heart hurting with every beat, she still could not bear that his mother should think him anything other than wonderful. She followed her into the library, arguing against her own belief, trying to make things seem right.

Lady Kirwan listened, but Rietta's reasoning didn't seem to persuade her. "Oh, but to marry you for your money and then to display his contempt so blatantly. I could hardly believe that it was my Nick being so cruelly mercenary."

"You know Nick would never . . . I'm afraid my father has a way of making things sound sordid when they are not."

"I saw how you looked, my dear," Lady Kirwan replied. "This business shocked you just as much as me."

"If I was shocked, it was only because my father had come, cash in hand, like a merchant instead of in a more gentlemanly fashion. I don't know why that should disturb me; after all, he is a merchant."

But it is different when you are the bargain in question. I know, Rietta. I—I remember."

It was then that they heard the raised voices of the two girls. Lady Kirwan raised her head as Rietta walked to open the door. The girls stood in the entry, so intent on each other that they didn't notice Rietta.

"You can't do that," Emma bleated. "I'll tell Mama."

"Tell her if you must, you beast, but at least wait until I'm gone. I must reach Arthur before Nick does something dreadful to him. If you were any kind of a sister, you'd come with me. But I suppose that's too much to ask!"

Emma started to sniffle and cry.

"Oh, stop it, you . . . you watering pot!" Amelia stomped her foot on the floorboards, then bit her lip. She heaved a sigh and put her arm about her sister's shaking shoulders. "I'm sorry, Emmy. I haven't been as sympathetic to you as I should have been, so it's unfair to think you'd support me now."

"I—I want to. But Nick will be so angry—"

"I don't care. We were doing splendidly before he came back to clip our wings. I almost wish—"

"Don't say it!" Emma said.

"No, I don't wish him any harm, but why can't he just be content with his own wife and stop interfering in our lives?

"I didn't choose so well," Emma admitted with a woebegone sniff.

"Well, I have chosen the best man in the world for me. What right has Nick to stick a spoke in my wheel? Mother doesn't object to my choice; why should he?"

"But I do object," Lady Kirwan said from behind Rietta.

"You do?"

She tucked her hand into Rietta's elbow and leaned upon her to walk up to her daughter. "I object strenuously to the idea of my daughter living the life of a farmer's wife, worthy though Arthur Daltrey undoubtedly is. I've seen a hundred blushing, sweet brides turn into hard-bitten silent women, worn out by the merciless and unending labor of being farmers' wives. Do you think I want that for you?"

"But you've never said a word of this."

Lady Kirwan sighed and gazed for a moment into each of the young faces above her. "I wanted you to have at least the memory of love to take with you on the journey that is a woman's life. Perhaps it was foolish of me not to look ahead, to see that you would want to keep your sweethearts, instead of letting them go, as you must. I suppose I forgot in my wish to see you happy in love, if only for a summer, that my daughters are so very self-willed."

"Is that why you didn't stop me seeing Robbie?" Emma asked.

"I knew he was a wastrel, my love. But you had a glow in your eyes when you thought of him, a tender smile when he was near. I thought that with his memory you could settle down to happiness with a worthy, if duller, suitor.

"You did say Arthur is worthy," Amelia said.

"Very worthy. But is it for his worthiness that you love him, or for his handsome face?"

"Certainly not. I'd love Arthur if he were ugly. Besides, he's never loved any other girl."

"Oh, so that's why," Rietta said. "I did wonder." Amelia's eyes flashed angry bolts, but Lady Kirwan gave her daughter-in-law an approving pat.

"It is flattering when you win the heart of a previously invincible man. All those girls whispering about you . . ."

Amelia's lips curved as though in a triumphant reminiscence, but she quickly shook her head. "It isn't like that. Maybe that's how Miss Blanche Ferris thinks of her lovers, but it's different for Arthur and me. We truly are in love. Won't that make a difference, Mother? How many of those brides you spoke of truly loved their husbands?"

"More than you might think. But love cannot survive when it must struggle against debt, indifference, and the tides of the world that sweep men away from their homes. Believe me, my darling; I know."

The protest Amelia was about to make died on her lips. She stared at her mother with wide, horrified eyes. Emma looked between them, uncomprehending.

Then Amelia backed away. "You are wrong," she said, her tone quietly defiant. "You are and I shall prove it. I love Arthur so very much that there is no way it will ever die. I will go and tell him that now. If Emma won't come with me, I shall go alone."

"I'll go with you," Rietta said, even before Lady Kirwan nudged her. "I should like to meet your Arthur, if you don't mind having someone who is almost a stranger with you."

Despite her emotional state, Amelia smiled warmly. "You're not a stranger; you're just a sister we haven't had very long."

Later, as they drove to the cottage, Amelia said, "I'm sorry about last night's scene. It never occurred to me that last night, of all nights, Nick would be prowling about the house."

"Does he prowl a great deal?"

Amelia nodded as she navigated a tricky blind turn in the road. "Almost every night we hear him pass our doors—sometimes earlier, sometimes later. I think he takes his horse out late at night when he can't sleep. I thought surely his wedding night would be the one night that I'd be able to slip out with nobody the wiser, and what happens? I come back to find you and Nick sitting in the kitchen!"

"We were hungry," Rietta said, and blushed.

"I should have foreseen that, I suppose."

"Why did you want to slip out, anyway? Couldn't you have visited him just as well in the day?"

"No. In the daytime, Arthur is very circumspect. Even when we hold hands, he worries about who will see. But, oh, at night! He even kissed me when we parted."

The Daltrey cottage had much to recommend it. Though on the same pattern as the dark and simple houses of the Claddagh with which she was familiar, the cottage had a large window in the front with glass panes and bright paint on the window frames and the door. There were flowers blooming under the windows, evidence of a loving hand that watered even when the sky didn't.

"Arthur says that being cooped up like a chicken at night after being outside all day makes him want to sneeze, so he added windows to every room."

"A trifle cold in the winter, perhaps?"

"He says not."

"Arthur says" had been the burden of the commentary Amelia had kept up during the drive. She handled the ribbons of the pony cart very well, despite her anxiety. Rietta didn't quite know what it was Amelia feared Nick would do, but that she feared something was obvious.

"There's Stamps," Rietta said as they drove into the yard. "But I don't see Nick."

"Oh, are we too late?" Amelia thrust the reins into Rietta's hands and jumped down almost before the cart had stopped. Her bonnet falling to hang by its ribbons down her back, she hurried toward the house. By the time the old woman had opened the door, Amelia couldn't speak.

Rietta tied the horse to a post in the yard and followed Amelia. "Good evening," she said. "I'm Rietta Ferris. Is Sir Nicholas Kirwan here?"

"Come in, miss. Stop your wailing, Miss Amelia, or I'll wallop you one."

"Oh, Granny Daltrey, is he very much hurt?"

"No harm's come to either of them. 'Sides, Arthur's not back yet."

"Not back yet?" Amelia echoed. She wiped her tears away, looking at her fingers as if unsure why they were wet.

When Rietta saw Nick, sitting comfortably by the spotless white fireplace, she realized for the first time that she had also been more than a little concerned. Though a cold fury still froze her heart, she couldn't help the sigh of relief that escaped her lips.

"Did you think I'd come to fight a duel?" he was asking Amelia, who'd cast herself upon him, heedless of his full hands.

Rietta relieved him of the mug and the plate before they spilled over Amelia's pelisse, and put them aside. His sister didn't answer him, being too busy sniffling into his lapel.

"Amelia felt some natural concern and I came with her." Rietta thought that covered everything very neatly, without exposing anything that should not be spoken of outside the family circle.

Nick's gaze told her that he guessed how much that statement concealed. "That was very good of you, Rietta. I appreciate your sparing my mother the journey."

He pushed Amelia firmly but kindly to a greater distance. The girl groped her way to a chair and sat down, clutching her handkerchief. "I don't know what I thought. I kept picturing one of you laid out, dead. I didn't know what would be worse—finding you like that or Arthur."

"Pair of fools they'd look either way," Mrs. Daltrey said. "There are right and proper things for men to fight over, but silly girls isn't one of 'em."

"But you know I mean to marry Arthur. My brother is adamantly opposed to any such future."

"I'm glad to hear he's no fool," the elderly lady said. "Wouldn't you care for some tea, Miss Ferris?"

Nick frowned. "You'll have to forgive my wife, Mrs. Daltrey. We were only married yesterday and she's not used to her new name."

"Yer wife, is it? Didn't you pick a pretty one, though. You know, dearie, my hair was just such a color—lit up like the sunrise, it did. Many was the man I ensnared in my long red hair. Who was it said it looked like Viking gold? To be sure, 'twas the lad what come to teach that summer. Poetical feller; died in a consumption. Tea?"

"Thank you, Mrs. Daltrey," Rietta said, smiling despite everything. "I should adore some tea."

Nick stood near to her, much too near for her peace of mind. Every shameless, impassioned moment from the night before stood there with him, colored now with humiliation. Her father had gone out and purchased her the best husband money could buy. Nick had fulfilled that promise last night, but now she felt empty, as though what she'd found in the night had proven to be a mirage in the morning.

He raised his hand and touched a fallen strand of hair. "That poetical schoolteacher had it right. I saw a tiny golden bowl once in the home of a collector, made in Munster a thousand years or so ago. The gold was just the color of your hair, too gold to be called red, too red to be anything else."

His touch lingered, curving down her cheek. Rietta closed her eyes, nuzzling her face into his hand. She scorned and despised herself for turning to melting femininity when she should have been standing like a marble statue, impervious alike to heat and cold. But when he touched her, so gently, owning her so completely, she felt her willfulness draining away. She'd do anything he liked, so long as he'd keep acting as if he loved her.

He tried to tilt her chin up so that he could kiss her. For a yearning moment longer, she yielded, tipping her head back to give him all he desired. Nick caressed her neck, gazing down into her eyes with such ardor that she almost believed she could warm herself at the fire she saw. But just before he turned his head to kiss her full on the mouth, Rietta turned away.

Of course, no one could be satisfied with a mere pretense. Rietta wanted to slap herself in the hope that that would break the spell he wove so effortlessly. The remembrance of two thousand pounds helped to break it. She stepped out of his arms as though he were a coat she had tried on and discarded.

Amelia sat with her head in her hands, the position of a gambler who had dipped too deeply and lost the family farm. "Amelia, do you still want to see Mr. Daltrey?"

"More than anything!"

"Nick, go find him. Don't fight with him just yet, if you please."

"No need," Mrs. Daltrey said, showing a nearly toothless smile. "That's his step. He'll be coming in after he's washed his hands."

He'd had the horses in the yard to give him warning. Mr. Daltrey walked in quietly, greeted his grandmother with all proper respect, and looked about him for an explanation. He found one when Amelia came running up to him. "Don't fight him, Arthur! Promise me that."

"Sit down, Amelia," Nick said. "Stop making a fool of yourself."

Arthur Daltrey made the same suggestion in a whisper and it was instantly followed to the letter. Rietta had come prepared to dislike Mr. Daltrey, but he certainly seemed to know how to manage Amelia. Firm kindness, keeping her on a long rein, and earning her adoration had been the necessary ingredients.

She studied her husband and felt a strange little thrill in the center of her body as a memory from last night bubbled up like a reminder of danger from a volcano believed dormant. Those lips had nipped gently at her thighs, tasted her body, sent her gasping in frenzy. Nick met her eyes and she was grateful that she stood in a shadowy corner.

"Let's set the ladies' minds at ease." Nick shook hands with his former tenant. "Well, Daltrey, what have you to say for yourself?"

"Myself, Sir Nicholas? Why, nothing whatever."

"My sister tells me she was out to an unconscionable hour with you. Have you compromised her?"

"Nick, no." Amelia pleated her skirt in embarrassment.

"Hush, now." Daltrey gave her a smile that combined tenderness and authority before facing Nick again. " 'Twas nothing at all like you're maybe thinking. Yes, we were together until long after midnight—so long I can't guess the hour when I brought her home. The moon had set. But we were only talking of this and that."

"Talking?" Nick's tone gave him the lie. "Does any man spend time 'talking' until all hours with an unmarried girl? If you were of rank, you'd have to marry her outright."

"So I will."

"I won't take you, not like that," Amelia declared, looking up. "If you love me, marry me. But not because my brother demands that you do it. I'll not be wed under such circumstances."

"Be grateful you at least have a sympathetic brother. It's more than I have," Rietta said. "Nevertheless, I agree with Amelia."

"Stay out of this, Rietta."

"Why should I? She's my sister, too. The only valid

reason for marriage is true love—on both sides. It may only be the foundation; one still must build well. But without that foundation, no marriage has a hope in Hades of surviving the inevitable hardships and misunderstandings."

"Well put, m'lady," Mrs. Daltrey said. "Now, who wants tea?"

The two men—one classically handsome yet wearing a smock with the sleeves rolled up to disclose powerful, sunburnt forearms; the other, his face too controlled to be idolized, faultlessly attired in a dark-green riding coat with moderately large buttons—faced each other. They ignored the advice and commentary of the women in what Rietta thought was a display of perfectly maddening masculine superiority.

"You see my difficulty," Nick said.

"I do, indeed. I'm what they call worthy," Arthur replied bitterly. "Worthy enough so long as I keep to my place and don't dare raise my eyes to the daughters of my betters."

He looked at Amelia. Even though Rietta caught only a glimpse of his expression, she knew she wanted someone to gaze at her with just that glow in his eyes. Then she corrected herself. "Not *someone*," she said softly. "Nick."

Arthur went on. "I'm as good a man as any in the country, but because my father was your tenant, I mustn't look at the loveliest, darlingest creature under heaven. I mustn't want her or need her, though I do."

Amelia held out her hands to him. "As I do, Arthur."

Holding her hand, he glared at Nick. "So you'll give her to some rich bastard who doesn't care tuppence for her. And all because there's good Irish soil under my fingernails. All because I wasn't laid in a grand cradle when I was born. Sir Nicholas, you must see how wrong and unfair that is."

"Well, damn it, man, I just fought a bloody war to keep the evils of republicanism out of this country."

"No, sir. You fought Napoleon to keep his breed o' tyranny out of this country and I don't blame you a particle for doin' it, no matter what the lads may say. But if Waterloo happened just to keep me from marrying your sister, then t'hell with it."

Rietta saw Nick's fists clench and the effort of will it took for him to force his hands back to his sides. "Don't say that, even in jest, Daltrey. I was there, you see."

The handsome farmer ducked his head, his fair cheeks reddening. "I see, Sir Nicholas."

"Very well."

Rietta let out the breath she'd been holding and Nick flashed a glance in her direction. "Speak up, my . . . friend," he said. "I'm sure you have the wisdom to pull us out of this morass."

Under this challenge, Rietta considered before she spoke. "You don't object to Mr. Daltrey in any personal way, do you? There's no family quarrel or anything personally amiss between you? No woman, horse, or hound that wandered from one hand to the other?"

Both men glanced at each other and said, almost in unison, "No."

"I see." She smiled reassuringly into Amelia's frightened eyes. "Since you object only to Mr. Daltrey's position, perhaps you can alter it."

"Alter it? How can I? I'm not that influential."

"Ask yourself what position he can fill that would be acceptable to you."

"Bearing in mind," Daltrey said, raising Amelia up to put his arm about her shoulders, "that while I minded my schooling, I'm not likely to make much of a success as a lawyer or a man of the cloth."

Nick took a turn up and down the room while every other person in it stared at him anxiously. Rietta alone waited for him to do the thing she had faith he would do—the right thing.

"Your brother lives out in Gortmore, so your granny tells me."

"That's right."

"Would he come back here to live?"

"That he would," Mrs. Daltrey said. "Nothing would please that wife of his more than t'be away from her mother, the ol' beldame."

Nick considered some more, rubbing his knuckles over his cheeks in thought as another man might pull his beard. "I'm not suggesting this is the only solution. What if Amelia were to go away for a few months, enjoy a season in town, meet more eligible men. Then, if her mind was still made up . . ."

Their protests drowned the rest of his suggestion. He held up his hands for silence. "Very well. Nothing will do but that you be married. Think hard, Amelia. You cannot change your mind once the deed is done."

Rietta knew that warning was meant for her.

"Nothing means anything to me if Arthur isn't my husband," Amelia said, standing proudly.

"As you wish." He came up close to the couple. "Mr. Daltrey, I have at present no agent. For all I know, my tenants are robbing me blind. I need someone to tend to their needs as well as collect what I'm owed. Someone to enforce the law when necessary and bend it when wise and the wit to know the difference. It's a difficult position and not one I'd offer to any man without a great deal of thought."

"Oh, Nick!" Amelia said, bobbing up and down in excitement. "The gatehouse?"

"You've always liked it."

"I don't understand," Arthur said. "Are you offering me . . . ?"

"At any rate, my last agent, Mr. Cane, died suddenly

some few months ago and I've not found anyone to take his place. Though having my agent as a brother-in-law may be slightly unorthodox, I'd rather have you handling my affairs than many another fellow. You're honest, you know the land and the tenants, and your affection for my sister means that I will never have to acquire another agent. I leave that task to my son, if any." He glanced again at Rietta and she crossed her arms under her bosom. What if she were already carrying Nick's child?

"There. I've stated my case, Arthur. What say you? Will you accept the position?" He looked around at the flabbergasted faces and Rietta wondered whether he'd staged the whole scene. He was capable of it.

Arthur tore his gaze away from Amelia. "Do you believe I can do the task you offer, and do it well? I'll not take charity of any man, not even a brother."

"I truly believe you will make an excellent agent."

"Then I'll take the position, the house, and the lady."

Rietta thought the least Arthur Daltrey could have done was shake Nick's hand, instead of instantly turning to Amelia and kissing the rest of the sense out of the poor girl. Poor Mrs. Daltrey staggered to a chair and sat down. "Windam's comin' home?" she asked dazedly.

"When did you think of this?" Rietta asked Nick, her eyes narrowed, while he stood back and surveyed the results of his triumph.

"Last night. I did have a little time to think at one point." His voice fell away to nothing but she was sure he'd added, "Right before you woke up."

"I'll shake your hand, so help me," Rietta vowed. "I will. That was a good piece of work."

Nick held her hand too long. Every nerve began to recall the ramblings of his surprisingly talented mouth. This time, knowing how easily such a touch could lead to something far sweeter and more dangerous, Rietta pulled free and crossed the room to congratulate the others.

He stopped her with one hand on her shoulder, just long enough to whisper, "Wait till tonight."

She looked him full in the eyes. "Nothing will happen tonight, nor any other night. The door between us is locked and it will stay locked."

Eighteen

Over the next few weeks, Nick learned, to his frustration, that not only was the door between their chambers locked, but Rietta had taken to locking her mind as well.

In the daytime, she fulfilled his every dream of a dutiful, charming wife. She smiled at him across the breakfast table, at luncheon, at dinner, the candlelight warming the firm cleavage revealed by her dinner gowns. When, beguiled by her smiles, he'd begun to talk to her, she'd listened attentively to all his plans for the future. Sometimes she'd even add a word or two, making him see things he'd not thought of for himself.

She proved a delightfully gracious hostess to all those who came to see his bride, whether titled neighbors or the grubby children of his most shiftless tenants. Judging by the comments he heard, he'd chosen a pearl among women, an ideal wife.

His mother and sisters, their heads full of plans for Amelia's wedding, came to rely on Rietta absolutely. If he heard them say, "Ask Rietta; she'll know" once, he'd heard it a thousand times. The hell of it was—she *did* know. She could answer any question, from which dressmaker should be entrusted with the length of satin for Amelia's gown to which wine should be served at the wedding breakfast to what he did with the book he was reading. Yet even as his respect and admiration grew, so did his frustration.

The only absolutely satisfying thing to come from his marriage thus far was that, since their wedding night, he'd not had a single nightmare.

After all, he rarely had nightmares while lying wide awake. Every night he retired, moderately sleepy. Yet within five minutes of lying down, when he should have been drifting away on an ocean of sleep, he would find himself lying broad awake, staring at the ceiling. The bed and the ceiling were the only things in the room that did not have some intimate acquaintance with Rietta.

The floor, of course, was where they'd made love. He'd thrown her petticoat over the back of the chair, later found a stocking draped behind a picture frame, and the windows had allowed in the light that had let him see all of her. Even the dressing table mirror had reflected her beauty when they'd stood before it, finding it a sturdy support for the two of them. He couldn't stand to look at any of it.

So he would lie there, hour after hour, trying to think of other things and returning helplessly to his wedding night. The knowledge that Rietta slept on the other side of the wall was like a flask of water just beyond the reach of a man dying of thirst. She was all he could think about. He fantasized about holding her, kissing her, and keeping her close to his heart throughout the night.

During the day, he managed to project an air of civility. He was as polite and charming as she herself. He could conceal all his yearnings, driving them inward to devour what they would.

One night three weeks after the visit to Badhaven, his mother paused on the way out of the dining room. She laid her fan against his sleeve with a playful tap. "You should strive to let Rietta get a little sleep at night, my son."

He had been staring after Rietta as she left the room with his sisters. The white gown she wore had silver flowers interwoven in the fabric so that she glittered like an unattainable prize as she walked away. Would she ever walk back?

"I beg your pardon, Mother?"

"Rietta doesn't look rested," Lady Kirwan said, her knowing smile a trifle forced. "I know you are a bridegroom, but she needs her rest."

Nick transferred his stare to her. How could his own mother be so blind? Rietta carried herself through the day with perfect posture, her face so smooth it might as well be a mask, while he staggered around, hollows burned beneath his eyes, from a lack of sleep and an excess of desire.

"I'll keep that in mind, Mother."

"Good. She's a dear child. I'm so glad you brought her into our lives, even if the arrangement was somewhat irregular. I've told my friends that you had an understanding with dear Rietta before you went away, but refrained from marriage because you did not wish to leave a young widow."

"That was noble of me, wasn't it?"

"They all know how noble and romantic you can be; I've told them often enough how proud I am of you. You've never done an ungenerous thing in your life, have you?"

"Not quite never."

Lady Kirwan patted his arm. "You can make it up to her. It will take a long time . . . but she'll forgive you."

"Mother, what do you know?"

"Everything. I know why you married Rietta."

"Do you?"

"I—er—overheard Mr. Ferris discussing the matter with you. Has he paid all the money into your account?"

Nick nodded. "Mother, it isn't the way it looks. Yes, Mr. Ferris offered me quite a sum of money to marry Rietta, but that isn't why I did it! I can't be bought like a hundredweight of potatoes in the common marketplace. Mr. Ferris threatened her—his own daughter—with a dreadful fate. What could I do but marry her?"

"And since you married her, you might as well accept his so-called reward?"

"We needed it; why not? Could I ask her to live in poverty because of my stupid pride? I'd give it back if I still had it all, but we've used rather a large chunk of it already."

"So what will you do? You can't go on making love to her and never discussing the matter." Lady Kirwan arranged the cobweb of her shawl over her elbows and missed the expression of blank amazement her son wore.

"I only wish making love was all I could do," he said, with heartfelt longing.

"Take my advice," she said. "If you don't mean it, don't do it. She's not likely to be fooled by any insincere protestations, no matter how much she'd like to hear them. She's not a fool, Nick."

"I know it. She's probably the cleverest woman I've ever met—present company excepted."

"No one ever thought me clever. I was lucky to have been beautiful." Something of that former beauty was in her eyes as she appraised him sympathetically. "Are you in love with her?"

He shook his head before he thought. She sighed and left him after changing the subject to the upcoming wedding. He was to be sure to have plenty of beer on hand for the tenants. Nick told her he'd discuss it with Rietta.

Nick sat alone in the dining salon, a diamond-bright decanter in front of him. He turned it meditatively, studying the play of light off its many facets. Like everything else, lately, it reminded him of Rietta. He'd tried several other methods of putting himself to sleep—maybe it was time to try intoxication.

An hour or so later, Bevans, the new butler, interrupted the ladies at the whist table set up in the drawing room. He'd only come to this decision after consulting the new valet, Everest.

"I beg your pardon, my lady," Bevans said in a low tone over Rietta's shoulder. "Would you be so good as to join me in the dining salon?"

"Is something amiss, Bevans?"

"Yes, my lady." Bevans had a deep voice and at times could sound funereal. Growing alarmed, Rietta excused herself, telling Lady Kirwan not to disturb her hand.

She became aware of the noise just outside the dining salon's doorway. "Almost got him that time," Nick said cheerfully. "I'll bag him the next shot, Everest, see if I don't!"

Rietta heard a respectful murmur in answer. "Has some animal come into the house?"

"No, my lady. I'm afraid it's Cupid."

Rietta's first thought was that the butler, despite his references, had been drinking. He withstood her scrutiny, standing as straight and unwavering as a soldier. Shaking away her suspicions, Rietta opened the door an inch and applied her eye to the gap.

Nick, his coat off, his hair disheveled, sat cross-legged in the center of the gleaming dining table, shouting instructions to the unseen Everest. The plate and crystal on the sideboard rattled in accompaniment to emphatic thuds. "Higher, man, higher. Jump to it. You'll never catch him like that."

Nick raised his hand and it was Rietta who jumped back.

"Where did he obtain that gun?"

"From me, I'm afraid, my lady. He rang for it."

"You didn't have to give it to him. You should have come to me at once."

"Sir Nicholas was most insistent, Lady Kirwan. I did, however, take the precaution of putting aside the ammunition and powder he requested. I told him that my unfamiliarity with the household precluded my finding any."

"Well done, Bevans. But why did he want it in the first place?"

"To shoot Cupid, my lady. Sir Nicholas seems to feel that particular deity owes him a certain attention he has hitherto withheld."

"Oh, I see. He's drunk."

Rietta felt the butler would have looked on her with sympathy, if it were permitted. "Fairly well to pass, my lady, indeed. Not a usual indulgence, I fancy."

"I've never known him to do so," Rietta said, not adding that she hardly knew Nick at all. For all she knew, he might be foxed two weeks out of four.

"He bears none of the signs of habitual tippling, if I may say so. Unlike my last master who was addicted to a vile French potion known as *crème de menthe*." He gave a delicate shudder.

"Pray call to Everest, Bevans. But please wait here. Sir Nicholas may require more assistance than I can give him."

When the salon's door had closed behind Rietta, the two servants sighed. "The mistress will soon have him sorted out," said Everest, panting from his exertions. "It's just pitiful how some can't see what's plain as print in front of them."

"The way of the world, Mr. Everest. Yet I would wager that the mistress will know how to manage him."

"Do the other ladies know about his condition?"

"On the contrary. The mistress showed nothing of her anxiety. Even Lady Kirwan remains in ignorance."

"That's good, or we'd have the whole scaff and raff of

them here offering t'put cold compresses on his head. If he needs 'em tomorrow, the mistress will give it to him, aye, and a hot plaster to his feet."

They'd settled the problem of having two women entitled to the name Lady Kirwan by reserving that title for the elder while Rietta was from their first day known as "the mistress." They implied no lack of respect. Rather, their experience taught them that Rietta would undoubtedly manage the household while Lady Kirwan retired more and more from the duties that had hitherto been hers.

In the salon, Rietta approached Nick carefully. "May I ask why you have that pistol in the house?"

"Almost . . . almost . . ." He raised the muzzle of the pistol higher, squinting along the top edge at something invisible at the height of the window cornice. "Blast! I wish the naked little halfwit would hold still for a minute."

"Nick? What are you doing?"

"Shooting." He raised the pistol and squeezed the trigger. Rietta couldn't keep from flinching, even though she knew there were no bullets. "He's trapped in here with me but I want him to stop flying around. He's giving me a headache. His quiver's empty; he's shot all his arrows."

"At you?"

"No, silly. I'm imp . . . impervious. Pardon me. Hiccups." He hiccuped again and added, "Must have been the mustard sauce."

Was this Nick's way of telling her not to hope for his love? She hadn't had very high hopes to start with. "Why keep him, then? You could open all the windows and let him fly out."

Nick's eyes were following the flight of something only he could see. "He's keeping that special arrow back. That's the one we want. Whoops! Watch out for the chandelier, old man, won't you?"

Though she knew it was but the wine working in him, giving his imagination free rein, Rietta began to have the curious feeling that she, too, could see some winged sprite zipping about the room. Nick raised his pistol, steadying on his forearm. "By the ranks . . . wait for it, lads, now, wait for it! Fire!" He even said "Bang!" adding, "Missed the blighter."

"Why do you want to shoot Cupid?" Rietta asked. "Is it so no one else can fall in love?"

"That's a silly reason," Nick said, gazing about him owlishly. "I want everyone to be in love. I want everyone to be happy. Are you happy?"

"Not very, perhaps. I've tried to fight against feeling this way, but I . . ." Rietta noticed that Nick was humming a march under his breath, one she recognized. It was called "The World Turned Upside Down" and had long been a favorite of hers, despite the Americans playing it when Cornwallis surrendered. Nick was not listening. Really, she'd been foolish to attempt any serious subject with a man half-seas over.

"You should go to bed, Nick."

"Hmmm? I'm not in the least sleepy. Wish I were."

In the course of an aimless look around the room, his vacant eyes fixed on her. He suddenly smiled and Rietta felt her heart squeeze, just as it had that first day.

"It's you," he said, pointing a finger that wavered despite his holding it with is other hand.

"Yes, Nick, it's me."

His smile widened. Straightening out his legs, he swung them around, then rested his cheek upon his hand, so that he was lying at full length on one hip. With his hair negligently tumbled and that gleam in his eyes, he looked like a wicked heathen from some gold-encrusted Arabic fairy tale. He patted the table invitingly.

"The table's remarkably comfortable. Why, if it weren't for you, I should go to sleep right here."

"Why don't you go to bed? You won't be disturbed and you'll feel much, much better in the morning. A bed's far

more comfortable than sleeping on a hard, cold tabletop."
Her experiences with her father, when he'd had a drop too
much, told her she was being too optimistic.

"On the con . . . contrary, I shall feel much worse in the
morning. As for hard and cold, you could give this table
lessons," he said, sounding quite sober. His tees would
have made an Oxford don cry for joy. His esses were clean
and crisp. But his words made no sense. Rietta decided to
humor him until she could persuade him to go to bed.

Rietta held out her hand to Nick. Without a word being
spoken, he helped her climb up. He draped an arm about
her shoulders, while he tracked "Cupid's" progress with
the muzzle of the pistol. He'd taken off his coat at some
point and unbuttoned his waistcoat. The hanging sides of
the waistcoat accentuated his flat stomach and narrow
hips. The heat of his arm penetrated her clothing, remind-
ing her of their one night of intimacy.

She had tried, often, not to think of that night and of all
they'd shared. For a time, she'd kept her anger hot by
thinking of how he'd agreed to an arrangement not only
scandalous but ruinous to her self-respect. When that feeling began to cool, she fanned the flames by recalling how
he'd avoided telling her the truth until after they'd con-
summated their marriage.

Yet her thoughts always turned to how she'd felt that
night when he touched her with such gentle hunger.
Whether it had been the aftermath of his ill-dreaming or
the end of a long period of celibacy, he'd needed her that
night. He'd needed her with an intensity that still hummed
in her body. She found herself often lying awake, listening
for any sound at all from Nick's room and hearing nothing,
not even a snore.

After he'd "fired" and missed again, Rietta asked, "Any
luck?"

"He's faster than a peregrine on the hunt. He's taunting
me, I think."

"What does his special arrow do?" Rietta asked, leaning into Nick's warmth. Funny, she hadn't felt cold, but she realized that she'd been freezing ever since she'd heard her father pay Nick. It was heaven to be this close to him again, even if he wouldn't remember in the morning. "Nick? What does it do?"

"It makes you fall in love. . . ."

"Don't all Cupid's arrows do that?"

"It makes you fall in love with me. And the little bastard won't shoot it!"

Rietta tried to wriggle away from Nick's clasp. Just as she was about to free herself, a beatific smile woke on his face. "He shot it," he said happily.

Then he kissed her.

It was impossible to push him away, to whisper "don't," not when she'd been imagining this moment for weeks. He tasted of the wine's mellow richness, intoxicating on his lips. The pistol dropped to the floor with a rattling thunk.

He pulled her closer yet, gathering her in his arms, his breath tickling her ear as he pressed his lips against her throat, her jaw, her mouth. She longed for him to kiss her deeply, adding those maddening flicks of his tongue and the incitement of delicate nips. But he rocked her in his embrace, tender, gentle, loving.

She tensed. Had "Cupid" shot Nick already? Could he possibly be in love with her? The temptation to believe it was harder to battle than that of his kisses.

Rietta slipped her hands inside his open waistcoat, skimming over the thin linen shirt. Nick groaned, returning with growing fierceness to her lips. If he loved her, she knew she would give herself to him without reservation.

Opening her mouth, she invited his tongue to dance with hers. A welcome heat began to burn in her body, even as she felt his harden. His hands moved restlessly over her gown, then he raised them to the sheer crêpe sleeves covering just the cap of her shoulder. In an instant he'd dragged them down, taking a good portion of her bodice with them. She wore the lightest of corsets, which he dealt with summarily.

"Nick," she gasped when the cool air touched her.

He gazed at her eyes, then down at his own hands overflowing with her breasts. "I'm sober—sober enough, anyway," he said in wonder. "And I'm more drunk on the taste of you than I've ever been on wine."

"Nick, we must talk. . . ."

"You're right. You're absolutely right." He hesitated, then, as slowly as if she'd been an unexploded shell, he took his hands away. He swung his legs over the edge of the table and stared at nothing.

Rietta felt cold again, the unfulfilled need in his eyes as chilling as the north wind. She glanced down at her uncovered bosom, at the soft nipple on one and the hardness of the other. "Do I please you?" she asked.

His answer was a groan. "You'd tempt a stone saint."

When she put her hand on his shoulder, she felt the quiver that ran through him. "I don't forgive you. I'm sure you had a hundred extenuating reasons for marrying me, but the truth remains that you let me believe . . ."

Suddenly her words dried on her lips. She wet them, and tried again. "I can't say that you let me believe you loved me. You said you wanted me and, if we are to have truth between us, I wanted you, too, Nick. From the first day."

Nick turned to her. "Yes, but . . ."

"Then if that's all we have, let's not spoil it by worrying about the why. If you want me, then take me." She smiled at him, offering him everything and demanding nothing. What could she demand? That he love her?

She was Rietta Ferris Kirwan. She could hardly recall her mother, the last person who had loved her. The others had only valued her so far as she was useful to them. Now she had a new value, as her husband's obedient wife. She would seize whatever benefits came with such a position and not ask for more. If she could not have Nick's love, she'd settle for his lovemaking.

Nick looked at her trembling mouth and wished to heaven that the befuddlement of wine was still with him. At least he understood the process at work then. If a man drinks sufficiently, he will be drunk. But the delirium that seized him when Rietta told him she wanted him defied explanation.

If all they had between them was wanting, why did he feel so triumphant when she expressed it? Why did he feel he could leap ten leagues without recourse to Finn Mac-Cool's famous boots? Why did he feel like ringing every bell on the island so that the whole country would know something unprecedented had occurred? This was certainly more exciting than an invasion.

Nick looked at Rietta, her sleeves around her elbows, her pink and white bosom revealed, a vision for a man to take to hell to solace a miserable eternity. He said no.

Her hands came up to cover her from his eyes. "No?"

"I can't let you, Rietta. I can't make love to you again under false pretenses."

"But I know what you did. It doesn't matter. So we are not in love with each other. We can have a happy, satisfying life without love."

"Perhaps you can. I cannot." He put his hands on the hard wood surface and slid off the table. He didn't dare look at her again.

"You won't make love to me?"

The pain in her voice all but broke his heart. "Not until we both feel more for one another than mere desire. It must be between equals, Rietta, or it won't be any good."

"It was good before. Wasn't it?"

He paused halfway to the door, spun about, and returned to her. "It was phenomenal," he declared.

Grasping her by the waist, he slid her toward him, hard

against his body. The kiss he drove into her startled mouth made all the others look like chaste pecks between romantic octogenarians in bath chairs.

His fine speeches were burned away in the roaring heat they created. Rietta should have been petrified, alarmed by his haste and his need. Instead, she demanded greater urgency as she tore at his shirt and trousers.

The touch of her cool hands on his hips was like a drug. Nick forgot about servants, sisters, and that the door wasn't locked. He laid his wife back on the mirror-glossy table and made a kind of love to her that approached worship.

"I can't . . . I can't touch you," she gasped. She ran her hands through his hair, the only part of him she could reach, teasing the sensitive top of his ears. Then her hands clenched as he found new places to kiss her.

With shudders of completion still racking her, he drew her hips to the edge of the table and wrapped her legs about his waist. "You have touched me," he whispered as he bent down over her. "This is for you."

He entered her very slowly, spinning it out, savoring every instant. She was his, and a feeling of triumph rushed through him like a typhoon, scouring him clean. Though he felt the strain of his restraint, the look of exquisite pleasure upon her face was his reward. Nick felt he could make love to her for a year and never need to find his own release, for hearing his name panted on her lips was nearly enough.

Nearly, but not entirely, he admitted silently as, lost in her secret clasp, he vowed with mock solemnity, "Soon, my lady, we'll try a bed."

She laughed and he was truly lost. The love he felt for her at that moment overthrew every idea he ever had of love. He felt as foolish as a man who brags of his fishpond until he sees the vastness of the Atlantic Ocean from the Cliffs of Moher.

Nick longed to tell her, but the pleasure that overwhelmed him made it impossible to speak. He could only hold her as tightly as possible as she twisted in harmony with him.

Later, when he could think, he realized that Rietta would have every reason not to believe him. She might ascribe a hundred different motives for him to tell her that he loved, adored, and worshipped her, and never come near the right one—namely, that he did. His task now was to build her trust so that she would believe him when he at last admitted his love for her.

Nineteen

Nick believed that if nothing further occurred to erode Rietta's trust, she would eventually forgive him. The understanding that they'd begun to create on their wedding night would soon have the opportunity to grow. Dimly, he could foresee a future of happiness. It seemed farther away than ever the day they received the invitation to her father's wedding.

At first, Rietta flatly refused to attend. "Ridiculous," she said the instant she realized what it was Nick held out to her. "Absurd. How can he even think to ask me?"

"He's your father."

"I don't care," she shot back. "I never want to see him again. I made that clear when he had the nerve to visit this house before, on business."

She flicked her big green eyes in his direction to see if her arrow struck the target. Nick half bowed to show that it had. "Still, he is your father and since he has invited you and me to attend his wedding to . . . to this lady, I think we should go."

"This lady?" Rietta couldn't sit still. She pushed her chair back from the breakfast table, her roll only half eaten.

"*This lady* is a notorious creature who has buried two husbands already, both of them elderly and infatuated."

"Your father isn't elderly, but in the very prime of life."

"But he is infatuated. He's been seen in her company for months—visiting her house, carrying her shopping through the streets and, no doubt, paying for it all."

"You seem very well informed of his movements."

"Every gossip in Galway has made it her business to keep me so well informed. I honestly don't understand how infidelity is possible in a city that permits no one to pass unnoticed by its indefatigable gossips."

"I trust you are not considering infidelity," Nick said lightly.

"I will introduce you to the gossiping ladies so that they may tell you when my foot slips. I'm sure they'll know it long before I do."

The thought of Rietta leaving him for another man turned something cold inside him—possibly his heart. Still, it might happen someday that her heart and soul would find a perfect mate, leaving him with the dilemma of what to do. He could be noble and relinquish her, or desperate and refuse to let her go. Looking at her now, the morning sunlight setting her hair into a blaze of multi-shaded red, he knew nobility was unthinkable. He'd married her; he'd keep her.

"You're looking very fierce," Rietta said. "Shall I give you my word to be faithful?"

"You already did that. At the ruined abbey."

Her face glowed pink as she turned away. "Be that as it may, I tell you Mrs. Vernon has only one interest in marrying my father and that is to spend his fortune as fast as possible. I don't really care what arrangements you've made with him, but if you have some hope of my receiving an inheritance, Mrs. Vernon will not increase it."

"I don't have any expectations at all."

She sniffed disbelievingly.

"It's true. Yes, I needed the money I received on our marriage, but I have no doubt that my investments will recover and we shall do very well without further help from anyone."

"Proud words."

"I suppose they are." Nick wanted her to look at him. "If I thought they'd mean anything to you, I should let you have a look at my accounts."

She gave him a startled and displeased glance. It wasn't the kind of melting glance he'd half hoped for, but at least she wasn't staring at a very murky landscape painting instead of looking at him. "I kept the books for my father's millworks as well as the household accounts since my mother's death. I think your estate books cannot be any more difficult than those of a thriving business concern."

Nick laughed. "You must tell Amelia. She hates doing the accounts. My mother's health doesn't permit her to spend long hours poring over ledgers so Amelia's done it since I went away. Not terribly successfully, I might add."

"I should be happy to do whatever I can to lighten Amelia's burdens. A bride has quite enough on her mind, I imagine, to trouble over mathematics. I, of course, wouldn't know what it is to plan one's wedding. . . ."

Nick enjoyed the thrust and parry of married life. Rietta had every right to be displeased; his motives for marrying her had been more mixed that he'd admitted. He should have protected her more by telling her everything rather than leaving her to find out so cruelly. Therefore, he did not resent her pointed comments; at least, not yet. He had the memory of how sweetly passionate she could be to bolster his courage. Soon, when she'd cooled, he'd awaken that part of her again.

"You should go to your father's," he said. "See whether he planned his own better than yours. Think about it, at least. Family is more important than anything else in life."

"I only wish my father felt that way about it."

Perhaps the matter of her attending her father's wedding would have been left in abeyance forever if the two brides hadn't met, quite by accident.

It was all a question of the satin for Amelia's wedding gown. Rietta wanted everything to be ideal for her, for she'd begun to feel great affection for Amelia. Lady Kirwan tired too easily to take on all the responsibility for the arrangements. Rietta, therefore, took on the planning of the menu, the ordering of the foodstuffs, the instruction of the new servants, and the decision as to which modiste would create Amelia's gown.

Rietta was happy to occupy her thoughts with wedding details, rather than filling empty hours with brooding over other matters. Only sometimes did she realize that she'd been staring for half an hour at the invitations she was supposed to be addressing, or gazing at nothing, dreaming of that wild night when she'd learned more about herself than she had in the previous twenty-three years. She found it difficult to look at Nick, even in the most sedate of circumstances, without suddenly blushing. He knew perfectly well why, too, drat him! It was even worse when they gathered for dinner. She found it difficult to eat there, with Nick's eyes, full of memories, upon her.

Some days she felt she couldn't turn around without tripping over him and yet, when business took him away from the house, she missed him. Nevertheless, she could only be grateful he hadn't wanted to accompany them into the city. Dressmaking details were much better left to the ladies. Besides, he had begun spending time with Arthur Daltrey, showing him the estate from the inside out.

Mademoiselle Brun had a reputation in Galway for *à la modality* second to none. Neither of the Kirwan girls dressed with much attention to the latest styles, delivered to Mademoiselle every third Monday by the *Ladies' Monitor of London*. Rietta, on the other hand, greatly enjoyed fashionable things—though she never looked as magnificent as Blanche, she knew what flattered her and what did not. She looked forward to helping Amelia and Emma appear to their best advantage.

True, Emma was, at the moment, too much like a drought-stricken bud to repay dressing her. She drooped, she sighed, or she stood like a schoolgirl denied a promised treat, stomach and lower lip protruding to approximately the same distance.

"Were Emma but happy," Lady Kirwan said, "I should match her in looks and vivacity with any girl in the kingdom. But as 'tis, watery eyes and die-away airs won't advance her, even if we can continue to safeguard her reputation."

Amelia, being happy, looked almost indecently radiant. Though she came in with the other ladies in her family, it was plain who was the bride. Greeting them, Mademoiselle Brun exclaimed, "Ah, *très jolie!* A woman happy in love has an unmistakable air, no?"

"Lady Kirwan, may I present Mademoiselle Brun?"

"How do you do, Ma'm'selle?"

"It is an honor, m'lady." She snapped her fingers at a pale assistant. "A chair here, at once."

Rietta thanked Mademoiselle with a nod. She'd been among the first to notice the woman's unerring sense of style as well as the delicacy of her designs. She'd encouraged Blanche to buy many things here. Her sister had looked so stunning in every creation that it wasn't long before the mothers of other hopeful young girls had come to this shop. Though it had never been discussed between them, Mademoiselle always made a discount for Rietta's personal, more sedate purchases.

"How may I assist you today, Miss Ferris?"

"Perhaps you've not heard? I've married Lady Kirwan's son."

"Oh! A thousand apologies, Lady Kirwan. I had heard nothing of this."

That was odd. Perhaps her father had felt more embarrassment over her hasty marriage than she'd believed. She would have thought he'd have stuck up posters and had the marriage announced from every pulpit.

Her doubts must have shown in her eyes for Mademoiselle Brun said, "I took to my bed three weeks ago with the grippe. I'm terribly, but terribly behind in my gossip. Gossip, you know, is the very lifeblood of a dressmaker's life. If I do not know who is marrying, who is contracting a betrothal, I may miss much custom. You did not come to me for a special gown, my lady?"

"No. I wore my green carriage dress."

"*Alors!* That is deplorable. I trust your hat at least—

"I wore a bonnet. I'm afraid I wasn't thinking of my clothes."

"As who could expect? I have always said so, haven't I, Marie? That when Mademoiselle Ferris marries it will be an affair of such ungovernable passion that there will be no time for us to make a dress. Ah, to know a love that waits for nothing—not even clothes!"

"Yeth, Madamoithelle," the pale girl lisped.

Rietta could now hope that, whatever gossip was making the rounds over her hasty, secret marriage, the ladies of this establishment would do their best for her. A passionate love match, heedlessly carried out, might be shocking to people with no experience in such matters. The rest would nod and sigh, recalling their own romantic interludes and wishing, no doubt, they had achieved happiness by using a little impetuosity.

She turned to Lady Kirwan. "I think you'll be pleased with Mademoiselle's work. May I show her the material?"

They'd no sooner removed it from its brown paper cocoon than the bell over the door jangled and danced. Rietta, and indeed all the ladies, looked up. They recognized Blanche at once, though she was wearing an old and shapeless pelisse as disheartened in appearance as Blanche herself. Her beautiful hair no longer sprang free in riotous ringlets but was strained painfully back from her face into a sedate bun. Her hat was too large for her kittenish face and a feather drooped disconsolately from the back. Even under these vicissitudes, Blanche was a pretty girl, but with her vivacity dimmed she achieved no more than the sort of prettiness any girl might possess.

Yet after greeting Blanche with a kiss, Rietta's full interest became fixed on quite another person. Behind Blanche, like a ship under full sail, came Mrs. Vernon. She wore a stunning costume of rich blue angora, cut with verve like a military greatcoat, even to the large brass buttons marching over her substantial bosom like soldiers taking a hill. With it, she wore scarlet boots, revealed by the shortness of her skirt, a large muff of swansdown, and a hat with such a high-standing crown it was a wonder a high wind hadn't blown her out to sea.

On a tall, willowy, and young woman, such a costume would have been startling but charming. As Mrs. Vernon was short, richly plump, and not in her first youth, the Kirwans could only stare.

Mrs. Vernon was not put out by their astonishment. "Well," she said, striking a pose on the threshold. "If it isn't my little daughter-to-be. How are you, Rietta?"

If her own mother-in-law had not been there, Rietta would have responded by a demand to be called "Lady Kirwan." As it was, however, she wanted Nick's mother to think the best of her. "I'm very well, Mrs. Vernon. I hope everything is well with you?"

"La, yes. I'm in the best of spirits." She advanced, her hand extended. "You must be dear Rietta's mama-in-law. I'm Lucinda Vernon."

"Indeed." Lady Kirwan did not rise from her chair and only briefly touched Mrs. Vernon's fingers.

"I'm to marry her papa, you know."

"Are you? My felicitations."

"Thank you, my lady. That's kindness." She turned with a kind of horrible parody of girlishness. "I haven't heard from you in reply to our invitation," she said to Rietta.

Rietta hadn't been paying attention. Rather, she'd been trying to interpret Blanche's eye twitches and jerks of the head. She'd just realized that her sister needed to speak with her alone when Mrs. Vernon addressed her.

"Haven't I answered? How remiss of me. I can only plead the press of my own affairs."

"That's right. I haven't expressed my pleasure at hearing of your wedding. I always knew you'd do well for yourself—so bright and pretty as you are."

Rietta wondered if Mrs. Vernon had known of Mr. Ferris's treachery in advance. She could hardly believe it, even of her, that one woman could concede to a plan to deprive another woman of her liberty.

Mrs. Vernon dropped her voice to a whisper. "You really have much to thank your father for."

"You knew what he planned for me?" Rietta took a few steps farther from the Kirwans and gave the impression of being vastly interested in a paste-diamond corsage that lay on a counter.

"Naturally he discussed it with me first," Mrs. Vernon whispered. "After all, it's my . . . our future as well as yours. You're a dear, good creature, Rietta, but there's not the slightest chance I'd live with you. I'm much too managing to ever drive tandem."

Aloud, she said, "Isn't that a pretty thing?"

"Yes, very pretty," Rietta agreed. Dropping her voice, she added, "Does my father know you mean to drive him?"

"If he doesn't, he'll soon learn different. I'll manage him so beautifully he won't even know it's being done."

"As beautifully as you've managed your finances? That should be something worth seeing." Having the satisfaction of at last seeing Mrs. Vernon left speechless, Rietta sat down with her family and, calling Blanche to her side, asked her advice about Amelia's wedding dress.

This woke Blanche's interest and she bubbled with what were some very interesting notions. She called on Mademoiselle to bring her sketchbook and together they created a dream of a gown that combined the dewy freshness of a bride with the charm of an evening party. Amelia was in raptures and even Emma took part, suggesting a modification to the sleeves that won Blanche's mild and Mademoiselle's enthusiastic praise.

Under cover of the ensuing discussion, Blanche leaned closer to Rietta. "I must speak to you. Everything's so horrid at home—Papa listens to nobody but *her*." A world of venom was encapsulated in that little word.

Rietta nodded. "Can you escape to Morton's?"

"Yes."

"Very well, then. Half an hour after we leave here."

Mrs. Vernon had been left to the ministrations of Mademoiselle's snuffling assistant while the proprietress attended to her titled customer. After a very short time, she seemed drawn to the round table in the center of the room.

"'Tis charming," she said, peering over their heads at the sketches of sleeves, bodices, and skirts. "My own gown is to be of ivory corded silk with a deep V neck and flounces around the hem. Bring it out, Mademoiselle."

"It is not yet finished."

"Bring it out. I want them to see it."

"I'm afraid we must be going," Lady Kirwan said, rising. "This will do very nicely, Mademoiselle Brun. Here is a note of my daughters' measurements. Kindly make up the blue evening dress for Emma."

"But, Mamma . . . ," Emma protested, thinking, no doubt, of the family coffers.

"It's all right, my dear. You must have a new gown for your sister's wedding day."

"Thank you, my lady," Mademoiselle said with a curtsey.

Lady Kirwan took Blanche's hand. "Won't you come with us to tea at Ranford's Hotel?"

Blanche agreed after a taunting glance at Mrs. Vernon. She went out with the two younger girls.

"A pleasure to have met you, Mrs. Vernon," Lady Kirwan said from the doorway. "Will you be coming with us, Rietta?"

"In a moment, Mother. Thank you."

Rietta turned to face her enemy. She noticed that Mademoiselle Brun and her assistant had vanished into the rear of the shop, but she had no doubt they were listening, agog, and that they'd not delay in spreading the story of this encounter. It behooved her to be careful.

"Very high and mighty, aren't you?" Mrs. Vernon said, twisting her lip into a sneer. "Yes, Mamma," she mimicked. "You'd not be calling her that if it weren't for me."

"You are responsible?"

"If I hadn't prodded your father into it, you'd still be living at home, bored to death. Instead, you've a handsome husband, a title, and everything pleasant about you."

"Then I must find a way to express my gratitude. What would be suitable?"

Mrs. Vernon snorted. "I'll bet you're grateful. So grateful you'd cut my throat, given half a chance."

"I'm not generally thought to be violent."

"No," Mrs. Vernon said, still sneering. "You haven't enough blood in you for murder. Murder takes passion. I think I feel sorrier for your husband than for you. And you needn't say you feel sorry for your father, either. I'll take better care of him than you have done."

"Judging by the life expectancies of your other husbands," Rietta said, and paused delicately, prepared to enjoy Mrs. Vernon's anger.

Then, suddenly, she realized how wrong she was to bait

Mrs. Vernon in this fashion. Like it or not, her father had decided to marry this woman. Though she was estranged from him, she could foresee the day when she would want him in her life once more. She could not, in good conscience, deny him the chance to be with his grandchildren, should there ever be any.

With that thought, she knew that she had committed to her unusual marriage. There would be children, she decided, and this woman would be their nominal grandmother.

She put out her hand and placed it over Mrs. Vernon's gloved one. "Let's not quarrel. I'm certain you will take excellent care of my father."

"I will at that," Mrs. Vernon said, looking down at their hands. Then she smiled at Rietta and Rietta saw her charm for the first time. "To tell the truth, it's not so easy to find a third husband. A woman starts to lose her bloom after the second one. I'll do my best by Augustus. Yes, and by that spoiled sister of yours, though the sooner she takes herself a husband the happier I shall be."

"I'm sure you'd be very good for Blanche but if it will please you, I shall invite her to stay with us for a time. No woman should have to take her husband's daughter on their wedding journey."

"We're not going any further than Tralee, but I confess I'd feel better about it if I knew she wasn't home alone. The girl's got no more discretion than a cat."

"I know it."

"Will your mother-in-law agree?"

"I think she will, if Blanche behaves herself."

"Very well, then. I'll tell Augustus."

Rietta turned to go. Mrs. Vernon stopped her with a hand on her arm. "One thing more—I don't know why you've changed your mind about me—maybe you haven't. Maybe you're just more of a lady than I am. Either way, dare I ask you one favor?"

"What is it?"

"Whether it's your concern to please me or not, I want you to think of Augustus and come to our wedding. He hasn't said a word to me, but I think it frets him that you've not answered our invitation."

"That was wrong of me and not very ladylike at all."

Rietta acknowledged the justice of one thing Mrs. Vernon had said. If it had not been for her father's interference, she still would have been at home, deluding herself that her family respected and needed her. Now, as she said, she had everything pleasant about her. True, there were still unanswered questions between herself and Nick, yet she had no doubt that her new sisters and mother did value her. Regardless of how hurt she'd been, of how betrayed she had felt, Augustus Ferris remained her father. She had to forgive him for her own sake, even more so than for his.

"Tell him that Nick and I shall be there."

If the marriage service of Mr. Ferris and Mrs. Vernon was sparsely attended, the marriage of Mr. Daltrey and Amelia Kirwan more than made up for it. Everyone, from farmers with mud still clinging to their soles to the Earl and Countess of Bellamy, hoping to make up for their departed, unlamented son's treatment of Emma.

The bridegroom was pale, with shaking hands that almost dropped the ring when the bride's brother, the best man, handed it to him. The bride, however, was serene and confident. After they kissed, something of her feelings must have passed to him, because Arthur smiled for the first time that day.

"Well, that's done," Nick said, coming up behind Rietta as she watched the newlyweds dancing.

"Yes. I never thought we'd make it this far," she said. "Amelia had an attack of wedding panic half an hour before she needed to be dressed."

"Did she, now?"

"Hmmm. She wouldn't listen to anyone—just went on and on about what a mistake she was making."

"Who convinced her otherwise? You?"

"Me? I was too busy writing out a speech for you to deliver to our guests explaining the cancellation. No, it was Emma. She marched up to Amelia, gave her a good shake and told her that if she threw away a man like Arthur Daltrey out of pride or fear of what people would say, then she'd marry him herself. That seemed to snap Amelia out of her funk quickly enough."

"Good old Emma. You know, Arthur was absolutely petrified. I had to send Everest to tie his cravat and make sure his boots were polished. If it had been left to Arthur, he'd have married in his smock and clogs. Of course, Everest made it perfectly clear that he was only lending a hand as a personal favor to me."

"I do like your valet, Nick."

"You were right; I needed someone to look after me."

For a moment, she gave him the opportunity to look right down into her beautiful eyes. "Not anymore."

He put out his hand impulsively. "Rietta . . ."

"I need more time, Nick."

"How much more? It's been almost a month. . . ."

"I'm sorry. I don't know."

He caressed her cheek. "Don't be sorry. I won't ask again. When you're ready, you'll find a way to let me know. Shall we dance?"

The cool of the late September evening made a shawl necessary, but it didn't stop young people from going outside when needing an escape from the warmth of the ballroom or from censorious chaperones. Rietta was afraid she fell into that category, for when she noticed Blanche was gone, she went at once to Nick.

"Who was she dancing with?"

"I haven't the faintest notion. You know Blanche—every man here put his name on her card."

"Don't worry. I'm sure she's just gone out to flirt in the garden."

"That's what worries me. She's been so quiet since she came to stay with us. That's not like her. I'm afraid she'll be even more foolish when she does return to normal."

"The way gunpowder explodes more forcefully if you tamp it down? All right; I'll go to the left, you circle to the right."

"What it is to have the military mind! Thank you, Nick."

As Nick walked quickly through the ballroom, he noticed that two men at least were missing. As both of them had a long connection with Blanche, he felt sure at least one was with her. She was not anywhere to be found in the house, however.

Circling around the square house, he realized that there wasn't a great deal of cover for a courting couple. The night of the party had been carefully chosen to coincide with the full moon. It shone softly but clearly down on the heads of the guests. Most of those who'd slipped out for 'breath' walked arm in arm or stood in charming attitudes, deep in a pleasant exchange of compliments. The coppice of trees alone stood dark and deep, offering refuge to less cautious persons. No one was less cautious than Blanche Ferris.

The filtered moonlight made the shadows all but impenetrable. Nick knew every stick by heart and didn't trip over the roots. There was a path to the heart of the trees. There, in the center, was a small clearing. Before Nick reached it, he knew this was where he'd find both Blanche and the two missing men. He knew it, because he could hear them. The sounds of a fight travel far.

Blanche stood by, her back against a tree, her knuckles pressed hard against her lips. A bandbox rested against her skirt. Even by moonlight, Nick could see her eyes flick frantically from one to the other of the combatants. They were still at the grappling stage, but even as Nick appeared in the clearing, one punched the other in the stomach, driving him back.

David Mochrie straightened up, his teeth glinting white. Then he launched himself into attack, but Niall Joyce had taken his instant to prepare. With a force that made even Nick wince, he threw an uppercut to Mochrie's jaw, unleashing a left fist more like a hammer than a human hand, and David Mochrie floated as gently as a fallen leaf to earth, landing with a thud that knocked him breathless.

Niall Joyce stood over him, both fists ready, panting hard. "Say it again."

Blanche came running over, her frail dancing slippers making no sound. "Oh, Mr. Joyce, you were wonderful!"

He paid no attention to her. "Get up and say it again, and I'll put you to sleep for a week!"

Mochrie sat up, a hand to his jaw. "It's true," he said thickly. "You can knock me down a hundred times and it won't change the truth."

"You're a liar."

Nick wondered if he had any business intruding on what was obviously a private quarrel when Mochrie said something that made it his affair. "I was there—I signed the book as a witness. Rietta's marriage is a sham. She was forced into it by her father."

Blanche was crying. "He said—he said if I went away with him, he wouldn't tell."

"Get up," Niall snarled.

"Wait a moment," Nick said. All three started in surprise as though a tree had just spoken to them. "I think it's my turn to knock him down."

Rietta had returned to the ballroom to see if she'd missed either Blanche or Nick while searching. It had been at least fifteen minutes since she'd notified Nick that Blanche was missing. Surely he could have found her by now.

Bevans found her standing by the fireplace, having been drawn into conversation with the countess and the elder Mrs. Daltrey. She excused herself, feeling considerable anxiety. She would have had an easier time reading the countenance of the Sphinx.

"I beg your pardon, m'lady. Miss Ferris would like you to come to her, if you please."

"Where is she?"

"Her room, my lady."

She had checked the rose-papered bedroom not ten minutes before. Now she found Blanche lying facedown across her bed, her pretty dress hidden under a cloak hemmed with leaf mold, her silver slippers stained with mud. The house echoed to the sound of the orchestra below, but here it was as quiet as muffled laughter.

"Blanche, where have you been?"

She started up, then relaxed back onto her pillow when she saw who it was. "I was running away with David Mochrie."

"What? Why on earth?"

Blanche put her hand to her forehead and sniffled. "Because he swore he'd tell the world about you if I didn't."

"Tell what? Oh, my marriage . . ."

"He swore he'd tell all his cronies how he found a husband for you. How Father bribed Nick into marriage without you knowing anything about it."

"I see. David Mochrie was there, but I didn't know he found me Nick."

Blanche nodded. "Something about him knowing how little money Nick had and how Father would be grateful . . . I don't know the full of it. He said he did it all just to have me."

"And you'd go off with him just for me?"

"Oh, don't make me out to be self-sacrificing. I probably would have gone with him anyway. At least he wants me." This last was a cry of the heart.

Rietta sat down with her sister. "What do you mean?"

Blanche sniffled again, her beauty only slightly dimmed by tears and a reddened nose. "Father doesn't want me to live with him now that he's married that woman. And I know you only want me here until they come back. You've got your new family; there's no place for me."

"There will always be a place for you under whatever roof shelters me," Rietta vowed.

"That's kind of you, but you know perfectly well Amelia and Emma can't abide me. And Lady Kirwan is all politeness, but she doesn't like me, either."

"That's not true. . . ."

"Yes, it is. Other women never like me very much." She continued over Rietta's instinctive denial. "No, they don't. They think I'm vain and rude and proud."

"You're not always as conciliating as you might be, Blanche."

"I know it, but how can I be? They dislike me before I even open my mouth. Naturally, I think 'well, if that's how you want me to be . . .' so I become just as mean and petty as they think I'm going to be."

"That's not a wise way to live."

"Isn't that what I'm saying? But it doesn't matter how I try, when I see them sneering at me just because I'm pretty." She drew a long, shuddering breath and flicked her tears away. "I don't know what I'm going to do now. I did like David."

"You still have Niall Joyce."

"And Mr. Greeves, don't forget. He proposed again and it would please Father if I . . . why do you shake your head?"

"Mr. Greeves was the other witness to my wedding."

"Mr. Greeves? But he's so upright, so proper. Imagine

that. I could understand David; he's so wild. And even Nick. . . ."

"Oh? What about Nick? He's upright and proper enough."

Blanche lifted her eyebrows and smiled knowingly. "He's the wild sort, all right. Oh, he's got to be in the right mood for it, but he could show a wild streak sure enough. Something about the way a man looks at you, like he knows all your secrets, gives it away."

Rietta thought about the look in Nick's eye when he'd asked her to come to him. It ignited a kind of deep smolder way down inside her, which frightened her even while it intrigued her. Not even finding out that he'd apparently plotted to meet her with leering David Mochrie's knowledge and connivance could put it out completely, though it damped it quite a bit.

"Never mind Nick," she said. "I'm concerned about you."

Blanche gave her a quick, hard hug. "Don't be. I know what I'm going to do." When pressed, she just smiled and stood up. "Never mind. You watch me."

Glancing in the mirror, she snatched off her cloak and began brushing at her gown. "It's not too bad, is it? Bring me my other pair of slippers, please, Rietta. I can't go down again in these."

Half an hour later, every trace of tears and soil gone, Blanche sailed forth to seize her prey. Rietta watched as she walked up to Niall Joyce. He met her with a hard, straight glance that stripped Blanche's self-possession away. She looked down at the floor, digging a toe into the wood, and an entirely natural blush rose into her cheeks. He spoke to her, his expression unsoftened. A moment later, she took his arm and he walked with her outside.

Nick appeared behind Rietta and said, "What's that about?"

"I don't know. I hope it's love."

"So do I." She knew he wasn't speaking of her sister. She wouldn't meet his eyes, but she asked him to dance with her.

When Rietta saw Blanche again, the younger sister kissed the elder and whispered, "There's to be another wedding come Christmas. . . ."

Twenty

Rietta awoke in the night to the sound of Nick's voice. She deliberated for a moment, then arose. Opening the desk, she pulled out the little key and a small vial of oil. Using a feather, she oiled the hinges and the lock. Just as she brought up the key, however, she hesitated. Biting her lip, she replaced the key in the desk and went around to his door by way of the hall.

The curtains of his room stood open, allowing what little light there was outside to come in. "Nick?"

His voice died to a mutter. He lay flat on his back, his arms spread wide. She saw that his chest was gleaming with sweat and that his breath came pantingly, as if he were running hard. His head tossed as his face twitched, lost in the reality inside his mind.

"Come back," he said, pleading throbbing in his voice.

"Nick, wake up," Rietta said, frightened. "Wake up."

She touched him on the shoulder, a gentle push intended to wake him. Too quick for her eye to follow, his arm came up and straightened.

Rietta found herself sitting on the floor, one hip aching from the impact with the wood. "Well, really . . ."

She stood up, rubbing the injured part. Nick lay more quietly, on his side with his knees draw up. The sheets were twisted around him, exposing the mattress.

Cautiously, Rietta sat down beside him. "Nick? Wake up. Please, Nick?"

Without warning, he sat bolt upright, pushing her once again to the floor. "Cashman!" he shouted. "God . . ."

Rietta sighed and clambered to her feet. "If you're going to beat me, kindly do it when you're awake."

"Rietta?" He rubbed his face vigorously, but she noticed that his hands trembled. "I'm not brave enough to beat you."

"Not when you are awake, perhaps, but you have no difficulty tossing me about while you sleep. I tried to wake you just now and you hurled me to the floor."

"Did I? Sorry." His chuckle sounded thin. "My batman used to prod me with a stick from a safe distance. I struck him a knockdown blow the first time he tried to shake me awake."

"I shall obtain a suitable walking stick first thing in the morning."

"A parasol, perhaps. Nothing with a spike on the end, if you'd be so kind. I want to wake up, and, in the wrong hands, a steel-tipped parasol could send me off to a permanent slumber."

She eyed him worriedly. Though he strove to keep his tone light, the bed shook to the rhythm of his hard breathing. He kept looking toward the windows, as if to reassure himself that the curtains were still flung wide.

Without being asked, Rietta poured him a glass of brandy from a tantalus on the dressing table. The snifter tapped against his teeth as he tried to drink. Rietta steadied his hand and guided it. "Sorry to be so stupid," he said.

After a moment, he threw off the tangled bedclothes

and stretched out his arms and legs to the accompaniment of an enormous yawn. "That's better."

Naked, he strode to the dressing table to pour water from a plain porcelain ewer into a basin. He scooped up water and liberally anointed his head, rubbing it through his hair to cool his brain. Some beads of water trailed down his back into the deeps of his shadowed body. Rietta tried to school her eyes not to look at him, but she couldn't help her curiosity. She'd touched his body but had never really taken the opportunity to see all of him. He was marvelous . . . strong and lean.

"I hate dreams," he said, toweling his hair.

"What do you dream?" Rietta only dared asked because he had his face buried in a towel. "They sound horrible from the outside; I can't imagine what it might sound like on the inside."

"Worse." His face emerged and he turned on her his most earnest expression. "It's not worth troubling over, Rietta. The dreams don't come often anymore."

"They used to?"

"Every night without fail. Since I married you, I haven't had any to speak of."

"What was that just now, then? It hardly sounded like a serenade for a young wife."

"I'll try again later. All I need do is learn the violin and I'll be ready. Give me three or four years, won't you?"

He went on jesting until Rietta gave up her attempts to worm the truth out of him. "I'll go back to my own chamber now."

"Why must you? Stay with me."

"I have too much respect for my neck, husband."

"Did I say I was sorry? If I didn't, I apologize again. I suppose I should have warned you that I am difficult to awaken."

"In some ways; not in others."

He laughed, though without his usual delight. "I've heard it doesn't take long for a virgin bride to become a hussy for her husband." He came to her side and tilted up her face. "Have you changed so much already?"

"Once the innocence is gone, it cannot be revived," she said with the lightest of intentions, but remembering the times when she'd been more than verbally shameless.

His brows came together and he seemed to look past her, though he still cupped her chin. "Yes, that's true. You can't go back to the way you were, no matter how you try."

Rietta put both hands around his wrist. "Is that what you are trying to do?"

"Once I was so free. . . ."

"And now I'm another burden to you. I'm sorry."

"You didn't have a choice, Rietta. If you are another responsibility, it is one I've taken on gladly. You've brought me . . ."

She held her breath.

Then he smiled into her eyes. "I needed distraction. You've provided that and more. It wasn't always what I believed I needed, especially these last weeks when I've suffered your displeasure, but I at least have relief from my troubles."

"The way a splinter takes one's mind off a sore tooth." She tossed her head free. "I will happily supply more splinters, Nick."

"Now, Rietta, I didn't mean it that way."

"What, pray, do you mean? You have made love to me on more than one occasion as if I'm the only woman you've ever wanted, but you will not share what is troubling you."

"Most women would take the lovemaking and let the troubles go," he said, turning to follow her.

"I don't believe that, and even if I did, what makes you so certain I'm like other women?"

"I've never accused you of that. If you're anything, Rietta, it's different. That's why I wanted you from the first. It's why I want you now." He stepped in front of her just as she reached the door. "Don't leave."

Her pride bade her refuse him again, but her need demanded a different answer. Softly, she said, "I need to sleep and I couldn't with you thrashing about like a wild beast with a sore paw."

"I'll lie as still as a bird in its nest." He smoothed her hair back from her face, his fingers tangling in the long strands. "I'll stay strictly on my side of the bed; I won't even touch your pillow."

Rietta looked at him with narrowed, distrustful eyes. "I don't believe a word, not a word."

"I certainly won't kiss you," he said, bending down to nip lightly at her lips. "And as for touching you . . . wouldn't dream of it."

Rietta felt the by-now familiar quickening in her heart. She'd learned already how very difficult it was to say no when he touched her with those seemingly tireless hands. Even now, she couldn't reconcile her idea of herself as a decent, respectable woman with the memory of the two of them on the dining salon table. It had to be a kind of magic spell that Nick could weave, making her not only amenable to his will, but a fully involved partner in his hot-blooded schemes.

Nick drew her close with his hands on her hips; close enough to feel that he, at least, was suffering from no conflict between pride and desire. If it was hard to say no before, it was all but impossible when he kissed her.

"Come to bed," he said. "It'll be a new experience. We've never made love like married people. Come to me."

The need in his voice was a faint echo of what he'd

called out in his dreams. Rietta blinked and withdrew her lips when he bent his head again. "No," she said. "No."

"You want to."

"Yes, I know."

"Come on, then."

"No.

"All right. No bed. We've done it on the floor before."

"No, not at all." Stepping away from him almost hurt her. "I can't do that again."

"Not the floor, then." He glanced around the room. "I think the bureau will support our weight."

"It's not that," Rietta said, realizing her departed innocence had nonetheless left her able to blush. "I can't make love to you again without knowing the truth. Nick, if you can't trust me then it's not making love at all, is it?"

"Did you ever hear of Psyche and Cupid?" Nick asked, his voice rough.

"All I know is you shot poor Cupid." Rietta's joke went unnoticed.

"Cupid had one rule that his wife had to follow—that she should never try to see his face. Her curiosity drove her to break that rule and it meant misery and unhappiness for everyone. Don't be Psyche, Rietta. Let well enough alone."

"But it isn't well enough. Something's tormenting you. What kind of wife would I be if I ignored that?"

"The kind I want. Someone sweet, obedient—"

"And stupid?" Rietta supplied. "Well, you should have married someone else."

"Perhaps. But you're what I have and there's nothing that will change it now."

"All right, then. Keep your precious secrets and your precious nightmares. But don't expect me to share your bed if you won't share yourself."

"Rietta, wait."

She paused, one hand on the doorknob.

"Rietta." He sighed. "I lived."

"You lived?"

"That's right. That's it in two words. I lived. I survived. I saw my dearest friends smashed into a heaving, bleeding mass that was so . . ." He shook his head violently.

"I can't tell you. These aren't things women need to know. It's better for you to think of battle like the paintings that are done of it. Fat, woolly clouds of cannon smoke, patient men with clean bandages lying about in artistically contrived groups, clean-shaven generals with steady horses, and silence."

"I've seen paintings like that. They're quite popular."

"Of course they are. A painting can't stun and horrify you with noise so incredible you'd give your soul for a single second's silence. But all you get is the roar of the cannon fire, the screams of the dying horses and men, and me, begging them not to be dead."

He walked to the window, naked and unashamed. "I can't stand the dark anymore," he said, apparently idly. "Comes of sleeping so long in a tent, I suppose. When I returned to Brussels, I had a room in an *appartement*, and slept with the curtains closed as one should. I couldn't stand it. I'd wake up in the middle of the night and think . . ."

Rietta came up behind him. Putting her arm around his waist, she leaned her head on his shoulder. "What would you think?"

He started to speak, but choked. Something wet fell to her arm, but she didn't know if it was water, sweat, or a tear.

"I'd think . . . I'd wake up and think I was dead. Buried with the others, as I should have been. I should have been." He made an effort to shake her off, but Rietta clung.

"You said some names."

"Did I?"

"Fox, Allenby . . . something Spanish?"

"Ribera." She heard the ghost of a laugh in his chest. "He was Portuguese. Hated the Spaniards like fire but hated the French worse. He had a way with the ladies, second to none. Used to make poor old Cashman half crazy the way he could choose the most starched-up female in a party and have her mooning over him in no time. Ribera would wink with one lazy eye and tell him that one merely needed sympathy."

Something of a foreign accent crept into his voice and Rietta could almost hear the voice of the Portuguese officer.

"Cashman was one of your friends?"

"My best friend. We joined up at the same time. God, we were young. We both thought it would be a pity to miss the adventure."

"The adventure?" she prompted.

"Yes, and it was, too. You wouldn't think men could enjoy war but I think we all have a sneaking liking for it. Not the battle, perhaps, though I've known a few who did enjoy the whiff of powder. But the rest of it—the travel, the camaraderie, the pitting of your wits against the world. Why, even the conflicts with some of the others had an enjoyable side. There was one captain who seemed to enjoy flogging his troops a little too much. We settled him. We . . ." He chuffed a sigh.

"What did you do?"

"No. Definitely not for your ears. It was all Allenby's idea, of course. He was the smartest of us. Foxy was always neat as wax. Didn't matter where we were or what was going forward; his batman would be ironing his ludship's neckcloths, or brushing the mud from his boots. Tompkins was just the opposite, yet you rarely saw one of them without the other."

She encouraged him to talk about them. She could almost see them in her mind's eye, young, playful, full of unspoken thoughts about duty and honor and the justice of the work they were doing that would have embarrassed them horribly if anyone guessed. He talked about his first time under fire, arriving in a coastal town to pick up supplies. He'd been cut by chips of rock when a bullet had just missed him.

"When I felt the blood trickling down, I remember thinking how jealous the others would be that I'd been wounded. They were, too. When I was shot at Vitoria, Fox had just escaped with his life as well when he'd stumbled over a Frenchie hiding in a ditch. There'd been a little back and forth with the Frenchie scraping Foxy's ribs with his bayonet. I remember him cursing because his coat wouldn't fit properly over the bandages."

"He was a dandy?"

"Don't let him hear . . . that is, no. He aspired to be Corinthian. He would have been, too. Top o' the Trees."

Rietta left Nick's side to sit down on the tumbled bed. "What happened with Napoleon's abdication?"

"We sat down at a *taverna* somewhere in the Pyrenees and had a carouse that they're probably still talking about. I hardly remember any of it myself—except for that girl with black eyes and large . . ." He gestured roundly.

"Quite a lot of this tale is not for my ears," Rietta said, glad that he'd had an opportunity to enjoy life after the tribulation of the long war in the Peninsula. Then she thought, *Good heavens, I'm not the slightest bit jealous of that girl he had. I must be more in love than even I knew.*

He laughed and joined her on the bed. "Almost none of it. After that, I came home for a time. So did Tompkins; his father was something in politics and wanted to show off his son. Then we rejoined the regiment in time to go to Holland. From there, we were sent to Belgium when word came that Napoleon had left Elba and was moving north."

"Then came Waterloo." She wondered if it would ever

be forgotten. She supposed it might be, one day, if there were more and bigger wars. No one had ever told her before that men could have a sneaking liking for war.

"Then came it all—Charleroi, Quatre Bras, Chateau de Hougoumont. Amazing how much of what we were fighting over was some respectable farm the day before. By the time we were through, they were roofless shells with holes you could have driven cattle through."

"My father read us the reports when they were published in the newspaper. He even sent for a fortnight's worth of the *Times*, an organ he ordinarily abominates."

"What did he think of it all?"

"What everyone thinks. A glorious action that threw down the Monster once and for all."

"Yes, I suppose it had to be done. Napoleon never should have tried to defeat us. You know, the first time we beat him, he was offered all of France to the borders of 1802, and he wouldn't accept the terms."

"He was a horrid man."

He laughed again. "To say the least."

"Don't laugh." She knocked her shoulder into him. "You can't deny he was odious. What's the use of being an emperor anyway?"

"I don't know. I've done with wanting to make more of my life than God intended. It would take a command from Wellington himself to move me from Greenwood now. If you're hoping to spend your seasons in London, you'll go without me."

"I have no ambition myself, except one." She didn't speak of it, but ever since he'd told her she might be pregnant she had wanted his child. Even when she was furious with him, that yearning still grew in her. She should have refused him in the dining room, but a combination of desire, maternal hopes, and pity had created an inability to refuse him. Thinking of those impassioned moments, the hard and gleaming table under her, Nick above her, his eyes closed in surrender, she pressed her hand to her mouth to stifle a moan.

Now wasn't the time to give in to her feelings again. Not when he'd finally begun to talk to her about the events of June 15, nearly a year and half ago.

"What part of the battle were you in, Nick?"

"I beg your pardon?" he spoke against the waves of her hair. He gathered the strands together. He dusted her neck with the thick end, as if he held a huge paintbrush and was painting her with light.

"Stop it. That tickles."

"Does it? I shall have to remember that. You wriggle so delightfully."

"Nick . . ."

"No more," he said, smiling. "The sun will be rising soon and I've yet to accomplish the thing I promised."

"What thing?"

"Making love to you in my bed. Call me reactionary, but I want a pillow for your head, a blanket to cover you, and a mattress to protect your soft buttocks." He grinned. "Don't be so shocked. They are soft, aren't they?"

"I wouldn't know." She strove to be prim once more, but how could she when he'd seen her passionate impulses?

"Then take my word for it. I've stroked more than a few and yours is the softest I've ever met with."

"Hmph. If you've had so much experience, you don't need any more tests. I'll go along to my room now, Sir Nicholas, if you don't mind."

"I shan't sleep a wink if you go. I've learned my lesson about that."

"I shan't get any sleep if I stay. My lesson is just as new as yours, but mine runs deeper."

"How much deeper?" He slid his arm around her waist and began to explore the skin exposed by the open throat of her nightdress. He seemed to have developed a fascination with her shoulder, one she began to share as he trailed his fingertips over the soft skin. He smiled down at her as her head fell back onto his shoulder. She reached up, above and behind her head, determined not to let an opportunity to kiss him slip by.

"Nick . . . ," she said dreamily as his hand dipped lower, seeking new territory to explore. He hummed a reply. "Did any of your friends leave widows?"

He took his hands away, leaving Rietta feeling a little empty and foolish. If only she'd waited to ask—waited until he was in a melting mood. Now he withdrew, not physically, for he still held her, but emotionally. Rietta felt a strange chill settle into the room.

"Yes. And even those without wives had sisters and sweethearts, all of them praying as hard as could be for their men to return alive. They wouldn't have cared if he came back missing an arm, a leg, or an eye. I tried to convince Cashman that his Anne wouldn't care if he lost his arm, but he was so sure he'd be an object of disgust."

"Cashman lost an arm?" Though she'd never met him, she suddenly felt as though she'd heard horrible news about her dearest friend. Tears stung her eyes. "How?"

"A shell burst. One moment he was there, on his horse, the next he was on the ground, holding what was left of a shattered arm. He died in a quarter-hour and said it was better that way. . . . I didn't tell her that when I wrote to her."

"You wrote to her? You wrote to them all, didn't you? That's how you know about wives and sweethearts."

He nodded. There were no tears on his face. She knew all his tears had dried up long ago.

"It was the only thing I could do for them. My . . . my penance, if you like."

"Penance? For what? For living?"

"You must see how unfair it is that I should be alive, living with my family in my family house, married to you, making love to you . . ."

"While they are dead."

She felt his back grow rigid once again. "Yes," he breathed.

Rietta sat beside him in silence. Platitudes, easy and quick, came to her lips but she had sense enough not to utter them. This was not the time for the gently thoughtless phrases that wrapped and muted grief. She vividly recalled the most un-Christian hatred she'd felt toward those well-meaning women who'd murmured, "she's in heaven now" and "you wouldn't have wanted her to go on when she was in such pain." Of course she had. She cared for nothing beyond the fact that her mother was dead.

He would hate her if she reminded him that they'd died for a great cause, or that they had suffered a hero's death.

Slowly, seeking the right words, she said, "I feel as though I've lost something precious that I never knew I had. I won't know them. They won't come here. I'll never meet their wives, dandle their children, hear their stories about you." She smiled, her face wet with tears. "I'll wager they had some marvelous stories about you—things you would have paid them never to tell me."

He laughed but it was cut short, as if he were afraid to be laughing now. Then, bravely, softly, he chuckled. "I would have paid it gladly. Anything rather than let you hear the story about the goose, the donkey, and the general's lady. Tompkins could imitate a goose better than anyone I ever heard of in my life."

They lay back together on the bed, Rietta's head on his chest, while he told her the little things that had happened in between campaigns. The struggle to eradicate the bedbugs and other vermin that accumulated every time they bivouacked in a Spanish household; the rage of MacMurray the batman upon discovering a cook using the last of his salt; a chance meeting with Wellington himself, were perhaps no more fit for her ears than stories of lusty village maidens, but they gave Rietta a clearer picture of war than any newspaper article puffing off the glories of the army.

She listened to him until he fell asleep, suddenly between one word and the next. Still she lay there, cherishing him, hoping by her presence to guard him from his demons. She did not sleep until the sky was streaked with red. He had not, so far as she could tell, dreamed.

In the morning, Nick woke late. Yawning and stretching, he knew the bed was empty except for him. Blinking, he felt a sense of disorientation, as though the bed had been spun around in the night, leaving him facing a new direction. He chuckled. Rietta had been having that effect on him since the day they'd met.

He sat up and rubbed his eyes. Then he frowned as he opened them. The worn green curtains in his room were pulled across the windows, blocking out the sunshine. Yet there seemed to be plenty of light.

Nick looked around and saw that the door between his bedroom and Rietta's stood wide open. He could hear her singing some Italian song and the sound of splashing. Swinging his feet out from beneath the covers and reaching for his dressing gown, he went to her only to pause on the threshold, spellbound.

The highly painted tin bath stood before a blazing fire. Rietta's hair hung over the lip, pouring down like a river of fire. He'd never heard her sing before and found her voice to be lighter than when she spoke. As she soaped her long, pale leg, raising it in the air to reach around with the sponge, she sang, *"Io sono docile, son rispettosa, sono obbediente, dolce, amorosa . . ."*

Nick laughed, despite the mouth-drying desire he felt for her. The water splashed as she twisted around to look at him. "Oh, you're awake at last."

"Docile, respectful, obedient, and sweet? That song was not written for you."

"I am loving, however, I hope."

"Mmm, that I can't argue with." He came around to the front of the bath to gaze in delight at the gleaming beauty of Rietta in her bath. At the same time, he became aware that he could probably use a good dose of clean water himself.

Rietta, despite the cooling effect of evaporation on her arms and chest, felt far from cold when Nick looked at her like that. The telltale evidence of his interest in her showed plainly beneath the clinging fabric of his dressing gown. "I'd invite you in," she said shamelessly, "but there's no more room."

"You could sit on my lap. . . ." He untied the belt and let the dressing gown swing open. Rietta couldn't control her eyes.

"I'll just get out, shall I?"

Nick picked up the towel warming over a rack near the fire. "Let me help you."

"Close your eyes, then."

"No." He grinned at her, cocky as the devil.

"Very well." Rietta stood up and felt a purely feminine satisfaction at the stunned expression on his face. He held out his hand to help her step over the edge of the tub. Then he pulled her into his embrace.

After a few minutes, Rietta pushed at his shoulders. "I'm all wet."

"I don't mind a bit." His hands slipped over her slick skin until she was gasping. Then he reached for the towel and took his time drying every inch of her body. After that, he threw the towel back on the rack. "Time for bed."

"It's broad daylight."

"We'll keep the curtains closed. One thing about being

married to you—so long as you are in my bed I will never feel less than alive."

"Nick . . ." Rietta stopped his headlong rush to the bed and gazed up at him worriedly. "I promised myself I would never ask, but now I must know . . ."

He took her hands in his and raised each to his lips, kissing them as reverently as though they were in church. "Yes, I do love you. In time, you'll come to care for me. I promise I'll make you care."

"I do already. You must know that. I love you."

"You do?" He stared into her eyes as if willing her to show him. "Are you sure?"

Rietta laughed. "Come to bed, husband. I'll prove it to you."

"You already have." Nick's eyes glistened with a sudden rush of tears. "I don't know what I would have done if you hadn't married me."

Sitting on the rumpled bed, Rietta reached out to draw him down beside her. "I think, you know, that my father's interference only advanced something that was bound to happen anyway. From the first moment I saw you, ogling Blanche, I knew—"

"I was not ogling Blanche!"

"I knew it would be you and me forever. I didn't really believe it would happen, but I knew it. Does that make sense?"

"Yes, perfect sense. I found that out later, standing in the abbey with you. It felt so foreordained, as though I at last had a reason why I survived all the battles. I dismissed the notion at once, but it was there."

Now Rietta's eyes filled with tears. "I will try to be all you want in a wife."

"Just be yourself. That is all any man could want from you. I need you, Rietta. Just you."

As they came together, Rietta's only thought was to prove, beyond all possible doubt, the truth of her love.

When they lay together in a rosy glow, Nick sighed and murmured, "That's one battle I don't mind losing. Just remember, like Napoleon, I will rise again."

Rietta muffled her laughter against his shoulder. "I'm so glad. How shall we decide who wins?"

"We've both won."

As she drifted off to sleep, Rietta knew it was a victory that would last a lifetime.

Epilogue

As it turned out, not all Blanche's wiles worked as well on Niall Joyce as those few minutes of genuine emotion. Though he confessed to Nick that he had every intention of marrying Blanche, he wanted to wait until she'd grown up a bit more. The year she spent with her sister and brother-in-law, watching them grow more and more involved with each other and the estate, completed the process. When Niall proposed again, she refused him.

"I'm not good enough for him," she said, storming up and down the drawing room while Rietta watched her from the comfort of an upright chair.

"Who do you imagine yourself marrying?"

"I don't know. I hear David Mochrie's back from England. He's low enough for the likes of me."

"Come now, Blanche. You're too hard on yourself."

"No," she said with deep sincerity. "What have I ever done to make him fall in love with me? I have a pretty face. Well, that won't last. I can't allow him to marry me for my face when in ten years I'll be a hag."

"Isn't that Niall's lookout?" Rietta had seen her sister become gradually less flighty and less vain. Why, just yesterday, she'd come in from a walk in the rain and did not check her reflection for half an hour. "What do you want to do? Turn into a bluestocking? Or a philanthropist?"

"That would be better than remaining a butterfly all my life."

"A butterfly?"

"Niall called me that one day. He said I was as pretty and insubstantial as a butterfly. Well, I refuse to be a butterfly any longer."

"It's not like Niall to be so thoughtless. When did he call you that?"

Blanche shrugged and sat down with a dejected thump in the armchair opposite. "Oh, last spring. We were out riding and there were butterflies in the hedges."

"Do you remember everything Niall says to you?"

"Every word. Don't you with Nick?"

"We talk so much I'd be hard-pressed to remember it all." She smoothed down her shirt and gazed in loving wonder at her infant, asleep with a trace of milk still upon her lips. "We've put Maire right to sleep with our chattering."

"Shall I take her to Nurse?"

"No, let me keep her a little while. Nurse will be down soon enough and I don't have enough chances to look at her."

Blanche came over and smoothed the baby's featherlight hair. "Will it ever lie down?"

"Some day. It's like Nick's—black, thick, and heavy. Much better than my red."

Rietta looked up at her sister. "You love Niall, but you're afraid to marry him because he might regret it when you lose your looks, is that it?"

"He deserves so much better than me."

"Then he should definitely marry Emma."

"Emma?"

"Why, yes. I like Niall and want to have him for my

brother. Since you won't marry him, it will have to be Emma."

"She's in love with him already, I daresay."

"No, I shouldn't think so. But why should that stop her?"

"I never thought I'd hear you express such heartless sentiments. Didn't you suffer enough from Father's plans?"

Gazing on her child, Rietta smiled reminiscently. "I'd hardly say I suffered at all."

Blanche resumed her hectic pacing. Rietta rocked her child and sang softly. True, Maire was asleep, but she seemed to relax into a deeper sleep when her mother sang. She could have slept a little herself; now that Maire was four months old, Nick and she had resumed their love-making and had a lot of time to catch up on.

"Speak of the devil," she said when Nick appeared escorting his mother.

"How are my ladies?" he asked softly.

"Very content indeed, except for Blanche."

Nick smiled at his sister-in-law. "And what's amiss with Her Highness?"

"You might as well know. I've refused Niall Joyce's offer."

"Refused it?" Lady Kirwan echoed. "And the poor boy half crazy with love for you?"

"I just can't bring myself to disappoint him," Blanche said. The tears came into her beautiful eyes and she bolted from the room like a half-tamed filly.

"Poor child." Lady Kirwan eased herself down into the unoccupied chair. " 'Tis a pity she hasn't more confidence."

"She's confident enough," Nick said.

"Not really." Rietta agreed. "She pretends to be, but I think she is honestly worried that he won't love her once he lives with her a time."

"She's afraid of losing her looks, too, isn't she? As if that were all that man were interested in."

"He can't love her for her mind," Nick said. "She's easier to have around the house than I would have believed a year ago, but she's not a clever woman."

"If Niall Joyce had wanted a clever woman," Lady Kirwan said "he would have been hanging out for Rietta. He wants Blanche and I must say I think it would be a very good match for both of them. He is too serious. He will steady her; she will enliven him."

"Undoubtedly you are right." Rietta gazed her fill on her child, for she'd heard Nurse's no-nonsense step on the stairs. "But as she has refused him outright, there's nothing more to be done until Niall asks again. If he asks again."

She watched all she could see of Maire over her nurse's shoulder until the door closed behind the woman's stiff-starched cap. Then, unconsciously, she sighed woefully.

Nick rose and came to her side. "If you want to dismiss the nurse, Rietta, just say so."

"Yes, please do," Lady Kirwan said. "She's a very good woman but the way she watches one! I picked up little Maire yesterday and from the way she acted you'd think I'd never held a baby before. I know Emma is simply dying to take care of Maire, too. But I think the nurse frightens her."

"She certainly frightens me," Nick said. "I don't believe she thinks a father ought to have anything to do with children, except to teach them to ride."

Rietta pressed her hand to her heart. "Here I was thinking I was the only one who was afraid of her. But I'm not afraid to dismiss her. I'll write an excellent reference, naturally. After all, I'm quite grateful for all she's done but I do so want to care for Maire myself."

Nick picked up her hand and kissed it. "That's settled, then. Now, about Blanche . . ."

"There's nothing we can do," Rietta said. "Her mind seems to be made up."

"Oh, I don't know," Lady Kirwan said, leaning back and smiling. "It seems to me that there's a certain ruined abbey that might prove just the thing."

"Mamma!"

"Mother?"

"Why not? It brought you two great happiness, didn't it? Why would it not do the same for Blanche? You can't imagine Niall would object, and it isn't really against Blanche's will, now is it?"

So, under a half moon that painted the roofless walls with silver, Niall Joyce and Blanche Ferris were married. The groom was point-device in blue superfine and biscuit-colored breeches; the bride less so in a draggled riding habit and a veiled hat leaning at a drunken angle. Her family, nearest and extended, were all present and cheered when the ancient monk stopped mumbling.

The bride was flushed and furious until the groom took her behind some tombstones and kissed her into submission. Blushing and bashful, she repeated the vows, gazing adoringly at the husband she felt herself unworthy to marry.

Afterwards, Nick walked with Rietta. "It is a pretty place. We shall have to come see it by daylight."

"Perhaps when Emma marries we can hold the ceremony at noon instead of at night."

"When Emma marries? Who is she to marry?"

"Your mother hasn't told me yet, but I'm certain she has someone in mind."

"Will you vow with me, here and now, never to interfere in the course of little Maire's affections?"

"Of course I won't. It's a mother's right to see her children happy. And a father's right, too."

"You believe that?"

"I do now that I have a child of my own. Perhaps my father's motives were not so high-minded as that, but I cannot deny that I am happy with you."

Nick kissed her long and deliciously under the moon. "A father's right to meddle? I don't imagine Maire will see it that way, but I will be more subtle than your father was."

Rietta laughed. "I will believe that when I see it."

"Are you calling me an overly protective father?"

"Yes. And I shouldn't want you to be anything else. As a matter of fact, though, I believe Maire would be happier if you had more children to protect. That way the entire burden wouldn't fall upon her. For her sake, therefore, I suggest we have at least half a dozen."

"As my lady wishes."

FRIENDS ROMANCE

Can a man come between friends?

❏ **A TASTE OF HONEY**
by DeWanna Pace   0-515-12387-0

❏ **WHERE THE HEART IS**
by Sheridon Smythe   0-515-12412-5

❏ **LONG WAY HOME**
by Wendy Corsi Staub   0-515-12440-0

All books $5.99